# MONDAY'S MEAL

## stories by
## Leslie H. Edgerton

University of North Texas Press
Denton, Texas

Permissions:
University of North Texas Press
PO Box 13856
Denton TX 76203

The paper used in this book meets the minimum requirements of the
American National Standard for Permanence of Paper for Printed Library
Materials, Z39.48.1984. Binding materials have been chosen for durability.

Library of Congress Cataloging-in-Publication Data

Edgerton, Leslie.
Monday's meal : stories / by Leslie H. Edgerton.
p.    cm.
ISBN 1-57441-026-1 (alk. paper)
I. Title.
PS3555.D472M66    1997
813'.54—dc21                                        97-6462
                                                          CIP
Cover design by Amy Layton
Interior design by Accent Design and Communications
Cover art, *Rain Dance* from the private collection of Ross Vick, is used by
permission of the artist, Lu Ann Barrow.

For my teachers—Elaine Gottlieb, Diane Lefer, François Camoin, Phyllis Barber, Wendell Mayo, and lots of others. You know who you are and I thank you. For the loves of my life—Mary, Sienna, Mike and Britney. For my family at UNT Press—Fran Vick, Charlotte Wright, Melanie Johnstone, and Barbara Heick. For my readers; without readers, writing is like having sex with yourself. The feedback you get for your performance is ultimately flawed.

# Contents

# Washday

# Blue Skies

E lise is not tardy; she is late. At a quarter of five I open the door and she comes in with a rush of Royal Secret perfume, dressed in a pinstripe and a hat and Ferragamo shoes, all different shades of gray. A hat! I don't remark on her little pillbox thing I've seen on women all over New Orleans since I drove up from Houma.

It turns out Elise still likes Dubonnet. I'd made a good choice and so I told her I liked her shoes and she lifted up her glass and smiled and said, "Blue skies, Ted, blue skies." I was sitting on the bed and she had elected the chair by the dresser. That, and the suit, were signals I could read clearly.

Then. Looking away and picking something I couldn't see off her suit with a shiny crimson nail: "You didn't ask about Celsi."

❊ ❊ ❊

We ended up at the Seaport Cafe and decided on bisque and a flounder for me and blackened redfish for her.

"I just had bisque last night," she said. "Otherwise, I would." Then, abruptly. "Look at that, would you!" There was an old, old lady on roller skates. As if that wasn't enough there were five half-grown ducks trailing behind her. After she crossed the street she ran smack into a light pole, her legs straddling it as she went down. The ducklings all waddled around her, quacking furiously. She got up in a minute and began skating again as if the accident was just a standard part of her routine.

"That's the Duck Lady," Elise said. "Remember?"

"Sure." She was on the Mardi Gras poster last year.

"Are you still painting?"

I was painting right then, the mental part. I was trying to engrave the Duck Lady scene into my memory. I was getting itchy to get back to Houma and get out a canvas. I tried to remember if I had

3

any stretched or if I had used them up in my all-nighters the past week.

"I'm doing something new. More commercial." I grinned and watched her reaction but couldn't see that there was any.

"I know you don't want to hear this—I really do think if you went back to what you were doing when we first met—"

"Look." She knew how to get to me, which button to push. "You think people *like* that shit nowadays, all that depressing stuff? I've got to make a living."

"They want art. Art that comes from the artist. They—"

I waved my hand for a time-out. "That's enough. Don't tell me what to paint."

We could have had a fight right then but she began talking about something else, both of us picking up the formal chitchat used on first dates: How was your day . . . we're due for bad weather . . . crapola like that.

We had both circled around it for long enough. Our conversations since the breakup reminded me of the Impressionists. Paint daubers. Once the daub was applied they never touched it again or blended it. That was us. Little islands of words that somehow made a picture.

The waiter came and cleared away our plates and asked if I wanted him to wrap up the rest of my fish.

"So," I said when he left, letting out my breath. "I've missed you."

"I've missed you, too," she said. "That's what makes this so hard to do."

She looked sideways at me, bits of light glistening in her eyelashes, but then she looked away, turning her head so I couldn't see her eyes. My heart was jumping and I felt light-headed suddenly.

There were some black kids down toward St. Peter Street break dancing on a big piece of cardboard they'd laid down, a crowd growing around them. M. C. Hammer was blaring from a boom box, one of fifty thousand sound-alike songs.

"What're you saying?" I said.

"Oh, Ted." That was all she said. *Oh, Ted.* We sat there in dinner party formality for a few moments and just sipped our drinks. After a time I looked over at her and she was looking down in her lap where her hands were folded. She hadn't touched her drink. Mine was half-gone, a wounded soldier.

"I thought for awhile that perhaps we might still make it," she started, and that's when I began to close up inside. "I kept thinking about something."

"What?" I said, before I could stop myself. I had the oddest feeling, identical to the time when I was ten and picked up a handful of change, maybe two bucks worth, off my parents' dresser and Dad walked in just as I was stuffing the coins in the pocket of my jeans.

"Remember when I was pregnant with Celsi?"

"Sure."

"No you don't. At least you don't remember like I do."

"Oh, well of course not. You're probably right, there," I said, starting to feel the booze a little, my speech a bit slower but clear. "I was just the ol' seed-giver, the party-guy. I got to have all the fun while you got the backaches. I remember now. You bet."

Another couple, obvious tourists, came out onto the balcony, sat down two tables away and began talking about how sick they were of seafood; where in town could they get a decent, basic steak, and how about all the filth and trash on the streets. They ignored the waiter who stood stoically beside them in his white jacket. Elise picked up a cigarette and her lighter, then laid them down without lighting up.

"I was so worried. I remember this nurse who came in and talked to me until you got there. You were on that job out of town then, remember? You couldn't be there with me. We needed the money. We desperately needed the money. I'd borrowed from Mother for the rent just the week before."

I guessed I remembered. Some of it, anyway.

The waiter came near and looked at me with his blank waiter's eyes and I held up two fingers and took out a twenty and put it on the table.

"I didn't know if you were even coming for sure or not. You stayed out all night some nights then. Even in my ninth month."

"Here it comes."

"You're the same, Ted. You just never change, do you?" Now, she picked up her cigarette and lit it, twisting her mouth as she inhaled.

"Hey, I did those things—I can't deny it, but good god, I was barely out of my teens and here I was with a wife and baby coming and no money, and . . . and, well I was just a kid. I thought I was becoming my father."

"Ted, I—"

"This is like getting a ticket. I know I did wrong, officer, but do me a favor, just give me the damned ticket and spare me the lecture."

She turned away. She wasn't looking at her hands any more. She was staring down at the street. A man dressed in a Santa Claus suit came by, a go-cup in his hand he kept lifting up to sip from. Santa was staggering a little, not picking up his feet. The rain had quit, I noticed, but the gray clouds hadn't. They were now the exact color of the sidewalk beneath us.

I remembered that night all right. When I came into the hospital, at a flat-out run, the nurse at the front desk shot down the hall screeching after me. *Mr. Gage*, the nurse said. *Mr. Gage, I have to talk to you. Before you see your wife. There's something you need to know.*

We went to this little room where a TV was playing, a waiting area for visitors. There weren't any visitors there, but "The Honeymooners" was on, the volume turned off.

"Elise—"

"You came in finally. I said, 'Ted.' That's what I said. 'Ted.' I was too scared to say anything else. I had a thousand speeches prepared, but when you came in all I could come up with was to just say 'Ted.'"

"I know," I said. I swigged a long drink and watched the Santa Claus shuffling into one of the strip joints, the famous one with the bare legs that swing out into the street.

"Do you remember what happened then?"

"Yes." My "yes" came out bent. I was drunk. There was an aitch on the end of my yes.

"You said something. Goddamn you. You said the only thing that would keep me married to you for nineteen miserable fucking years. I still love you for what you said. No, I hate you for saying it. It's kept me in a holy prison. You said—do you remember what you said?"

She wasn't slurring her words like I was, but she never said *fuck* unless she was totally smashed. She must have had a few before she came by the hotel. Probably why she was late. She was looking away from me again.

"You said, 'Honey, God sure knew what he was doing here didn't He? Look what He has gone and done. Anybody can love a perfect baby,' you said. 'But only a real God would know who to give a poor, sick baby like this to.'"

I guess she was crying now, I don't know. I wasn't looking her way. I just sucked hard on that drink and wished I was anywhere else. I wished I was back home in Houma with a Grumbacher #3 in my hand. I guess I had said what Elise said I did, that thing about God and all, but I honestly didn't remember. The person I was now wouldn't say such a thing, *couldn't* say such a thing. Elise thought that person was still around someplace, maybe hiding inside me somewhere, only needing some magic or other to bring him out.

That, finally, made me sad.

Across the street was a sagging giant Santa and eight *huge* reindeer action-stretched across several balconies, lifting and falling in the breeze, faded reds and blues only weathered plastic can achieve. In the fierceness of the New Orleans sun they were achieving it faster. Christmas decorations from Christmases Past. Dusty, bleached bells and gray-green pine boughs. Celsi would squeal at the Santa if she was here. My poor, *challenged* Celsi. That's the word they use nowadays. Challenged. Her challenge is mental. I wonder what mine would be called.

"What changed, Ted?" Her eyes were red, beginning to puff, but she wasn't crying.

I sipped my beer and looked down at the street. *Get down to brass tacks*, that had been her way as long as I could remember. If Elise painted, she would fall into the Andy Warhol camp. Just slap that tomato can, that cartoon of Marilyn up there and call it art. I'm of the old school. Lush and complex backgrounds are important. My canvas would have the can sitting on a Penncrest stove with a copper pan and wooden ladle, a Duncan Fife table in the background, saltine crackers spilled out onto a plate and a glass of milk with droplets of condensation. A curtain and a view beyond, some trees and a lawn. A small crack in the oak table. I want the viewer to smell the tomatoes, feel the heat from the stove, know there's a mother in the room somewhere and a sick child waiting.

At least that's the way I used to paint. Now it's all trick shit, commercial stuff, loose, floating, soft, shapeless abstract muck.

"You can't tell me can you? Remember what you told me one time when we were going together? You were talking about painting, and you said that it was only the mind that really sees—the eye only looks. You said you can only see what the mind knows. You need to use that in *your* life. All you do is look, Ted. You haven't connected up your mind with your eye yet. Not with us. Not with Celsi. You're a phony. I bet you haven't painted anything worthwhile in a long time either." She reached for her purse and pulled out another cigarette, lit it, then turned her head away from me to look at the street below. She took short, furious puffs.

"Sandwiches."

I didn't plan to say that, had no idea that was what was going to come out of my mouth, hadn't even really *known* about the sandwiches until that very moment. It just flashed into my head complete and entire, and for the first time, I knew exactly when I'd dropped out of our relationship.

When I'd dropped out of my daughter's life.

There was this *thing* I'd noticed when Celsi was only about three years old. We were in this coffee shop up on Magazine, and had all ordered tuna fish sandwiches. They had these great tuna fish sandwiches, with apple chunks and celery and lots of parsley and mayonnaise—they didn't even smell like fish, but clean, apple-cidery, *fresh*. They always cut the sandwiches diagonally. On this day—probably before too, although this was the first time I noticed it—Elise and I bit off the sharp tip of the sandwich but Celsi—Celsi took a huge bite out of the middle.

I don't know why that struck me but it did. From then on I began to watch whenever others bit into sandwiches cut that way and the oddest thing was that every adult ate the tip off first but every single *child* took a bite out of the middle. I think I even pointed it out to Elise. Or maybe not. It was something she would have forgotten and I had myself until another day years later when we were sitting in that very same coffee shop and ordered tuna fishes all around. We had just celebrated Celsi's sixteenth birthday the week before. I think she even had her birthday present with her that day in the coffee shop, one of a never-ending series of Barbie dolls.

We were talking and laughing and maybe I had a beer, I don't know, and our order came and Celsi picked her sandwich up first and took a bite. Out of the middle.

That's when it came over me that Celsi had become an adult, biologically, was now a woman. And it came over me at the same time that she was never going to change the way she ate a sandwich. She still went on talking in her private language, the language her parents had learned to understand, and she still hugged her Barbie to the inside of her neck the way she had yesterday and the way she had when she was three years old and I knew as perfectly as you can know something that this was it, this was the way she was going to be forever and longer than forever and it was at that precise moment that I withdrew from them, from Celsi and Elise and from the private planet we three had been living on for sixteen years.

It was a year later that we separated, but it really began with that sandwich. When the lines began to curve and intersect in ways I wasn't able to comprehend. Or control.

Elise was saying something. The Santa had lurched out of the bar and was coming our way. I kept my eye on him. His shuffle, that was the thing I'd need to capture. Mr. Thierry's words came floating up from out of the past. "Now, people, to capture the action of the figure remember that the center of balance for the whole figure is the center of the head and all action points are related to the pit of the neck." I took a mental snapshot of the figure below and closed my eyes to develop the film.

"—*do you mean*, sandwiches?"

I don't know why I didn't explain. She looked at me, obviously expecting an answer, and when she saw none was forthcoming, went on.

"What are we going to do about Celsi?"

"Huh?"

"Ted, I can't have her with me anymore. Not with my job. You know that. I've explained my situation. Oh God, this is hard."

She was looking away, showing me the back of her head, but I knew she was crying.

"What do you want from me, Elise?" I said stiffly, looking away, aware that others on the balcony were staring.

"I don't know Ted . . . I guess . . . dammit, I want *help* in making this decision. I think we should put her in the Huntley Home. She'll get excellent care there. The kind of care she needs. Don't you think so?" She had that vulnerable look now.

"Do what you think best." I was starting to feel more sober than I wanted to feel.

"You see?" It sounded like a scream and it took a second before I realized she was whispering. "This is you. This is you all the way. You never make a decision. Well, this time you have no choice. You have to make a decision on this. Yes or no, Buster, which is it going to be?"

She straightened her head and leaned forward, eyes unblinking, something in them telling me that we were finished as of this moment. "You *won't* make a decision, is that it?"

I couldn't look at her. Not directly. Not into those eyes. I held my gaze slightly to the right, where a piece of her hair stuck up like a C. Stared at that alphabet hair as hard as I could like it was a life buoy she could throw to save me, if she wanted.

"Can't, won't, don't. What's the difference?" I downed the rest of my drink and lit a cigarette, holding my lighter with both hands to keep it from shaking.

There wasn't much else. We were both quiet for awhile and then the waiter came by again with his Little Orphan Annie eyes and I ordered both of us another one and she got out her compact and worked on her face and told me some about her job, how exciting it was and what a wonderful opportunity especially for a woman her age and then it was time to leave. I had the feeling all along that if I could only come up with the right combination of words everything would be all right again, we would go back together and be married and a family again, back on our planet. But whatever those words might be they weren't in my power to imagine and so they never got said and I guess that's the way it's supposed to be, or else I would have come up with them wouldn't I?

It began to dawn on me that the artist part of me had changed too. Before the sandwich episode I used to think God was working His Grand Design out through me, through my paintings. Not now. God only works through those who've managed to hold on to their sense of humor.

"Goodbye Ted," she said, one foot on the streetcar step. I watched until it turned off Canal and then I went into the hotel and up the elevator.

I had drinks, more than a few, and thought about leaving, going to another hotel. Maybe out to the Days Inn in Kenner. Maybe even go back home to Houma, start painting. Do a street scene with that Santa Claus. Maybe I could work in the Duck Lady, do something surreal. Trying not to think about Celsi.

Hell. I couldn't do the Duck Lady. Her face had changed. It was overdeveloped or underexposed; it was Elise's face. No it wasn't. It was Celsi's.

I could maybe do the Santa.

What I did was I just kept sitting on the bed in my clothes and dialing room service for drinks, and smoking cigarettes one after another down to the filters until dawn and I had drunk myself around to being sober, and then I went back down in the French Quarter with its streets left black and glistening by the street cleaners and did some more drinking in the white New Orleans morning sunlight. Drinking in the French Quarter in the early morning, after a night of booze, I found to be a unique and strangely delicious feeling. Like some Parisian a hundred years ago sitting with his raw umber and linseed oil before a virgin linen canvas, idly sniffing his armpits and working his wrist to loosen it.

Waiting for the perfect north light before he begins.

# I Shoulda Seen a Credit Arranger

A thousand to one longshot, I figured; the odds on Sam "The Bam" McMurtney finding me here, clear out in Fat City, but when Tommy LeClerc waltzed right up to me, I knew my goose was ready to be a Thanksgiving Day feature. Tommy was quick, had some street smarts, but he was only in Double-A Ball compared to Sam. If Tommy could find me, Sam wouldn't be far behind. I sighed and pointed at my glass, which the girl behind the bar filled with Jack then splashed water in it with her little gasoline pump.

"Keep the change," I said, pushing a five her way. I could have ordered the same for Tommy and he would have drunk it, being a Wild Turkey man and not knowing the difference, but I thought, what the hell, let him buy his own. Whatever news he's got has to be bad for me. And so it was.

"Turkey and Coke," he said, waiting until she poured the drink and named the price before he came up with three singles. He took one of the quarters and put it in his pocket.

"Sam's been looking for you."

"Well, if it ain't the *Times-Picayune*," I said, shaking my head and turning to look out over the pool tables. I was wishing one of them would open up. Shooting eight ball helps calm my nerves.

"I guess you know that already, else you wouldn't be out here in the boonies, in a Yat bar."

I didn't say anything. Whatever was on his mind would be on his tongue in five seconds, maybe less. Maybe he was the finger man and soon Sam or one of his assistants would walk through the front door and up to me and put one in my arm.

"I got a deal for you."

That got my ear, but I tried not to show it. "Yeah? What kind of deal? Robbing parking meters?"

13

Now he acted superior. "No, shithead, not parking meters. A real deal. Fifty, seventy-five big ones, maybe more. You owe Sam nine. Ain't no secret you could use a score."

Ninety-five, to be exact. That much was public knowledge. Any barkeep in the French Quarter could have phoned that bit of info in to the paper.

"That any a your business? I shoot my mouth off about how much you owe people?"

I was mad but that didn't stop the little roach from acting superior. I couldn't hide the fact I was interested, at least a little bit. I hated the little worm, just like about everybody else, and if he dropped the figure seventy-five K, it probably meant closer to twenty or thirty if even that, but he could be in on something. Hang around enough sewers, you find some quarters that fell in.

Tommy liked to act tough. He'd spent two years in some backwater prison up north before he'd come to New Orleans, and was forever yakking about it. Try and watch a movie with him!

"Naw," he'd say. "Whoever wrote this shit don't know from spit about the joint. In the joint they never say 'screws.' It's always 'hacks' or 'the Man.'"

Like I care.

"I made it my business," he was saying. "'Cuz I need a partner for this deal, and I said to myself, who is it needs money bad? Why, ol' Pete, that's who." (Now, Pete's not my real name, it's my middle name. Peter, actually. But when your first name's Evan, and you hang out where I do, you want to use something else.) Tommy still had his mouth going.

"Yessir, ol' Peteroo, that's who. Ol' Peteroo, who's gonna get his dick crushed when Sam th' Bam gets holt of him."

I got up, taking my drink with me. A table had just opened up. I walked back, stuck two quarters in the slot, and placed my drink on one of those little wooden racks on the wall.

"I'm not shitting you, Pete. This deal's worth at least a couple hunnert thou, almost half for you." He was right on my heels, yapping.

I racked up the balls and picked up a cue. "Tell you what, Tommy. You break. You put the eight ball in on the break, I'll talk to you." He curled his lip, sighted down the cue, and drew back. Damned if the eight ball didn't ricochet an inch from the corner pocket. Face-saving break for both of us.

"Okay, Tommy. What's the deal?"

\# \# \#

He made me go into the other room to hear his scam, but not till after we finished the game. I won and he still had six balls on the table.

"You buy the drinks, chump," I ordered, and damned if he didn't. The deal started to have a legitimate smell. The girl wasn't going to let us go into the other barroom since it didn't open till midnight when the music started, but five bucks took care of that. I paid. "Business conference," I said. She looked like she'd seen twenty, maybe thirty "business conferences" that week, and from the nobody's-home look in her eyes, had probably taken part in ten of them herself.

"Okay, Tommy," I said, once we'd sat down. "Make this quick. I'm kind of not waiting for someone."

\# \# \#

Fifty cents or so of gas after we left the bar, we were walking into this house somewhere in the Ninth Ward, in a part cops shy away from, and it was just like Tommy said.

"Holy Mother of God!" I say. "Holy fucking Christ!"

There he was, just like Tommy said, all tied up in a chair in the living room, a gag in his mouth. Tommy was ear-to-ear smiles.

"I told ya." He looked like he'd just hit his first trifecta.

"I'm leaving, Tommy. You're insane. I want no part of this. They electrocute you for this in this state. They don't let go of the switch till your brain looks like a Camelia Grill omelet." I turn to go and he grabs my arm.

"I ain't gonna kill him, man," he says, in a whiny voice. "Just cut his arm off, then let 'im go. That way, worst happens, we get busted for aggravated assault."

See what I meant about Double-A Ball? I was thinking hard about my car parked down the street, glad I'd made both of us drive. I tried to reason with him, knowing it was just a bad use of oxygen.

"Tommy, it doesn't matter if you ransom his hand, his balls or his whole self—it's still *kidnapping* any way you cut it. You think this'll get you a five-hundred-dollar fine and thirty days in slam? Who's your legal counsel—Peppermint Pattie?" I tried to leave again, but he jumped up in my face, eyes pleading.

"Just listen, Pete. I need money too. Sam's got me for three big ones. Listen!" He put his hands on my shoulders and leaned in close, spraying me with Wild Turkey. "Sam told me he'd take five hundred off my tab, I find you and turn you in. You owe me something for that. I coulda made a phone call for a quarter and got five bills erased and off the hook for another week."

I knew he spoke the truth. He wasn't slick enough to make that up, and besides, it was standard operating procedure for Sam. I'd almost turned in Fenton Brown for the same amount one time.

Besides, I recognized the man tied up in the chair. Not from traveling in the same circles, but from the paper. The man was Charles Lacy Deneuve, socialite, heir, and any other damned adjective you could tie to money. Old money. Uptown money. There was a story about Deneuve that showed how much money he had. He had this big yacht he kept out at Pontchartrain that he used to give all these big to-dos on, and one time he had this big dinner party with the mayor, the governor, the Mafia big-shot, even the Metry sheriff—that's how big the gig was—and it starts to sprinkle. Well, the head maître d' leads all the hob nobs downstairs where they see the exact same spread laid out, and another whole crew of coloreds was down there, throwing away courses in tune with the upstairs crowd as they finished up. It was set up just sos in the event of a rain like we get here in New Orleans from time to time, the honored guests wouldn't have to miss a bite of their Oysters Bienville. Somebody once told me that Aristotle Onassis did something like that too, only he got the idea from Deneuve, least that's what the guy that told me the story claims. Anyway, Deneuve was always pulling high-browed stunts like that to show he was the real thing, all right.

How Tommy'd got him here, tied up like the Marquis de Sade's best girl, spit dribbling from the corner of his mouth where a white rag protruded, I could only guess. Some said Deneuve was an old queen, so that was probably it. Tommy had been known to do some part-time hustling, just as he had been seen busting into parking meters for change. There wasn't a whole lot he drew the line at.

"Tommy, I'm telling you the truth. This is some bad shit here, man. You're gonna get fried and I'll get my face melted off just standing this close to you. I pass. I'll take my chances with Sam. Most he's likely to do is break a couple fingers, put a bullet in my instep. This here is serious shit."

I don't know why I'd even come this far, coming here in the first damned place. Greed, I guess. Most of us will sit up at the smell of a buck, and back at the bar, I'd seen where Tommy might have a way to some serious green. That was before I saw he had a real person here. That was there; this was here. I looked at that old man trussed up in the chair, eyes bugged out like a poodle giving birth to a litter of Great Danes, and I decided to depart. With haste.

"Hold on, pal. You're in this now. You're an accessory." He planted his body in my way and I saw how it was. Only exit was through him. That wasn't any concern; I could deck Tommy, but the noise might bring company. If someone saw me here with Tommy and Deneuve, I was going to be on a free bus ride to Angola State Prison, sure as birds fly south to Argentina and mechanics take Greyhounds to Detroit. I wasn't exactly up for Citizen of the Year, and it would be my word against Tommy's that I wasn't his rap-partner, and I knew already how that wind'd blow. Hurricane Tommy, that's the way it'd blow. Three months from this minute, we'd be sitting in a cell on an army blanket wondering who was gonna get to play the guy and who was gonna get the prom queen role. I sighed, thinking that my mother certainly never figured this for her baby boy. It's funny how you can just be minding your business, staying out of trouble, and it just comes and looks you up, no matter where you are. I could be in Timbuktu and just having a little cup of rice wine, shooting a little nine-ball, and here would come some jerk named Tom Won and get me in some fix.

"Okay, Tommy. When you gonna do it and what do I have to do?" I walked over and sat down on a sofa with brown flowers on it, across from Deneuve. It smelt like urine, but what the heck. I was already in the shit; what's a little piss? Tommy saw I wasn't going to make a break for it and came over and sat next to me. Near the door, though. I guess he didn't trust me that much. Deneuve gave out some kind of little moan, but I didn't look his way. If I didn't make eye contact, maybe I wasn't really here.

"Tonight. We'll do it tonight. Don't worry. I'll do all the hard stuff. Look at this."

He went over and grabbed a large grocery bag from the corner and brought it back. He dumped it out on the sofa. "Everything. I got everything here." He wasn't stretching the truth this time. Hacksaw, kite twine, pliers, soldering iron, box of baggies like you use to put dope in, a bottle of some clear stuff, rags that looked like old diapers, and a bottle of Wild Turkey. Some other odds and ends and that was it.

"Wild Turkey? That how you're gonna put him under? Oh, I'm going, Tommy. I'm really going now. See you around." Only I didn't get up. I should have.

"No, no, man. The Turkey's for us. I got chloroform for him. That stuff." He pointed to the bottle with the clear liquid.

"Okay, then what's the pliers for? I thought you were gonna cut his hand off. You gonna twist it like a piece of copper pipe?"

He laughed. My blood froze in the veins; I could feel it.

"You're a riot, man. Naw, I don't know why I got that. Just thought it might come in handy. I ain't never done this before, y'know. Hard telling what we'll need. Might as well be prepared."

"He's gonna bleed t'death, Tommy."

"No, man. No way. That's what the solder iron's for. To cauterize him. I read this story once that big-time wrasslers, like in the Olympics, use a hair curling iron to cauterize their nose if it gets broken so they can keep on wrasslin'. Figured you needed more heat for a cut-off hand, so we're gonna use the solder iron."

I was beginning to feel grateful that I wasn't some wealthy person of Tommy's acquaintance. If I was going to be part of this, I was at least happy to be sitting on the sofa with him and not across the room, facing him, all trussed up in a chair. I heard a kind of animal noise from Deneuve, through his nose, and even though I didn't look, I was pretty sure he'd come awake for a minute then just passed back out. All that talk about cauterizing must've upset him.

"Lookit this." Tommy shoved several pieces of xeroxed paper at me. They had drawings and a lot of words. Most, I had never seen before.

"Campbell's Operative Orthopaedics" it said in the corner of one of the pages.

"You read all this?" What I meant was: Did he *understand* all this.

"Sure. Well, most of it. Don't make much sense, though. They use a lotta college words and stuff. I can pretty well dope it out, though. Copied it in the library over at East Jeff Hospital. Told 'em I was a writer, doing an article on amputations."

I was wondering how Tommy could carry that scam off, when I remembered Mr. Moneybags Deneuve sitting six feet from me. If he could get a sharp dude like that up to this room in the Ninth Ward, he could sell pork rinds to a hog farmer.

"Ex-ten-sor dig-i-tor-um com . . . communis muscle," I read, tripping over the words, but proud I had learned phonics. I'd bet that was the first time those words had been uttered in this house, or even on this block.

"Ah, don't worry about that stuff. We don't have to know what it's called. All we gotta know is how to whack it off and how much it's worth to him."

"Tommy, what comic book did you get this idea out of?"

"It was in the *Times-Picayune*. Some guy over in East New Orleans got his hand caught in a conveyer belt or something. It was noon and everybody else was out chomping on a po-boy sandwich, so he grabs his mitt and walks four blocks t' the hospital and they cross-stitch it back on. It's as good as new, the paper says, and he goes back to work in six weeks, arm-wrassling his co-workers and everything. I got to thinking. If you was to snatch some rich dude and cut off his hand and hold it for ransom, it'd be better than the regular way. There's more advantages.

"First off, a guy what's got his hand detached ain't gonna go to the cops. He's gonna come up with the money, get his hand back, and then go to the cops. That gets rid of the dangerous part of kidnapping someone."

"What part's that?" I wanted to know.

"You know. When you kidnap a kid or a wife or something, they always call the FBI and you always get caught. Watch TV, learn something! See, you'd call the cops if they had your old lady and wanted a couple of million dollars—I mean, a *couple of million-fucking dollars*! But, if it was your right meathook, the hand you diddle your girlfriend with, the hand you pick your nose with, the hand you stroke your trouser worm with, well, hey buddy—are you gonna dick around with that? No way. We're talking a different story here now. You ain't gonna fart around with that hand, not like you would with the better half. You're gonna get the money up and get it to the kidnappers before it rots and you can't sew it back on."

He was grinning at his logic, and damned if I didn't have to agree with his flash of insight into the human heart. I knew he was right, though there were still a few details I wasn't too clear on.

"He'll go into shock," I said.

"Naw. . . . Well, prob'ly not. The guy in the paper didn't. He walked four blocks to the hospital, stepped up to the doctor and said, 'Shake, partner.'"

"Tommy!"

"Well, maybe he didn't say 'shake'—I just made that part up. But he did walk four blocks—that's in the paper. 'Sides, look at ol' Deneuve there. He's strong as a horse, especially for an old geezer. You wouldn't believe what he had in mind when we got here. I bet your ticker wouldn't take it!"

I didn't want to know, so I didn't inquire. Instead, I said, "Okay, smart-ass, you got this all doped out. But there's one thing you didn't figure."

"What?"

"How long's he got before it can't be sewn back on? I bet it's not very long."

He had been waiting for that question, like a kid for chocolate. I hated the smug way he answered.

"Eight hours. That's max. After that you got some minor problems. Like if you get it back on, it falls off in a stiff handshake. That's the gist of what the librarian at East Jeff said. I figure an hour after we whack his hand, we'll be on the road for Disneyworld, the back seat full of money. 'Sides, what's it matter he dies or his hand turns black? It's not like we was Doctor Kildare or something."

※ ※ ※

He planned to do it that night, when it got dark, though I don't know why it had to be at night. I guess probably it wasn't a bad idea—it'd be a lot harder for someone to see an old geezer stumbling into his mansion holding a bloody stump—but I think the real reason was Tommy's stomach. He wanted to get fried before he started working out with that hacksaw.

I still wasn't too clear what my part was going to be. Moral support, I suppose. We were going to ask for two hundred and fifty Gs, we decided. A hundred for me and the rest for Tommy. His idea, he said, so he deserved more. That part sounded fair.

This was all duly explained to Deneuve, but in small doses, as he kept passing out on us. Tommy read him the article he'd clipped out of the paper, and I'm damned if he wasn't telling the truth. I read it myself, soon as he was done using it for the Kidnap Story Hour.

Deneuve took this all in, the whites of his eyes bulging and little snorting sounds coming from his nose. He couldn't comment too much as he had a handkerchief stuffed into his mouth, but he got the drift, you could tell.

"We gotta let him know the score," Tommy says, while we wait for Deneuve to wake up from his latest nap. "I think he's got the picture, don't you? He wants his hand back, he's gonna have t' play ball with us." I started to make a joke about how's he gonna play ball with his throwing arm minus an essential part, but I let it go.

The deal was that he would be released in front of his house and we'd wait fifteen minutes for him to come out with the money. His hand would be back in Tommy's house in a baggie in the fridge. I wondered what would keep Deneuve from just riding back with his chauffeur and getting his hand back his own self, but Tommy said he'd already covered that, having blindfolded Deneuve a few blocks before they got to the house on the pretext of some kinky game. Tommy ran this all by Deneuve and made him nod that he understood, even though he was trying to say something. The gag in his mouth kept that from happening.

It looked like I was in this for good or bad, so I decided to help Tommy out with the Wild Turkey.

※ ※ ※

I must have caught a little nap 'cause when I looked up, I was lying on the floor and Tommy was lugging Deneuve over to the sofa. The old man was making a kind of high-pitched whining noise, sort of the sound a jet makes when it's warming up, getting ready to hit the skies for the Bahamas. I sat up and rubbed my eyes.

"Whatcha doin'?"

Sweat was falling off both their faces, Tommy's from exertion and Deneuve's from concern.

"What's it look like I'm doing? I'm putting 'im on the operating table, ass-wipe. Your arm broke, you can't help?" His words had that Wild Turkey mush to them.

I got up, a little wavy, but he already had Deneuve on the couch, legs and arms both tied, arms in front. Tommy wiped his face with his sleeve and reached over for the bottle of chloroform, keeping his knee on Deneuve's chest. Deneuve hummed louder.

"He wants t'tell us something," I said. Tommy gave me a drop dead look I wasn't too crazy about, and said, "No shit he wants t' tell us something. He wants t' tell us not to cut his hand off and he'll be so grateful if we just do him that favor that he'll run along home and get the money for us and we won't have to go to all this trouble. He wants t' tell us he'll throw in another hundred thousand, free, just for us being so kind and benevolent." He snorted. "You sure you're not a Sunday school teacher or something? I swear t' God, Pete, some-times I think you just got your first pair of long pants."

He turned back to his work and I stepped over to see if I could be of help—not that I really wanted to. Tommy got the lid to the bottle off, soaked a rag in it and shoved it in the old man's face. You could see Deneuve struggling like a girl on her first date, and then quicker than I would have thought, his body just sort of went *whoosh*, like the air'd been let out, and he was under.

"This is some good shit," Tommy said. Good shit; it was great! I was feeling a bit better seeing Deneuve out cold. He didn't mean nothing to me, but I hate to see any man suffer. The chloroform stunk terrible. I stepped over and grabbed the rag and threw it as far as I could. Unfortunately, when I threw it, I knocked over the jar of chloroform which Tommy had neglected to close. All of a sudden, it stunk to high heaven and I was getting hazy.

"Jesus Christ!" Tommy yelled. "We'll all be out!" He had a point. My peepers were already feeling heavy. The fumes were everywhere. Tommy was screeching something about grabbing the bottle and some rags. The room was going in slow motion and it was hard to concentrate.

"Just shut up," I said, murder in my thoughts. Murder must have been in my voice, too. Tommy glared at me and I could see his bad eye drooping and I wondered which one of us was gonna fade out first. He tried to say something else, but he must've forgot cause nothing came out. I waded through what felt like swamp mud but what I could see was only thick air and fumbled through the things Tommy'd thrown on the floor and got hold of one of the diapers and soaked up as much of the spill as I could. I left the rag there to soak and put the lid back on the bottle, but it was more than half gone. I was really getting woozy. I threw the diaper over in the corner with the first rag and the air seemed to clear a little. Then I remembered Tommy and he wasn't there. He was gone.

I have to admit it. I panicked. There was Deneuve lying on the sofa, out like Ali's sparring partner, chloroform flooding the air, and no Tommy. I did the only thing I could.

I screamed.

"Tommeeeeeee!"

"What?" he said in this normal voice that made me jump about as high as the ceiling, and there he was, over at the door, inhaling the oxygen from the outside. He just shook his head at me and closed the door and went back over to the sofa. I worried for an instant about somebody hearing my yell and decided it didn't matter, not in this neighborhood.

Tommy was already busy with the task at hand. He sat next to Deneuve, who was still nodding out on the couch, and cut the ropes. He grabbed the old man's left hand and slung the arm over the couch, then reached for the hacksaw.

"Wait a minute, Tommy," I said. "Does it matter which hand you cut off?"

That gave him pause. "Yeah," he decided, after a second. "The right hand, I think. He might hardly never use his left." He flung the first hand back and grabbed the other one, bringing the ax to Deneuve's wrist.

"How do you know for sure he's right-handed?"

The action stopped again. Tommy looked at the hand he held, glared up at me, then glared at the hand. "You're a son-of-a-bitch, Pete," he said. He put the saw to the wrist, took it away, put it back again, and withdrew it once more.

I could see the fury in his eyes. He let go of the hand.

"You're a bastard, Pete. Why'd you have to bring up something like that for anyway? How the hell should I know if he's right or left-handed? I fucking sure ain't gonna wait for him to wake up and ask him." He picked up the other hand and placed the blade to the wrist. "Sometimes you got to take chances in life, Pete. This is one of those times. I'm cutting this one."

It was the left hand. I pointed that out.

He stood up, thrust Deneuve's hand from him like he'd seen all of it he wanted to, and stomped out of the room, into the kitchen. I could hear him slamming drawers and cupboards around and something fell and broke and then he came back out, a water glass in his hand. He found the bottle of Wild Turkey and poured himself half a glass and went back into the kitchen. I decided not to join him. It got real quiet in there.

After awhile, I went in to check. He was sitting at the kitchen table, just staring at the empty glass. Before I could say anything, a thumping noise came from the living room, like the front door banging. Tommy looked at me and the same thought struck both our brains at the same time.

Deneuve!

He was gone. The room was empty and the front door wide open.

"Oh, God," says Tommy. "OhGodohGodohGodohGod!" Over and over he said it. I sprinted to the door and there he was, halfway down the walk, pulling himself along with his hands. He must've still been too groggy to think about untying his feet.

"Tommy! Here he is!"

We flew out the door and grabbed him. For someone half dopey from chloroform, he sure put up one hell of a struggle. We lost him once, he broke completely away, and then we just picked him up like a sack of uncooperative potatoes, and hauled his ass back inside, looking every which way while we're doing it, checking if any of the neighbors was out.

We were in luck. There didn't seem to be anybody out on the street except us—a couple of star-crossed kidnappers and their victim. We hustled him back inside and threw him on the couch again and Tommy tied his hands back up while I closed and locked the door. He had to bust him in the chops to quiet him down a little. Worked about as good as the chloroform, 'cept for the trickle of blood that ran down his nose.

"Jesus, Tommy," I said, standing by the door and peeking out to see if the cops were coming. "Can you believe it! Is this just not our night, or what?"

All you could hear was the rasping of our breath, Tommy's and mine, and Deneuve wheezing through his nose. He hadn't thought to take the handkerchief out while he was loose, which was a good thing for us. One more good yell and it didn't matter what neighborhood we were in, somebody would've got nosy and called the cops. The blood running from his nose had saturated the gag until it looked like a six-year-old girl's washcloth after her first self-taught lipstick lesson.

"Hell, I hope he don't bleed t' death from his nose before he does his hand," I said, attempting to inject some levity into the situation, which didn't work.

Deneuve started making movements again, so Tommy went over to where I'd thrown the rags and brought one back and put it over his nose and Deneuve relaxed right away.

"Let's do it, Pete," he said. He went into the kitchen and brought back the whiskey bottle and took a huge pull and handed it to me. I took one about as big. I looked at the bottle and figured we'd better go ahead and do it. The bottle was seven-eights gone. Once we started sobering up, it might be a bit harder to go on with the operating. For Tommy, that is. There was no way I was capable of cross-cutting that hand, even if I had the blind staggers. That was Tommy's department, all the way.

Tommy gave Deneuve another hit off the rag and cut his hands loose again. He picked up the hacksaw and tested the sharpness on his thumb, then reached over, swigged the last of the Turkey and announced he was ready to commence. He also started talking out loud to himself.

"Asshole don't understand how hard this is. Had to psyche myself up for hours to be able to do this. Think know-it-all-jackasses'd have the guts to do this? No way, José! This is a very delicate operation. Takes the courage of a lion."

He paused, peeking at me out of the corner of his eye, to see if I'd been listening and was properly ashamed. He took a deep breath and clenched his teeth, the words hissing as he continued to mumble to himself.

"Fuck it, Tommy. Just do it."

He drew the saw in a backstroke to get the teeth started, the way you do when you saw the barrel off a .12 gauge. I had come over and was standing in front, not a foot away, and at first there was nothing, not even a line. Then it turned white and then pink, and then, man! The blood began to seep like water over a kid's wading pool when you forget to watch the hose. The booze I'd drunk began a slow boil in the pit of my stomach, like a belly dancer workshop going on in there.

"Harder. Got to do it harder," Tommy hissed, and put more wood into it on the downstroke. That's when the juice really started to come, not spurting but flowing. Heavy-duty flowing.

"Shit!" Tommy yelled. "I forgot to plug in the solder iron. Where the hell is it?"

I found it on the coffee table and ran to plug it in. The cord wasn't going to reach to the couch—I seen that right away. I left it plugged in, dropping the iron to the floor, and ran around looking for a closer outlet. There wasn't any. Tommy had dropped the saw and was holding Deneuve's forearm in both hands, applying pressure. His face was whiter than the sheet of a Klansman at an induction meeting. Beads of sweat were popping out all over him. He wasn't smiling. The blood continued to run, but not as much, and just then Deneuve moaned and tried to sit up.

"Holy shit!" Tommy screeched. "He's comin' to! Get the fuckin' chloroform!"

"Which you want, the chloroform or the iron?!" I yelled. The organization of this job was not as tight as it could have been.

"The fucking chloroform!"

I ran across the room looking for the rags I'd tossed. I found one in a jiffy and ran back with it. Tommy was trying to hold the bleeding arm with one hand and punch Deneuve with the other. I stuck the rag over Deneuve's nose and mouth. He opened his eyes, wide, not six inches from mine, and then they slammed shut. At the same instant, he tensed and then slumped back into the sofa. Tommy's face was soaking wet and there was blood everywhere. It looked like an Indian massacre.

"Get the iron," Tommy ordered, his words high and reedy. "We got to cauterize him as we go."

I looked at where I'd left the iron and both of us saw it at the same time. You couldn't actually make out the iron itself, as it was hidden in smoke. The carpet was on fire.

Not actual flames, but sort of smoldering.

"Holy fuck," was all Tommy could say. "Holy fuck."

I must not have given Deneuve as good a dose of the chloroform as I thought, cause he shot straight up, eyes big as canteloupe halves. Tommy just smacked him, sucker-punched him and he went as limp as the gay caballero's handshake. I ran over and grabbed the cord and snatched the iron, stomping on the burning rug. There was a red glow in the carpet, but now was not the time to put it out. I gave it another stomp, sending sparks flying, but I couldn't stay around playing fire department. Tommy was shrieking and acting generally like Sybil with all the personalities turned loose at once. I ran the iron over to him. It seemed to be what he wanted most, though it was hard to tell. He was yelling about everything—me, Deneuve, the fire, his ex-wife, everything. I thrust the iron at him and he grabbed the business end.

"Fu-uuuck!" He was in some kinda pain, seemed to me. "You stupid!"

Me! He was yelling at me! Like I was the blind idiot what had latched onto the wrong end.

"Listen, Tommy," I said. "There's no sense getting mad at me. Open your eyes and watch what you're grabbing."

I was getting more than tired of his screeching and his orders, and especially his constant panics. "I just might leave."

"No!" he screamed, his voice hysterical. "Don't go! Don't go! It'll be all right. We'll hit him a shot with the iron and then you run back and plug it in again. Do that two, three times, we got it. Next time lay it on a plate or something from the kitchen."

It was hard to concentrate with the smoke and everything. I ran in the kitchen and got a glass of water and came back and threw it on the embers.

Tommy had the iron in one hand and Deneuve's bloody paw in the other. He laid it on the cut. It was still plenty hot enough. Flesh sizzled and a picture of fast food steakhouses flashed in my mind. Then, the smell hit me and it must have hit Tommy about the same time, since regurgitating Wild Turkey hit the deck in two different places at almost the same second. We couldn't have been more precise if we was the Rockettes or the Saints' cheerleaders.

Just then, Deneuve decided to take a crap, being as how he'd missed his morning constitutional, and things were getting spicy. There was a regular smorgasbord of smells in that room, including the puke up my nose. This was not the way I'd envisioned the proceedings.

✄ ✄ ✄

I was halfway down the block by the time Tommy caught up to me.

"Where the hell you goin'?" He yanked at my arm but I pulled away from him.

"Come on back, Pete. We're not done. You're kissin' away a quarter of a million bucks." I just stared at him and went on walking. I didn't have a clue where I was walking to and I didn't much care. Let Sam eradicate me. It was just too much trouble. I was fresh out of ambition and energy. Tommy clutched at my arm again.

"Touch me again, Tommy, and I'll kill you. I'll hit you so hard I'll wipe out half your family. Just get the hell out of my face."

He didn't say anything, just turned and walked back toward the house, head down. I watched him for a minute. I could tell which house he was making for. It was the one with all the smoke coming out. He began to run the last few feet. I waited until I saw him go inside and then I began walking away.

Six blocks I walked before I became aware of a car creeping alongside me, just behind. Cops, I thought, not looking, and then I heard sirens. A fire truck came hurtling around the next corner and turned toward me. Oh, sweet Jesus, Angola here I come!

But it wasn't cops behind me. It was Tommy.

"Get in," I heard him say, his voice weary. Windows were popping open on both sides of the street and people were starting to come out of their houses. Another fire engine raced by, sirens blaring. I had no choice.

Soon as I was in, he accelerated. Neither of us spoke for awhile, and then I had to know.

"What happened?"

"What happened where?"

"Back there. With Deneuve. Did you go back?"

"Yeah."

That's all he said. I waited a minute and then said, "Well?"

"Well, what?"

"Did you do it?"

"What do you think?"

"No," I said.

"I almost did. He was comin' to and the smoke was really gettin' thick. If I'd had a *partner* (the word came out like a curse word), I could've done it. How's it feel to blow two hundred fifty Gs?"

We were quiet for a long time. I had no idea where he was driving until we were on the Causeway. Fat City. He was heading back to the bar he'd found me in. My car was there, but Sam knew what it looked like and I didn't think it would be a good idea to be seen in it just now. If Tommy had found me, that meant others weren't too far behind.

We went into the bar and a different girl was bartending. The joint was jammed now, even the other side, and heavy metal music made it hard to talk. Not that we were doing much of that anyway. I ordered both of us a drink and Tommy laid his keys on the bar, searching through his pockets.

"Got a quarter?" he asked, sullenly.

I handed him one.

"Gotta call the wife," he said, getting up and heading to the pay phone in the lobby.

While he was away, I took the ignition key off his key chain.

He came back and I took my turn, excusing myself to go to the bathroom. Before I left, I ordered another round and laid a ten on the bar. The bathroom was in the other room, where all the dancers were. I went past it without looking and on out to the parking lot, where I jumped in Tommy's car and hit the juice. Ten minutes later, I was paying the toll-taker a buck and heading north across Pontchartrain.

I wondered what Sam the Bam would say when he walked in and Tommy told him I was in the bathroom.

I couldn't help laughing.

I didn't know what I was going to do. It was for sure that New Orleans was too hot for me now, what with owing Sam nine thousand five hundred, and Deneuve getting ready to go through mug books and chat with a police artist within an hour. Florida, I thought. That was the one good idea Tommy'd had. I had a few bucks in my jeans and knew a girl in Sarasota who'd take me in.

Coming off the bridge into Covington, I saw a billboard with a cartoon figure of a guy with a worried look on his kisser, cartoon sweat peppering the air around him. The caption said, "Money Worries? In Debt? Call The Blarney Credit Arrangers For Help! Get Out From Under That Mountain!"

The guy in the billboard's face stayed with me clear into Gulf Shores.

I shoulda seen a credit arranger. I shoulda seen that sign six hours earlier. I shoulda looked at the gas gauge sooner, cause just then the little red light went on and I had to coast over to the side of the road.

# It's Different

As a boy, he had watched his mother grow bigger with the child that would become his sister. The larger her belly grew, the more repulsed he became, shrinking from her touch, afraid to touch her skin. Two reasons. She might explode, expel the thing inside her. Her skin, the skin on her upper arms that had gotten thicker, felt cool, clammy. Skin that enveloped fatness.

Now, he had one himself. A pregnant wife.

It's all right, he'd say to her. I think you're beautiful. You're not fat, you're just pregnant.

Do you mean it? she'd say, several times. Do you really mean it? I remember when we were going together you said you thought pregnant women were gross.

I was kidding, he'd say, flashing his teeth. That was *other* women, not you. It's different.

Then, he'd feel as though he should make love to her. After, he'd say to her: See?

Take me to a movie, she said. They never went to movies. Hardly ever. They'd skip a year, sticking to television, and then go on a movie frenzy, one or even two a night for two weeks. Then, it was back to the TV for awhile, six, seven months, sometimes longer.

Now it was her eighth month and she craved movies.

They went. They saw Richard Pryor in the movie where he was blind and Gene Wilder was deaf. Richard Pryor looks skinny, he said, leaving that movie. I wonder if he's on drugs again. They saw Robin Williams as the English teacher. He laughed at the end, even more when she cried, but that didn't mean anything; anymore, she cried at lettuce wilting.

Take me to a movie, she said. I would like to see a movie. You choose.

We just went, he'd say, concentrating on the crossword puzzle. He made himself do all the "down" words before he'd even start the across words, even when the across answers leaped up at him, demanding to be filled in. He was secretly proud of his discipline.

Watch TV, he said. That show you like is on tonight. *Thirty Something.*

You hate that show, she said.

I didn't say I'd watch it, he came back. I just said you should watch it. You like it. You like shows about people without real problems that think they have real problems. You even cry at it these days. You even cry at the Bob Newhart show these days, when Steffi can't find anything to wear.

You think I'm fat, she said. That's why you don't want to go in public with me.

⁂

There were cars everywhere at the mall, all scooting around looking for spaces to park. He let her off at the movie, in front of it, and went to look for a place and to have a last cigarette. He had to park a long ways off. He could have parked closer but somebody in a Corvette took up two spaces, angling across both. It made him furious. If he'd had a church key, he'd do something to it, he thought.

They went in and got their seats first, down to the left, halfway down, early enough to get seats in the middle. She went to get the popcorn and soft drinks; only after she had been gone for awhile did he think about feeling guilty for allowing a pregnant woman to go instead of offering to do it himself. He wondered if anyone noticed. The thought made his eyes narrow and he looked around, belligerently.

It was a matinee and the theater was only half-crowded. In front of them and to the right was an older woman and beside her a younger version of herself and a young man. They were all three talking. Mother and daughter, he decided, and son-in-law. He wondered where the older woman's husband was. Probably smarter than me and stayed home, he guessed, smiling.

His wife returned, with one box of popcorn to share, as well as a single drink, and with a box of JuJuBees, his favorite.

She chattered as usual, and then the lights went out and they were given a film lecture about not smoking in the theater and asked to please throw trash in the trash bins and not on the floor. Feeling the stickiness under his shoes, he figured there hadn't been much attention paid to that one during the showing before.

There was a commercial, showing all the things that could be purchased in the lobby, and he said to his wife in a loud whisper, if I'd seen the pictures of that stuff first, I'd never buy it—it looks terrible. Then, there were two previews that didn't look too good and then they were into the feature.

He saw his wife was flushed, giddy almost. Her craving was being satisfied. She smiled and whispered to him, her hand on his forearm. For a minute, he thought maybe he ought to put his arm around her shoulders, but he didn't. He nodded at her questions and smiled back at her with his mouth, one eye on the movie, and then the older woman in front of them turned around and said in a loud voice,

"Would you guys be quiet?"

The woman didn't look either of them in the eyes, but stared school-teacherishly along a plane to the left of him, and then turned back around.

At first, they didn't respond, other than to stop talking, and then they looked at each other, the red creeping up his neck. Not that anyone could see it in the dark, but he could *feel* it, and his wife got the same expression on her face she did when the child had kicked hard against her ribs, her eyes round and luminous.

What'd she say, he said.

His wife lifted her hands and shrugged.

It's a fucking adventure, he said in a loud whisper. It's Indiana-fucking-Jones, not a goddamned French art film.

He thought of all the things he'd wished he'd said, but it was too late. The moment had passed. He kept thinking about what he should have said, and when he had two or three clever ones, he began whispering to his wife again, but the woman didn't turn around.

The movie was ruined for both of them. They tried to get back into it, but all either could think of was the woman shushing them.

He kept imagining scenarios with the woman. He'd get off one of the retorts he'd come up with and the man on the other side, the son-in-law, would turn around and say something. Then he'd say to him, *don't fuck with me, country. You don't want to fuck with me.* Only he never got to say it. The woman spoiled it by ignoring their whispering.

Then, the credits were rolling and they were walking up the aisle.

In the lighted lobby, packed with people leaving the three theaters and other people standing behind a rope, waiting to take their place, he looked around for the woman.

Come on, his wife said. Let it be.

He started to say something to her when he spotted them. The woman was just coming out, around the corner, stuffing something into her fat mouth. Her daughter and son-in-law were just behind her.

And then, an odd thing happened. The woman stopped dead still, and the people behind her, her daughter and son-in-law and everyone else, ran into her, the ones farthest back streaming around the sudden island.

She's choking, said his wife. She's got something in her throat.

Yes, he said. It looks like it.

You know Heinlich, she said. You used it on Wayne at work. That piece of white chocolate. Remember?

It's *Heimlich*, he said. Heimlich with an M. I remember. Yeah.

The daughter and son-in-law were standing around her and some other people too, but farther away. The son-in-law was patting her on the back. She just stood there, her eyes buggy and her skin turning blue, her hands sort of waving up and down at the wrists, like a little kid does when they get out of a swimming pool into the chilly air.

She's choking to death, his wife said. You know the Heimlich thing.

He looked at the woman. Her eyes, darting wildly in either direction, locked with his.

He turned and grabbed his wife's hand. Let's go, he said, and pulled her toward the door.

They were through it and outside, and he thought it was strange how, with all the people, inside and out, it was oddly quiet. People were standing around in little pods, whispering, talking quietly, their hands over their mouths, all staring back through the glass doors at the woman choking. Word spreads fast, he said to his wife, and started to pull her towards the car when he stopped and let go of her hand.

Well, shit, he said, and began to walk back toward the theater doors. She stood there a minute and then followed. He shoved the door open and stalked toward the woman, but a man in a maroon jacket, an usher, came at a run and got there before he did. The usher stepped up behind the woman, whipped his arms around her, making a fist in front, and yanked the woman back towards him.

Something dark and slimy expelled itself. It missed him, where he was standing next to his wife, but some of the goo that came with it landed on his shoe. He turned on his heel and went back out, grabbing his wife's hand on the way, his eyes dark and jaw muscles twitching.

When he got to the car, he dug around in the glove compartment, while his wife stood and waited, until he found an old napkin from Burger Chef, which he used to wipe off his shoe. He threw the napkin on the ground and only then stood aside to allow his wife to climb into the car. He walked around to his side and got in and drove home, not asking his wife if she wanted to stop on the way for some ice cream or a soft drink.

After the ten o'clock news, they turned off the television and went to bed. He finished the crossword with the night-light on and then flicked it off.

Lying in the dark, both silent for a while, and then his wife reached over and put her hand on his penis. It didn't respond.

You think I'm fat, don't you? she said.

No, he said, staring up at the ceiling. You're just pregnant. It's not the same. It's different. Really.

Oh? she said, withdrawing her hand and turning over on her side, away from him.

I mean . . .

I know what you mean. I know exactly what you mean.

It was silent in the bedroom for long minutes.

When he finally had it together, the words he wanted to use, he spoke her name softly, once, then again. There was no response. He listened to her breathing, realized she had fallen asleep.

He got up, went out into the living room, fished through the pile of yesterday's newspaper sections until he found the crossword. Number one, down, read, "The ___ We Were." He inked in "WAY." This was going to be an easy one.

Tomorrow, he thought. First thing when we wake up. I'll talk to her, explain.

"Unattended" was the second one down. It wasn't until he got to "Pathetic one," number seven down, that his pen paused even briefly, but then he got it and moved smoothly on, swiftly writing in all capitals, until he had filled in all the down blanks. Filling in the blanks across went so effortlessly he had to laugh. Theme puzzles were a no-brainer.

# Broken Seashells

He tested each shell between his fingers. Those about to break he placed in a plastic sack. Those too strong to break between his fingers he returned to the sand.

He had walked nearly a mile and the bag was just about full.

After a few more yards the bag was filled as much as it would ever be. He walked over to a large piece of driftwood, sat on the sand and began taking the shells out, one by one, placing them in neat rows of three each.

Suddenly, a small boy appeared and asked, "What are you doing that for?"

The man smiled, a small reflection of a smile, as he lifted his gaze to meet the boy's.

"Because I always do this now, that's why."

The boy was silent. The man could see he was thinking.

"That sounds crazy to me," the boy said, after a time.

"It sounds like a very sane thing to me," the man said. Neither spoke for a space as the man went about his task of placing the shells where he wanted them and the boy looked on. When all the shells were in rows he stared for a long moment at his creation and then he started putting them back into the bag, very gently and very carefully.

He began talking to the boy again as he worked.

"How old are you?"

"Nine. Nine and a half."

"Can you remember when you were four?"

"Sure."

"So can I."

"You can?"

"Sure. You know what I remember?"

"Going to the beach?"

"No. I'm reasonably certain there wasn't any beach. We couldn't afford the beach, I don't imagine."

There was another silence and then the boy spoke.

"Well, then, what do you remember?"

"I remember something tragic. Something extremely tragic and sad."

"What was it?" The boy's brow furrowed.

"I don't know, exactly. It was something I did and was punished for, I think. Broke something or other, I expect. Or sassed my mother. Something like that."

One of the shells the man was handling broke. He stopped talking for a moment, staring at the delicate pieces in his hand until his eyes grew moist. The boy looked at him and then away, uncomfortable. The man held the pieces to his cheek tenderly for a second and then put them in the bag. It was the only broken one.

"Anyway, my mother punished me. Spanked me and yelled at me. I remember a very intense feeling of rejection and wanting her to kiss me and say she was sorry." He thought for a minute, seeing past the years. "She didn't. She ignored me completely. You see, she was angry with me. Does your mother ever get angry with you?"

The boy answered instantly. "Sure. Lots of times. Boy, I'll say!"

"What does she do when she's angry?"

"Different things. Sometimes she smacks me and sometimes she just yells. Sometimes she doesn't do anything but look mad and not talk to me. You know."

"I know. I especially know. I decided to run away."

"Now?"

"No, not now. Then. When I was four."

"I ran away once."

"Did you go back?"

"Of course. Didn't you?"

"I ran away. I told my mother what I was going to do and she said she'd help me. She asked me what I'd need and I said all I needed was some food. She said to take whatever I wanted. I took a full loaf of bread." The man paused for a picture that formed in his head. "I took my jacket, too. And I was crying. You see, I wanted her to say she loved me and was sorry and ask me not to run away. Only she didn't. All she did was say she hoped I'd be very happy wherever I was going.

"I went to the front door of our apartment and looked back. She wasn't even watching me. I waited a long time but she never once turned around. Then, I went out the door and closed it behind me. I didn't know where to go."

The man's words came closer now, with fewer breaks between sentences. He wasn't looking at the boy or even at the ocean before him, but farther away than that, a long, long distance away.

"I went downstairs to the front door of the building and sat on the bottom step. I decided to wait there until she came out to look for me. I waited three hours and the door never opened. It was snowing." The man took a moment to draw air deeply into his lungs before he plunged ahead.

"I waited three hours and I ate some bread. I ate the whole loaf. I wanted her to open that door so badly. I don't know how long I would have gone on waiting or what I would have done eventually, but it was decided for me. My father came home from work. He asked me what I was doing sitting on the step. I told him and he laughed. He laughed! Then, he got angry. He jerked me up, said my mother was probably worried sick, and hauled me up the stairs. I was kicking, fighting him, but I didn't scream or anything. I didn't want to go back there. I wanted my mother to come after me. I *needed* her to come after me."

The man stopped.

"That's a very sad story, sir. What happened then?"

"Nothing. I don't know. Oh yes. My mother laughed and my father did too and then she said, 'Well, I guess you've found out that your home isn't as bad as you thought, haven't you?' And that was all there was to it. Except . . . " He paused and looked out at the waves. "Except, my own son ran away once. I don't think I'll tell you about that."

The man straightened up with his bag of shells and the boy stood as well. They both looked out at the water for a few minutes, and then the boy said good-bye and walked away. The man stared after him for a minute and then seemed to decide something. He hurried after the boy.

"Wait."

The boy looked up. He had forgotten the man. He hadn't heard him coming across the sand and it made him jump a little, his voice coming up behind him like that.

"Yes sir?"

The man looked at him and the boy thought; lost *eyes*. He wasn't exactly sure what that meant, it was just something that came into his head.

"I didn't explain that very well," the man was saying. "I told the wrong story."

He didn't know if the man was dangerous or not, one of those people he was always getting warned about, but something said he wasn't. He decided not to take any chances, however.

"I live right over there," the boy said, crooking his head. "Right behind that dune. See? You can see the top of my house. The white one. My mom's probably out in the yard hanging up clothes. She'll come to the top in a minute and wave at me. She usually does."

"We'll wave back," the man said. "She'll see it's all right. I . . ."

He paused, then put his bag on the sand and sat down beside it. The boy remained standing, facing the dune behind which his house stood.

"That wasn't the story I wanted to tell. That wasn't the right story. The story I wanted to tell was about Lord Ha-Ha."

"Lord who?" He thought he saw his mom's head appear for just a second at the top of the dune, but then he knew it wasn't her, just a swirl of sand in the wind.

"Lord Ha-Ha. During World War Two. He was a guy, a propaganda guy for the Germans. Like Tokyo Rose. You've heard of Tokyo Rose?"

The boy didn't say anything, just kicked at the sand with his bare foot and continued to stare at the dune.

"I suppose not. Anyway, that's not the important thing. What's important is what my father did. He was a bomber pilot."

That got the boy's attention.

"He *was*? Jets?"

The man smiled a little.

"No, this was before jets, I think. Prop job. B-17s, I think. They flew across the Channel from England, dropped bombs on the Germans. It was a war, so it was okay."

"Did he get shot down? I saw a movie once where the pilot got shot down. Bermuda, I think it was. No, Burma, that was it. It was a jungle, like in Africa. Was that about your dad?"

The man reached over and lifted the front of his bag and peered inside. Satisfied, he let it fall.

"No, that was a different part. A different *theater*. That's what they called them, *theaters*. Theaters of war. Like it was a goddamned play or something."

"Sir, I—"

"I'm sorry. I usually don't curse. Excuse me. I won't do it again."

The boy looked in the man's eyes and saw that he was telling the truth and then he looked back at the dune.

"What happened was, my dad bombed an orphanage. By mistake."

"Why would he do that?"

"I told you, it was a mistake. He didn't mean to do it. They got the wrong coordinates, whatever they steer by. The navigator, the man who tells the pilot where to go, he made a mistake. Or, maybe intelligence screwed up. Whatever. The thing was, it was one of those

things everybody feels bad about, but they happen. War is hell."
Hurriedly, he added, "That's not cussing, son."

The boy considered this, noting the man's anxious expression,
and then he nodded.

"When they got back, that's all Lord Ha-Ha talked about. For
weeks. On the radio. He even named names. He named my father's
name. Called him a baby-killer."

The boy got tired of looking at the dune. It looked like his mother
wasn't going to show up for a wave, but he didn't care now. He
wanted to leave this man, walk down farther and see if he could
scare up a fiddler crab. You could throw them up in the air and a gull
would snatch it. It was the coolest thing. He didn't know a good way
to excuse himself from this man, though.

"You've got things to do, places to go, I can see that," the man
said. "It's okay. I'm just about done."

Now the boy really wanted to go. He began hopping from one
foot to the other, looking down at the sand. He made his feet land in
the same spot each time, making the footprints deeper each time he
came down.

"I think what happened was my dad felt so guilty about those
kids, he felt like he didn't deserve to have any himself." The man
stood up, reached down and picked up his bag.

"That's all I wanted to tell you," he said. "Now you understand
it all. Listen," he said, suddenly sticking his hand out. The boy understood the man wanted to shake his hand. He felt it would be all
right so he brought his own hand up. The man's hand felt soft, mushy,
and surprisingly, *small*. It felt like a kid's hand, not a grown man's.
He withdrew his own hand first, as soon as he felt he could.

"You see your mom, you give her a wave for me. Okay?" The
man threw his bag of shells over his shoulder and walked down to
the edge of the ocean and struck out along the shoreline, gazing out
occasionally at the boats far out on the horizon as he hurried along.

The boy walked on and on, in the opposite direction, looking back every hundred yards or so, until he could no longer see the man.

Then a woman came along and hallowed to the boy.

"Yes ma'am?" he said when she neared.

"Have you seen a man on the beach wearing a pair of blue bathing trunks?"

"Maybe," he said.

"Collecting seashells?"

"He was here a while ago."

"Did you talk to him?" she asked.

"Yes ma'am. He told me a story."

"About the kidnapping? When his son was stolen when he took him to the park? When his son got mad and told him he was running away? When they found him later, dead?"

"No, ma'am. Not that one. He told me a story about when he ran away from home. When he was four. He ate a loaf of bread. Then, one about his father dropping bombs. On little kids."

"Oh. That one. God."

The woman said something else under her breath the boy couldn't quite hear, but it sounded like cursing. He thought she said a "Jesus" and then *the word*, the worst word of all, and then she asked him a question.

"Which way did he go?"

He pointed.

"Are you his mother?" he said.

"Sometimes," she said. A brief chuckle escaped. It didn't sound cheerful to the boy. "Sometimes I'm his wife. It depends on the day of the week and how many he's had."

"Are you looking for seashells, too?" he said.

There was no answer, for the woman was already moving away, striding at a brisk, unswerving pace.

She'd been crying, the boy thought.

*Grownups*, he thought, and then he thought no more about the man and the woman, but ran down to the edge of the beach, making footprints in the wet sand. He stood and waited to see how long it would be before the waves washed out the marks his feet had made.

# Princess

W e had just come out of the Royal Sonesta when I looked up and there he was. I don't know if he saw me or not, and I looked the other way the second I recognized him, and the next time I peeked, he was gone.

Teddy had just picked me up at the Fairmont. Ché had just highlighted my hair; he's the best in town, and we decided to have some étouffée at the Sonesta.

Boy, did a chill go through me! I hadn't seen Evan since the annulment. Once, I thought I did, right after I got back from my Aunt Desderada's (Dee Dee), in Virginia, at PJs on Magazine. They have the best coffee in New Orleans. Everybody goes there.

I had just come out, after buying some dark roast, and I saw the back of this man's head. He was standing outside PJs with his back to me, and my little heart just jumped up in my mouth! He turned and I thought I'd faint, but it wasn't him. Even so, I dropped the coffee and the package broke. I had to go back and buy another. That was just like Evan. Even when he wasn't there, he was causing me grief!

My momma told me right from the start that I shouldn't go out with him. His family wasn't right. He'd been born in New Orleans, but both his parents were from up north, Chicago. Well, his daddy was from Chicago, but his momma! She was from Cleveland! Have you ever heard of anyone being from Cleveland? I can't imagine anyone ever admitting it! But she did. She was even proud of it.

They had money; that was in their favor. Evan's daddy did something with electronics, had a company in Metairie. Came down here to get cheap labor, he said. He said that right in front of my momma and daddy. I thought I'd die! He even laughed! Daddy just turned away and left the room, but Evan's daddy, well, he's just too crude to get the point. If Evan had laughed when his daddy did, we might never have gotten married. Now that I think of it, I wish he had. I would have seen right then and there that he was common.

I lied to Momma, that's how crazy I was about him at the time. I told her he went to some private school in Mississippi. If she'd known he went to public school, she'd of packed me off to Europe in a New York second! Now that I think of it, I wish she had! I only got to go the one time, when I was sixteen, for just two little itty bitty months. I never even got to Germany. Not that I'd want to, actually. I mean, Germans! Paris was dirty, but fun. I got some wonderful clothes. Except Daddy cut me off. Daddy's my sugar, but he can be mean sometimes. I called Momma though, and she wired me what I needed. I think Daddy knew, but he never said anything.

And the men! They were gorgeous. Sensitive. Arty types, you know? I think that's why I went for Evan like I did, later. He was kind of like the French boys. The first date we had, he took me to his home and played a Miles Davis album. *Sketches of Spain*. He said Miles Davis hit such a high "C" on one song that he split his lip. He said this one song was so perfect it made him cry. That's when I fell in love with him. That's something a French boy would say. I'd never met anyone who liked jazz music. The boys I knew liked rock mostly, except for a few twits who said they liked classical music, and all they wanted to do was plunk me in the back seat of their cars. "Plunk" is a word I use for the F-word. Nice girls hardly ever say the F-word, so my girlfriends and me say "plunk" and we know what it means and can have the most sexual conversations and no one knows what we're talking about. Oh, I suppose they know, but it sounds ever so much nicer than the other word, and refined. I mean, listen to people around you at a rock concert and you can tell in a second that they're common and cheap and never had a proper home life or anything. It's not that they're bad people exactly; some of them aren't, but your language can say a lot about what kind of person you are, and who wants people to think you're from the Ninth Ward or somewhere horrible like that? And it's not that Ninth Ward people are bad or anything; they're just poor and can't help it, and, you know!

After we got married, Mr. Palmer, Evan's daddy, asked my daddy to get him into Endimion, and Daddy rolled his eyes, but, bless him, he tried. There was no way. I mean, Mr. Palmer was a yankee! What did he think? Daddy did help him get into one of the other Krewes. I won't name the Krewe because it's not very good. It's only ten or so years old and they take just about anyone, as long as they can afford the dues. Their ball is a joke, more like a sock hop or something, and they have the worst throw-things during carnival, and although I've never been—can you imagine!—they say the women have the most disgusting dresses, bought right off the rack. They allow Jews.

That sounds bad, doesn't it? I didn't mean it that way. I even have a friend that's a Jew. Jewess, I mean. JAP, actually. She actually calls herself that, a Jewish American Princess, get it? Half of Tulane seems to be JAPs. I guess I'm a NOP, a New Orleans Princess. I'm from New Orleans and my name is Princess.

Marsha Gold. That's my Jewess friend's name. She said it used to be Goldstein, but they shortened it. We even went to school together, which Momma says would never have happened in her day and just goes to show you what the world has come to, but I'm not as prejudiced as Momma and I don't see what all the fuss is about. I mean, Marsha's daddy isn't even into banking or loan-sharking like most Jews, he's got horse ranches in Texas and a paper mill over in Covington, and I've been to her house lots of times. They do have those funny noses; it's a stitch. And once I told Marsha she had hair like a pickaninny, but it was only in fun and she laughed too, so I know she didn't take offense, but only took it in the lighthearted way it was meant. One thing I didn't believe for the longest time, I even argued with Momma about it because I just didn't believe it. Christmas. I just couldn't bring myself to believe that of Marsha, she seemed so regular and intelligent and all. It used to drive me crazy. I thought of just asking her, but always chickened out. So, one year, I went over, just to see. At Christmas. I think it was the day before, but I figured you could tell, even if it wasn't the day itself, being that close. I said I just came by to borrow a book for school we were supposed to read over vacation. I never even read the book afterwards, I was so shocked! My Mammy, Inez, says they're heathen, don't even believe in the Baby Jesus. After I found that out I always felt a little awkward around Marsha. On the surface, she seemed all right, but when you got down to it, she was strange. Like from a different planet or something. I wonder what happens to them when they pass from this life. I guess they go to H-E-Double-Hockey-Sticks. I feel so sorry for Marsha. Imagine never getting a Christmas present. Why, I'd just die!

Evan needed a haircut. When I saw him in front of the Sonesta. I remember now, Evan always needed a haircut. I took him to Ché's once, but he made such a stink about a measly sixty-five dollars that I never took him back. I heard Evan calls himself "Pete" now and hangs around with low-lifes, even street people. God!

I wonder what he's doing now. For work, that is. He worked for his daddy when we first got married, at his place in Metairie. It's a truly horrible place. Mostly women, Chinese, I think, or maybe Vietnamese Communists, walking around in white, like waitresses, some with masks on their mouths. I always had to giggle, the few times I went there. They make some kind of electronic stuff you can't even breathe on.

When Mr. and Mrs. Palmer died, in the wreck, Evan never went back. Sold the whole thing for six million dollars. That, and the insurance money and some other things, stocks and things, gave us almost eight million dollars. I only got two when we separated. I could have gotten more, but Momma talked me into getting an annulment instead of a divorce, and she said it wouldn't be proper to take half, under the circumstances. I don't see what the difference would be, but what could I do? Go against Momma? Ha! Go against the Red Chinese Army!

I'm glad Daddy was able to arrange the annulment. He never said what it cost, but I'm sure it was enough! I'm glad he did, though. It's almost like I've never been married. Like being a virgin, almost. Ha! I'm sure Mister Brad Sonier from my eighth grade class would find that highly amusing!

Momma was a mess. A divorce in the family, especially from her own daughter, would have sent her straight to St. Louis Cemetery! There's never been such a thing in our family, ever. I suppose in Evan's family and with people like that it's quite common, but they're yankees and barely know who their grandparents were, for pete's sake! Momma says Palmer is an English name and they probably came over here because of the potato famine or something. Or was that the Irish? It was the Irish. I can never keep those kinds of facts straight. It doesn't matter. They probably rowed the ship or worked in the kitchen or something.

I just wish I hadn't seen Evan, that's all. I stayed in Virginia for most of a year just to forget him and all that nastiness, and here he comes along to ruin a perfectly good day; sunny, just a little humidity, and a new hairdo and highlights, and we'd just had the most marvelous étouffée and were on our way to Bart's out by the lake.

We still went, and I never said anything to Teddy about seeing Evan, but my day was ruined, regardless. Boy!

I wonder if he's working somewhere.

He's probably laying in bed most of the day, listening to that record album of his. Miles Davis, the jazz trumpeter. Awful! When I first heard it, it was all right, but please! After the ten thousandth time, it gets old. I could listen to some of that stuff, jazz, if some of us went out to a club or to the Blue Room, but to sit and listen to it by myself! I'd rather snap green beans on the back porch with Inez!

I can see him listening to his record. He just has the one. In the annulment, the only thing he was worried about losing was his "jazz collection." Ha! A collection of one!

*Sketches of Spain.* Concierto something, is all he ever plays. Music from Mars, I call it, but he didn't think that was funny. Evan has a retarded sense of humor, not retarded dopey, but retarded as in cut off. It makes him dream, he always says, and his imagination takes flight. Dream Flyer, is what Momma calls him. She'd call me up and hear the record going in the background, and say, "Is the Dream Flyer at it again?" And I'd have to laugh, and say, "Yes, Momma," and we'd both giggle, and Evan would say, "Is that your mother?" And I'd say, "Yes, Evan," and then he'd say, "What's so funny?" and I'd have to make up something, and then he'd say, shaking his head, "I don't see how that's so funny," and walk away. My face would be as red as a coonass's underwear, from holding it in, and Momma, being sarcastic, saying things like, "Well, is the Dream Flyer flying off?" Geezum! I mean; you talk about funny!

I suppose there's a chance we might still be married if he hadn't drove by that night, up at 4141 and saw me in the back seat of Timmy Demarest's Jaguar. We weren't doing anything, not really, just a little kissing, but try to explain that to Evan! He was always one to jump to conclusions! We must have argued and fought for days. I was so sick of the whole thing and his acting like an Italian waiter or something, that all I could do was go on up to Aunt Dee Dee's and let Daddy take care of everything.

He beat me up, too. I never told a soul about that, not even Momma and Daddy. Especially not Daddy! I just told them I didn't love him anymore, and it's the truth. I don't. I don't know if it's hate I feel; I just know I wish that boy was on Mars or Neptune or something. I don't wish he was dead—you should never wish that on someone, no matter how low-class or despicable they are—it's not Christian.

I felt sort of bad about everything since it was so soon after his parents' unfortunate accident, but it's not my fault Evan has no understanding, and has to assume the worst about a person all the time. I felt just as bad as he did about his parents, maybe even worse if that's possible, but all I was doing was a little innocent flirting. I've known Timmy Demarest since the first grade, and there's no way I'd ever let him plunk me, not in a thousand years.

I think if Evan was a decent human being, he would make sure he kept away from the places I'm at. It was unsettling, seeing him again like that, and the more I think about it, the more upset I become. It's got me in a state. I may call Daddy and see if he'll let me go stay with Cousin James in Houston for the summer. I don't want to run into Evan again. I couldn't stand it if he came up and wanted to talk to me! Imagine!

I just thought . . . I wonder . . . I wonder if Evan felt anything close to the hurt I did.

I wish I didn't feel like crying so much, sometimes. I just hate that man.

I wonder if Evan has a girlfriend now.

I wish I had a party to go to.

# Hard Times

Once, in Miss Wexler's third grade, Amelia Laxault won the arithmetic prize. She got a certificate from Miss Wexler and a bloody nose from Arnold Critchin who caught her on her way home, jumping out from behind a thicket of blackberry bushes along Boudreaux Creek about a mile from her place. Before she knew what he was about, he grabbed the paper and ripped it in two.

"Why'd you do that?" she said, getting back up, brushing dirt off her shift with one hand, wiping blood from her nose on the back of the other arm. She doubled up her fist and took a step toward the boy.

"Cause." Arnold said. "Stupid girl." He glared at her and threw down the pieces of certificate and ran back the other way, toward his own home.

Later, out in the privy, she taped it back together and put it in a shoebox she'd hidden out in the woodshed. The next morning, which happened to be a Saturday, she worked in silence with her mother, taking the shirts her mother kneaded on the scrubboard to squeeze out in the rinse tub and put in the basket to be hung up. When her mother leaned back on her stool for a moment, legs splayed, wiping her forehead with the hem of her dress, she ran to the shed and got the certificate.

"Here," she said, thrusting the mended paper at her. Her mother wiped her face again and pushed up off her stool to stand and read it, a smile gradually softening her mouth as she labored through the words.

Later that night, after her father'd shoveled the last bite of red beans and rice into his mouth and scoured the plate with a piece of cornbread, he told her she was done with school.

"What boy would marry a little smart-aleck?" he said, cheeks bulging with cornbread. "You can read, that's enough." He crumpled up the certificate and stuck it in his pocket. She knew better than to say anything. On Monday morning, she went out to the fields with him. He never knew she had cried herself to sleep the two nights previous. She did everything he asked, once accidentally slicing the back of her forearm with the machete, cutting sugar cane. He laughed and told her to spit on it.

"Rub it in, it'll quit. I ain't gonna kiss it and make it well like yore teacher does," he said, in that voice of his like a saw biting through thick oak planking, and she did. She didn't cry then, and she didn't cry after that.

✣ ✣ ✣

Way it started off, way he looked when the two deputies came in the front door of Roy's Tap, they didn't even unhook the clasps on their gun holsters, just walked over and bent down to lift him up, one on each side.

"Asshole didn't look like he weighed more'n a hunert ten, hunert twenny pounds," said one of the deputies at the jail an hour later. "Li'l ole scrawny arms, bout as big round as your Slim Jim, Faustis."

"Wasn't his arms did the damage. Lookit this, Billy. Probly gimme rabies. I got to get a shot now, mebbe stitches." The one named Faustis held up his forearm. Blood still flowed, seeping into the torn khaki sleeve.

Four other officers crowded around them, looking at Faustis's arm. The oldest, a heavyset man with captain's bars on his shirt, peered at the wound from under the bottoms of his glasses and said, "Hell, y'all don't never get outta town much, I reckon, get up in the hills. Y'all did, y'all ud known that was ol' man Critchin. Arnold Critchin. He's usta hunting wild hogs with a Bowie knife, couple little bitty city boys like y'all ain't nothin t' him. How long Roy say he bin there drinkin? Lessee." He walked into the cell, which hadn't been locked yet, and with the toe of his boot pushed at the lump lying in the middle of the floor. The lump stirred and gave out a little moan and curled itself into a tighter ball. Smiling, the captain walked back out and clanged the door shut behind him. "All day, and probably all last night, I'd say. Left his ol' lady agin."

He walked up to the desk near the front of the room and picked up a ring of keys hanging on a nail and tossed it to Billy. "Lock 'im down. Soon's he sobers up, find out what he's doin' in town. Ask how his ol' lady is. I went to grade school with her. Smart woman. Too good for *him*." He put on his hat and pulled it down low on his forehead, put his hand on the doorknob. "Tell this asshole he earned hisself six months this time, minimum. Fine out if his wife has any food or money. Last time he went on a binge he left her up there all alone with all them damn dogs and kids and nothin' in the house."

"Lord!" the other deputies heard him say, going out the door. "Ain't it never gonna rain again in this damn place!"

✕ ✕ ✕

Sixteen miles away, accessible only by a dirt road, was a pine board cabin, divided into two rooms by brown burlap bags sewn together and strung on a clothesline. No back door and only one window, in the front, but it had a porch of sorts, on which lay panting half a dozen black and tans and one large Walker, mostly white with dark brown mottling, and five or six other black and tan hounds scattered around the yard, all lying down in whatever bit of shade they could locate. If you could call it a yard. Nothing but brown straw that used to be grass, and red dust that swirled in little lazy tornadoes.

The woman sat in her cabin staring out at the hill that was a deeper red than the rest of the land and brushed a fly away, buzzing near the back of her head. A praying mantis of a woman, arms and legs protruding sharply at right angles from her body, cheekbones sticking out in stark relief against the lines of her face. In her mid-thirties, although a stranger might have guessed twice that.

"Mama, did daddy go away?"

Amelia Critchin pushed a long strand of gray hair back into her clumsy bun, looked at the girl and then away from the sight of skin stretched over the outline of her ribs.

"He went to look for work."

"Mommy, I'm hungry." Three-year-old Abby, the second-youngest, came wandering out of the other room where she had been playing with the baby, a bowl in her hand.

"Me, too."

"Mommy, I am too."

"Mama, I'm hot."

James, August, and Mary all piped up, crowding around their mother. In the other room, the baby began a staccato wail and Mandy ran to pick her up.

"Children. Please. I'll fix something in just a little bit. Go play."

She continued to stare out at the hill that was a little redder than the rest of the landscape and tried to remember the color green. Even the milkweed and lamb's quarters had turned brown. The oleander bush looked like it did in the winter. Sixty-two days in a row without moisture. A few weeks back, she'd seen the dogs out in the early morning, licking dead grass, puzzled at first before she realized they were trying to get something from the dew before it evaporated. No dew now—the air was as close at midnight as it was at noon. All she could get from the bottom of the well was mostly a watery silt that had to be strained through cheesecloth to make it drinkable.

She remembered one other year like this one, the year after she'd married Arnold Critchin. The year when he'd sold most of the land his daddy had given him.

※ ※ ※

"Oh, Lordy," Amelia's mother had said, when she finally told her. "Amelia, yore daddy is goin t' kill yore poor sweet self. Oh, child!"

He didn't, although there were times since she wished he had; he only slapped and cuffed her, kicking her hard enough in the side she thought she'd maybe lose the baby, but it was only a busted rib that eventually healed on its own.

The worst part was marching over to the Critchin place, one of her daddy's hands twisted in her hair, the other grasping the stock of his rifle. They got married the same day, soon as the hubbub and cussing died down, over at Justice of the Peace Dunfield's, who did the officiating, drunk as a cow on sour hay, the bridegroom glaring at the floor the whole time, spitting just before he mumbled "I do." Three days later she turned fourteen.

Their baby was stillborn six months later. She never told her father the baby was seeded with a rape. Less than two months after they buried the infant, she was pregnant again. That one lived. A little girl she named Mandy.

⁂

Yesterday, she'd cooked all but a little of the rest of the mule, which had lasted almost a month. The meat wasn't beef, but it could be choked down, rank and strong-smelling; it sustained life and that's what was needed. The children stopped playing tag and hide 'n seek in the yard, any game which required energy or much movement.

Gathered around the table, too exhausted to even whine, her brood just sat staring at their plates.

"Mama, it's spoilt. It's nasty," said one.

"Hush up and eat it," said Mandy, older than her ten years. "It's all we got. Don't be such a baby."

"We can't," they wailed, and Amelia picked up a spoon and ladled a bit of the gravy from her own plate into the eighteen-month-old's mouth. The baby promptly threw up.

That was when Arnold Critchin stood up and snatched up the plates, stacking them in a pile. He carried them out to his dogs, who came whimpering up to the porch, their tails trying to wag down between their legs, one or two of them growling from behind grinning teeth.

"That's the kids' food," she cried, running out behind him and bending down to snatch one of the plates back from the biggest of the hounds, a black and tan he called Brownie. The dog almost casually reached over and sank his teeth into her wrist at the same time her man was swinging his fist at the back of her head, knocking her off the porch onto the ground. Back inside, she rubbed the arm she'd used to break her fall and wondered if it were broken or just bruised. She wrapped it tightly around a piece of kindling and tried to ignore the ache. It was the same arm the dog had bitten.

This morning, when Arnold sat down to the table, he stared at the plate she put silently before him. Save for a bit she had hidden, it was the last of the mule meat. He took one bite, chewed in moody silence for a moment, and then spat it out. He picked up his hat from where it lay on the table, clapped it on his head and spoke to the woman, his voice china egg brittle.

"I'm goin t' town, fine some work."

She watched him from the window until he was just a tiny brown insect, far away in the vastness of the red dust. He had gone like this before, and stayed away one or two days, even one or two weeks, but the woman knew this leaving was different.

The kids slept till noon. There was a little flour left, about two cupfuls. She took what there was and brown water from the bucket that stood beside the stove and mixed the flour into dough. There was no yeast for leavening, or salt for taste. She was careful with the water.

She molded the mixture into six tiny cakes and relit the fire and baked them in the cast-iron skillet, slowly and carefully, as if cooking them too fast would somehow diminish their bulk. When they were done, she put them on a piece of oilcloth and cut each in half. That would be two meals for the children.

Besides Amelia and the kids, all that stirred on the place were her old man's dogs. A baker's dozen mangy, long-limbed, thirst-tempered hounds, all males save one pregnant bitch.

That night two things happened. The children ate the last of the flour cakes and what was left of her tiny hoard of meat, and the bitch gave birth to a litter of four pups. Surprisingly, they were all alive.

There was no food left in the house.

After she put the children down that evening, humming to quiet the smallest ones' whimperings, she scoured the house in a vain effort, looking for food. Even insects. There weren't any.

✖ ✖ ✖

"They just fine, Cap'n," Arnold Critchin said. "That ol' woman's toughern all y'all put t'gether. It's the dogs I'm worried about. She don't care squat about them dogs and they's all champions, specially my Walker. Don't fuckin' sweat how my ol' lady is. Hell," he laughed and leaned back in the chair, hands behind his head. "She's always hidin' stuff. Prolly got enough food to start a restrint."

The Captain pushed the paper he'd been writing on into a folder and walked over and opened up the filing cabinet. He came back and sat on the edge of the desk, facing the prisoner.

"Critchin, what makes you such an asshole? I remember you in school, always pesterin the girls and hittin' the little kids. How the hell you ever git a fine woman like Amelia t' marry you? Specially Amelia. She wuz the smartest kid in the whole school."

Arnold looked up, jaws working. His voice was tight. "I wuz smart, too."

"Sure you were," said the captain, a smirk on his face.

Arnold stood up.

"Yore daddy give you candy bars when you got yore report card, dint he? Well, my daddy give me whippins. My daddy said I had to quit school once I made sixth grade, start helpin' him on the farm. Become a *man*." He snorted. "Hell, I *loved* school. You know how hard it is to get F's when you know that stuff inside out? You ever wonder why I kept flunkin' third grade? You remember when Amelia got the math prize? Yeah, she wuz smart, but I wuz smarter. I knew the multiplication tables inside out. That prize shoulda been mine.

Only thing, if I'da won it, that woulda been my last day in school. Might as well a been, though." He stared out the window behind the captain, his eyes fixed on some point outside. "Daddy made me quit the next year. Tricked me. Asked me to help him on his tax form. Did the whole thing in ten minutes. Too smart for my own good."

He stood up.

"You kin put me back in my cell," he said. "You know, Cap'n? Things ever git rough for you? You ever have to sell your home to feed yore kids? Naw, I don't guess so. Long as they's people t' pay taxes you git yores."

"So, that makes it okay to beat yore wife? That makes it okay to treat those dogs better'n yore family? I ain't buyin' it, Critchin. Sam! Put this piece of crap back in his cell," he said to the deputy over at the filing cabinet. "Tell Faustis to get on over to his place, check on things."

"Captain, Billy and Faustis took that prisoner on down to New Orleans. They won't be back for two days, minimum."

"The minute they get back, then. First thing. Tell them if she ain't got any groceries t' git her some. Take it out of Discretionary."

He picked up his hat. "First thing when they come back, hear?"

"How 'bout my dogs? Y'all gonna check on my dogs? My dogs is hungry, too."

He went out, ignoring the man in the cell.

✖ ✖ ✖

One of the pups, the runt of the litter, died early in the morning.

The woman looked out in the yard in the first hours of the new day just in time to see the other dogs tearing it to shreds.

"You dogs git!" She rushed out and swung wildly at them with her broom. Yelping as she connected, they finally scattered and stood a short distance away, growling softly and watching the woman out of the corners of their yellow eyes. The woman snatched up the mangled pulp and carried it back to the house. One of the dogs made a run at her back, nipping her heel as she opened the door.

Inside, she stripped the remaining flesh off the dog's bones and dropped it into a pot. She poured four inches of water in the bottom, and put the pot on the stove. When it was done, she took it from the fire and placed the meat, bones and all, on a tin plate and placed it on the table. The water she poured into six tin cups. There was about four swallows of broth in each.

"Get up. Get up," she said, moving from child to child on their pallets. "Food." The smell of the meat nauseated her and she had to sit down for a minute. Then, she took a tiny sliver of the meat she had put aside and forced herself to chew and swallow it. The taste made her lightheaded. She picked up the baby and went out to the porch to sit down. The baby fussed until she set her down to crawl on the ground.

The rest of her brood came straggling out, some to sit hunkered down on the porch beside her and one or two of the others scattered out in the yard, heads down, kicking at rocks, making marks in the dust with twigs. Before long the dogs began circling the baby, who had made her way out into the yard, nipping at her body, the same way they had the puppy's.

"Stop it! Stop it, stop it, stop it!" Amelia screamed, running at the pack, apron flapping, arms windmilling. The dogs skulked away, tongues lolling in their mouths, their eyes yellow and unblinking. Snatching up her baby on the run, screaming at the other children to get inside, she cradled her in her arms. Breathlessly, she slammed the door behind them. The girl was miraculously unharmed, except for one arm oozing blood from half a dozen teeth marks. She cleansed the wounds with spittle and wiped them with the hem of her skirt.

"Mama, I'm hungry."

"Mama, my head hurts. My tummy, too."

"Mama, what's the matter with Daddy's dogs?"

They kept inside the next two days. The waiting dogs, always there, even at night. Why don't they go away, she thought. She watched the dogs circle the bitch and her litter early one morning before the kids wakened. Once the first puppy was attacked and killed, the bitch joined the others in ripping the flesh off her own offspring and choking it down. Amelia took the children to the back of the cabin and tried to get them to sing a song, so they couldn't watch or hear. On the third day, the morning sun toasted the cabin even more, bringing with it nothing but heat and more suffocating air.

Arnold wouldn't be coming back; she was certain of that. Everything outside was brown and red, and even if there had been some weeds to dig up or pick, the dogs wouldn't let them out. They guarded the house, waiting, making it crazy to even think about opening the door. She had tried to go for water and they were waiting for her, one hurling his body at the door as she started to open it, clawing at the screen, teeth tearing at the wooden frame.

Well, she thought. So.

The water was down to a tepid three inches in the bucket. She had been rationing it for days, allowing only tiny sips for the children, one small sip a day for herself. Finally, she began moistening a bit of a rag and letting them suck on it.

When the baby died, the eldest, Mandy quit talking. "Let's sing a song," Amelia said. "'Rock of Ages,' it's your favorite," but Mandy just sat in the corner, sucking her thumb. Amelia bundled the baby in a blanket and put her in the pie safe. The other children seemed not to notice.

The sound of the dogs was very clear now, as they waited by the porch, sending up thin wolf-like howls, as if they were waiting for an answer from inside the house.

❉ ❉ ❉

"Faustis," the captain said. "I want you and Billy to go on out to Critchin's place, check on his wife."

The two deputies had just parked the car, hadn't gotten out yet.

"Oh, Captain," Billy said, leaning over and looking up at his boss. "We just got in and we're beat. Can't you send someone else? That's an hour ride, on those cowpaths. If we can even find it."

"Cap'n, Billy's right. We're beat, and besides—I think we're about to throw a rod. Somethin's not right, anyway. It's been knockin' the whole way back. I bin puttin' oil in it every two hours. I better take it down to Smiley's, have a look at it. The AC's not workin' right, neither. We been sweatin' like whores in line on Judgment Day."

They both got out of the car and stretched in unison, as if to show their superior just how hot and tired they were.

"I'll say one thing," the captain said. "Y'all sure smell like y'all been working. Workin' the French Quarter'd be my guess! Well, shit . . . " He paused and took off his hat and ran his fingers through the few strands left on the top of his head. He put it back on and squared it with his fingers. "I guess y'all better take it on down to the garage. We sure can't afford a new engine. I can't send anyone else—we're all tied up with Crawfish Days. I'm worried about that woman, though. Oh, hell . . . " He fumbled in his shirt pocket and took out a pair of flip-ons which he snapped onto his eyeglasses. "Guess one more day won't make much difference. Take the car over t' Smiley's and then git yore asses on home, see your wives. And for godsakes, take a bath. First thing in the morning though, y'all git out there and see about that woman."

"Yessir," they said, climbing back into the car.

"You want a beer?" Faustis said, as they pulled away.

"Hell, Faustis," Billy answered. "The only part you got wrong is the 'a' part. I want me about a *case*!"

✖ ✖ ✖

"Ma," the children begged. "Mama, I'm hungry. Fix us something to eat, please Ma." A ringing began in her ears and then she realized another day had passed and they weren't whining at her. She tried to remember when she had heard them last ask for food and thought it was the previous day.

Roots, she thought. Maybe somewhere out there in the dust she could find some roots. She had to try. She had to get water, at least. She went to the door and opened it a crack. The dogs ran up on the porch. She pushed it closed, just as a hound's body slammed against it.

"Get into bed," she ordered the children, lost for any other course of action. "Try to sleep. It'll take your mind off your stomachs."

The rest of that day and through the night the children kept waking up, calling her name. Once, she went in and put her hand on James's brow and pulled back in a rush. She dipped a rag into the precious remaining water and wiped his forehead. It seemed to help at first, but an hour later when she checked on him, he felt cold, and after that she didn't feel him again.

There was a hole in her own stomach, and she felt something strange on her face. When she touched it with her fingers a door opened, a memory came floating up. The same wetness on her cheek. She thought back to that day when Miss Wexler called her name, had her come stand before the class, and said those things about her. "Best math student I've ever had." Nice things. And the way she handed her a piece of paper as if she were presenting a queen's gift to her devoted subject. Her name was on it, and a gold seal, raised and shiny. As she made her way back to her seat, heart thumping, Miss Wexler got a laugh out of the whole class, when she said, "Arnold, if you'd pay attention like Amelia, perhaps that glorious day will arrive when you'll finally master the multiplication tables and find yourself in the fourth grade."

"Six times six," she said aloud, surprised at herself. "Thirty-six." She went back into the other room and stared out the window. "Seven times seven." She went through the entire multiplication tables, never missing, never hesitating, and she realized what she was doing was a wonder. Since that long ago day, she had not once multiplied a single number, even in her head.

You do what you do, she thought to herself; you just do, and then she dismissed the multiplication tables entirely and concentrated on the situation at hand.

Maybe Arnold would come back. Maybe in the next twenty-four hours.

She had to get something into the children's stomachs. She thought of the baby in the pie safe and then she thought of James, and a terrible inspiration began to form itself. That made her get down on her knees, bow her head low, but the proper words refused to take form. Her thoughts were as dry and empty as the landscape outside the cabin.

Then, in a flash, the thought became whole. The notion made her legs begin to shake so that she had to sit down, chest heaving as she gulped lungfuls of air, fighting dizziness. She just sat there in the chair looking out onto the moonlit yard, until the murmurs from the other room settled and died down, and then, in the near, small hours of the morning, while the children slept, she walked over to the pantry on legs that cramped with every step to gather what she needed.

A stewing pot, a length of stout twine, and the kindling ax that lay by the stove. She poured the last of the rank water into the pot and started a fire in the stove. Using her teeth and right hand, she tied the twine as tightly as she could around her left forearm. She picked up the ax. "Eight times eight," she whispered, and raised her arm. "Sixty-four," she grunted and swung.

⁂

Three days later, two men dressed in the khaki uniforms of the parish sheriff's office walked up the lane, cursing at the dust that settled over their shoes and filled their nostrils.

"That's a shame," said one of the men, stepping onto the dead grass of the yard. "Look like these was prime dogs." Only the Walker moved, raising its head with an obvious effort, the others beached and bloated on their sides. The deputy lifted the rifle in his hand and slowly squeezed off a round. The dog's body jerked in the red dust and was still. The men walked past the dog and entered the cabin.

The stench made both men step back at first, and then the scene—children lying on the floor on pallets, faces white and full as harvest moons. The woman lay sprawled on the kitchen floor, blood everywhere.

"Looky here," said one of the men. In a pot on the wood stove was a hand. A fly buzzed near it.

Faustis ran for the door. The other man came out behind him, eyes wide and glittery, and spoke to no one in particular.

"Goddamn," he said. He shook his head slowly from side to side. "That woman." Faustis bent over, spitting, and said, "Tell you a secret about smells, Billy." He wiped his mouth with his forearm. "Force yourself to take it in. In three minutes, you can't smell it anymore. Doc Polton tole me that. Some kind of defense thing the body does."

Suddenly, Faustis grabbed the revolver in his holster, and fired at the sky, shooting rapidly, pulling the trigger even after it began clicking. Billy looked up and saw a buzzard circling. The shots didn't seem to affect the creature as he continued in lazy circles.

"We'll need some body bags," he said, holstering his gun and walking down the road toward where their car was.

"Oughta make Critchin come up here and do it," Billy said, catching up.

"I don't think he's gonna be able to," Faustis said. "Captain hears about this, I gotta feeling Critchin's gonna get shot trying to escape."

Billy slowed a step or two and then hurried to catch up. "Yeah," he said. Then, "I don't know about that, Faustis," he said, drawing his revolver and pointing at some spot down the road, eyes squinting as he aimed. "I want to think about that, some. Y'know? I just don't know about something like that. I mean . . . godamighty, Faustis!"

The two men walked faster and the dust swirled briefly, then settled behind their feet, and the sun arched higher. Now there were two buzzards drifting overhead and the first gray clouds in weeks and weeks began to move up from the northwest as the wind, which had blown steadily for as long, stilled and seemed to hold its breath against the sudden chill in the air.

# Sheets

While we were passing the hash pipe back and forth, somewhere in Arizona, she confessed her indiscretions. That's what she called them—*indiscretions*. She hadn't even changed the sheets the morning she picked me up at LAX, seven months ago, and that, she seemed to feel, was the worst of it, not that she'd actually screwed another man in what was to be our bed and not told me until now.

I agreed. She should have at least changed the sheets before I laid on them with her.

Maybe you shouldn't have gotten me out there in the first place, I suggested. I gave up a good job in New Orleans just to come be with you in California, you know.

By the time we were going over the Mississippi at St. Louis, I figured out what I would do. She liked the idea, the part I told her. I didn't tell her the whole deal.

You're a crazy man, she said. I'm glad I told you. I feel so much better now.

Yes, I said. I can see that you do.

We got the marriage license at the courthouse in Goshen, Indiana and then went to a motel, paid for a room and made love. After awhile, we gave it a second go, only I couldn't come this time. The next day we both got jobs, me as a barber and her as a dog groomer and arranged a weekly rate at the motel. Put our money in a checking account, unloaded the car, figured out how to get the different channels on the TV. On the third day of the waiting period, I drove her to work. She had already asked her boss for permission to get off work early so there would be time to drive back to the courthouse and have the judge deliver our vows at five.

An hour after dropping her off at the groomers, I had gathered all of my clothes from the motel and stopped at the ATM and cleaned out our bank account. By 10:30 A.M. I was passing the exit for Anderson, Indiana, on Highway 69 South.

She'll remember me, I thought, making a mental note to stop somewhere at 5:00 and have a glass of wine. Celebrate. Think about her looking up and down the street, waiting for me to drive up.

That California bedroom kept appearing between the hood of the car and the North American Van Line truck in front of me. I could see the dresser and I could see the sheets and I could see the tiny Rorschach pecker tracks. A single pubic hair. His or hers? It's impossible to determine.

Outside the California bedroom window is a swimming pool that needs cleaning. You can see the mold clearly.

When I passed the semi, the pool disappeared. Then, the dresser and then the bedroom itself. So did the sheets, but the pubic hair became a squiggle in my eye, making it difficult to see.

Then the corn fields vanished. The cars ahead, on both sides of the four-lane, drove out of sight. There was just my car and the open road, stretching forever off into the distance. Then it too, disappeared. I looked down at my speedometer and the needle was over as far as it would go. The gas pedal seemed to be stuck. I looked back up to find that I had disappeared as well. So had the car. Except for the taillights. When I tapped the brakes, they lit up but the car didn't slow. I could see their glow in my peripheral vision. It must have looked strange to the cows standing in the fields, sucking on their cuds, seeing a pair of naked taillights disappearing and reappearing as I whispered past on silent and invisible rubber tires.

# Lights and Darks

# The Jazz Player

On the day Miles Davis died, it was what Jake defined as a "soul's gray day," and he instinctively knew the instant his brain processed the words coming over WNOL, that this was going to become one of those "Kennedy moments," the kind of memory wherein he would be able to recall exactly where he had been and what he had been doing at the time, one of those epochal frozen tableaus he would always be able to bring back with perfect clarity and precision, right down to the smell of the room he was in at the time.

Pine Sol.

He had just wiped down the stool in the bathroom, chipping away dried pieces of barf from the previous night's revelries. He'd brought the little clock radio in with him to listen to while he cleaned and the newsman was halfway through the announcement before what he was saying penetrated, at which point Jake said in a very clear and loud voice "Oh no!" the most banal remark he could have uttered, he realized later upon retrospection, and then, illogically, he struck at the radio perched there on the sink, knocking it back and off, busting a large chunk of the plastic casing loose, which didn't seem to affect the quality of the announcer's voice other than to render it slightly tinny. The speaker must have torn slightly.

That was what he remembered the day Miles Davis died.

Oh . . . and that later on that evening Paris came to the club where he was playing to let him know she was getting married and moving to Chicago and did he want Josey's clothes or what should she do with them.

"Do? What the fuck should you *do* with them? What do you mean—what do you *do* with them. They're her clothes, what have you *been* doing with them? Can't you just . . . keep them, or something? I don't understand. I don't know, Paris. Give me a minute to think. This is kind of sudden, isn't it?"

It had been more than a year since he'd seen her. More than a year since the divorce was final. Long after the inquest, the statements given, the questions asked, the police, the reporters, the stares from shoppers in the supermarket and the dry cleaners, the steadily lengthening silences between he and Paris, the estrangement, then the separation and inevitable divorce. They'd never fought, never even brought up the slightest reference to their daughter, never discussed the circumstances of her death. An unspoken pact of silence. Funny that on the very day Paris would come back into his life, break the silence, remind him of their daughter and all of that history, that would also be the day Miles Davis would die.

But the radio was what he remembered most from that day, which was often the way life was, he thought. Big, important, critical stuff was often subsequent to secondary experience; it was almost as if ghost images were primary, and the foreground of his mind's memory-photo inconsequential, instead of the other way around. Sort of a parallel universe churning around inside one's skull, seen through a frosted shower door. Like the man he had seen at a party one time, after a lot of drinking as he remembered, drugs, too, probably, and the man talking about getting wounded in 'Nam, shoulder shot all to hell, but all he could remember was the sun and how hot it was, bringing this little drop of sweat that had collected by his eyebrow and sat there for what seemed forever. His arm was hamburger, but all he could ever remember was that little bead of sweat.

All he could remember was the acrid scent of Pine Sol. He'd wanted to do something, commemorate the occasion somehow, solemnize it, but all he could come up with was to go into the living room and put the "Ah-Leu-Cha" side of the *'Round About Midnight* album on and listen to it while smoking a doobie. He thought he should do something else, get drunk or something . . . hell, *Miles died*, but he just couldn't get it going, couldn't get up and do what it took to get himself ready to go out to a bar, get connected to other human beings who probably wouldn't even know who the hell Miles was or what he meant anyway . . . oh, maybe they'd know him from his marriage to Cicely Tyson or from some appearance on the "Tonight Show," but his passing would mean little more to them than the passing of any other celebrity, probably less than if the jazzman had been a movie star or TV personality.

So, he got last night's paper and did the crostic instead.

It seemed to help.

No, it didn't. Not really. Who was he kidding? It wasn't as if he knew Miles Davis or anything; that wasn't the case. He'd never even seen him play in person. Miles represented *something* in his life, something big and important and *crucial*, but why or how or in what manner he wasn't sure or maybe he'd just forgotten. It had something to do with where he was on this pathway he'd chosen or had thrust upon him, and it had something to do with who he was, not "he" the personality; no, it was not that superficial, it was more embedded inside, in the center that was who he really was. Miles or something Miles represented to him, something *centrist*; that was it. That was a good word. *Centrist.* That was the right word. Always there, a rudder in the sea of disorder and confusion, the guidon not only in his art, but in some way in his very life.

It had something to do with that night in Yazoo City more than a year before. With his daughter and Paris. Miles was in there, someplace, right smack in the midst of it all, germane and important to it all, to the meaning.

His daughter Josey. Dead now a year. Josey and Paris and Miles, all wound together, a ball of life-stuff twine, all mixed up; yes, mixed was the right and only proper word when *Miles's death* was what he remembered, was what leapt to the forefront of his mind and not what should, not, for God's sakes, Josey's death, brought back by Paris and her inane nattering about their daughter's clothes, not even the man lying there, choking on his own blood, cursing him in a steady, monotonous stream of invective until he could stand it no longer and put another one in him, in the throat, this bullet silencing the man's nasty, foul, blasphemous words, Paris screaming, beating herself with her fists, and his own daughter, his own baby lying over there in the other part of the room, silent and still, so still that he didn't have to go to her to know that she was dead too, but he did, he looked at her and shook her, a little at first, and then hard, and they said later he was moaning and crying and cursing at her to wake up, and he couldn't really remember that, only that it felt like those times when she was an infant and he was constantly terrified of SIDs and had gotten up four or five times in the night to go into her room and peek into her little bed, ending up putting his head down close to her face until he could discern her tiny, whispery breath and know that she was all right, for a little while at least, and Paris told her mother, later, he overheard her, that that's what he was doing when they came, the police, the detectives, he was holding his ear close to Josey's silent mouth, and Paris told them, the police, that he was listening for her breath like when she was a newborn baby.

And then, from that point, then it was like parties all the time, a long way from Yazoo City, a long way from marriages and families, parties and drugs and booze and noise, lots of people around him, parties like the one the night before Miles died, but mostly it was being alone, even when others were surrounding him, chattering at him. Days, he found he slept a lot, awakening around noon, making a toasted cheese sandwich, listening to Miles Davis, trying to get something back he'd lost, something he thought he'd shared with Miles at one time, something he couldn't quite define but felt missing from his music. From his life. He lives in a second-floor apartment now and the sounds of this city are all around him, but he doesn't filter them out and work up stories for what he hears. He is in New Orleans now. He has lived in other cities and they all sound much like one another he thinks, but New Orleans has a different sound, like noise underwater. It was the city men would have chosen Morpheus for had men still believed in such gods and assigned them places of residence. Kansas City and Trenton, New Jersey, on the other hand, sound exactly alike—like traffic; horns honking, tires screeching, people yelling, things like that. If towns were music styles, New Orleans would be a trumpet with a mute, the way Beiderbecke did it in the twenties and Bird and Louie did later on. Detroit and Philadelphia? Drums and microphones that squeal.

A divorce then, filed scant weeks after, was there a choice? . . . and then that apartment that wasn't really one, way down yonder . . . it was only two small rooms, and the sounds of the city, and he, Jake, thinking it somewhat of a pity he didn't make up stories about the sounds or even little capsule biographies for the voices that drifted up to his bedroom, sometimes quiet, sometimes shrill and accusing, sometimes full of lust and desire and hopelessness and unbearable, smothering heat, but he didn't. He appreciates the sounds, and he enjoys them, in a passive way, but he doesn't do anything with them. He leaves them alone. He has problems enough, problems with his playing. Problems with Josey's death and his divorce from Paris, and something else, something that flits around the edges of his memory that he can't bring to the surface but which he understands to be important—more than important would be defined by a job interview or applying for a bank loan—but important, as in cataclysmic, and perhaps that is why he has difficulty bringing it to the front of his mind.

Neon red splashes and bathes his room at three-second intervals and "'Round Midnight" and "Ah-Leu-Cha" repeat and repeat, and he pays homage. This record player has always stuck, playing the record over and over again unless he gets up and turns it. He doesn't. He fires up a joint and the joint and the music work like window pane acid on his soul. He conjures up his own flashbacks, deciding to start with colors. They fingerpaint the inside of his skull, he and Miles, and pretty soon an hour has passed in twenty minutes and he has to get up and go find some human beings. He leaves the radio where it has fallen, in the bathroom.

This is on the day that Miles Davis died, but that is not the important thing. The important thing is coming up, later that evening, when Paris will show up, but the radio account of Miles's passage is how he will recall the day.

He decides he will go to work even though he doesn't go on until midnight. The Mockingbird Cafe. Not the famous one. The other one, just a few blocks from the famous one, but worlds removed in character.

The Mockingbird Cafe where he is working is not a place a tourist would be likely to be found sipping a drink. It is a place for serious jazz fans. It is a place where they will cut your throat and worse. That is because they have serious jazz and blues in this place. Not what is offered up for the tourists in the French Quarter, but the real thing. In a place where they have the real thing, a human life is not a big deal. Jake has seen a man killed in this place simply because he was staring at the man who killed him. Shot in the throat. Jake can relate to that. The man who was killed was not being impolite. It was a misunderstanding. The man who was killed was not even aware of the man he was staring at; he was experiencing deep chest pains and was practicing deep breathing and focusing on what turned out to be the other man's forehead. That's what Joe Duplaissair said, and Joe Duplaissair should know; he was a friend of the dead man's and Joe said the man did that often; he had a bad heart.

That didn't matter to the man who shot him. He just assumed the man was being rude and so he killed him. He went to Angola State Prison for awhile and then some other inmates raped him and stabbed him with a straightened-out laundry pin. In the throat. So, in a way, justice was served.

When Jake gets ready to leave, he picks up his trumpet and tries it, tries the high C Miles does in "'Round Midnight." It is technically the same C, but it sounds different. Like he is playing underwater. Before the thing with his daughter, even before his daughter, when it was just him and Paris, when he had been with the big band, when people knew his name and his photograph was behind glass in front of nightclubs, his C had a different sound, sharper, cleaner. Crisper.

After wiping the mouthpiece, he puts the horn back in its case. He looks around the room, searching for something. He does this every night. There is always the feeling he has forgotten something, but he never can see what it is. This is what happens when you live alone, he thinks. You always think you have forgotten something.

He blinks. Once, then again. It is the bartender. He has asked him if he wants another and Jake nods that he does. He likes this bartender. He knows when to talk and when to shut up. He is supposed to charge him half-price for the drinks, even though Jake works here, but he never does unless the owner is poking around nearby.

He gave Jake some good advice a few months back, this bartender did. About Paris. You can't forget them, he said. What you have to do is pretend they're dead and then you'll be all right.

He did what the bartender recommended. He buried her, threw dirt on her coffin, even tossed a white flower on top of the casket. He doesn't know the names of flowers, never did, but something white, and then he was all right. Of course, Jack Daniels and a joint now and again didn't hurt, and Miles Davis helped turn the ache into a positive thing, a physical thing you could deal with and handle, and things were not bad for awhile. He was maintaining, could at least talk to people decently and cash his check and shower daily and keep clean. He could do pretty much everything except hit that C the right way. It was mushy, undervalued.

Jake likes this bartender, respects him. He's an old pro, knows drinkers. He leaves the old ice in the glass and just adds more. Bartenders you get most places these days throw out the ice each time, like they're doing the customer a favor. They don't understand old ice. They're the guys who say things like "Have a nice day," when you slide off the barstool. When Jake hears things like that, he wants to say something like, "Likewise, shit-for-brains," but he doesn't.

The bartender says something about the Saints' latest football loss and laughs, and Jake says something back and it begins to look like a pretty good night to him, and he's coming out of his depression over the news about Miles and his head is starting to clear from the combination of last night's hangover and the joint he'd smoked a short time ago. Small crowd, but the right ones, the ones that know Oscar P. and Dizzy and Sonny Rollins, and don't have a clue who the pseudo acts like Spiro Gyro are and walk away when names like Kenny G come up. The warm-up group is playing now, and they're okay Jake thinks, though not in his group's league yet. The guy who plays their bass who can cook though. They'd like to get him for their group, but he likes the guys he's with. He thinks they have potential. Jake thinks the bass player stays with them because they like to run shit, smack mostly and speedballs. Jake's group, they don't mind a joint at all or even a little coke, but the hard stuff they don't allow.

He is cooking himself, Jake is, warm with the Jack and water and the anticipation of a good set, Miles's death is just starting to work up a little heat, inspire him, when she walks in. Paris. By herself. She walks right up to the bar where he sits, like she has been looking for him on purpose. He guesses she has.

Buy me a drink, she says; I'm getting married. All in the same sentence and while she's getting up on the barstool, never mind it's months and months since they've seen each other. The bartender is smooth. He's already whispered what will you have and she's told him and he is mixing it and Jake is not even sure there was such a conversation, but he guesses there was because here he comes with Anisette and that's what she drinks. His skull is buzzing and he feels slightly nauseous and he drinks some of the water the bartender has put beside her drink, not even caring it's "New Orleans poison," tap-water.

I wouldn't bother you with this, she goes on, eyes everywhere but on his; rattling along like she's prepared for this meeting. Except there's something, she says. It's Josey's things, she says. Jake hasn't said a word yet, and when she says *Josey* there's thunder in his ears and he sees her again, a mind-picture that's thrown up there, of their daughter, a black-and-white photo that's etched in acid, and he realizes he hasn't allowed her picture in his brain for months. Josey's.

*That's it*, he thinks. *That's what I couldn't remember.* He's fought thinking about Paris so much that's all that's in his head, even though he was doing pretty good with her in an imaginary grave and all, but Josey had just disappeared until that second.

Her things, she keeps saying; what shall I do with her things? He doesn't know what she's talking about at first and then he begins to understand that it's Josey's clothes and toys, stuff like that, dolls, that she was going to get rid of unless he wanted them. No, he said, and then; wait, I have to think. She nods and drinks the rest of her Anisette and the bartender comes up without asking and puts another in front of her.

That's okay with me, she says, but make up your mind soon. She was your daughter, too, you know, and I don't blame you, not any more, and then she was saying something else but Jake wasn't listening because he was thinking: *Josey's dead and I didn't go to the funeral.*

He should have been at the funeral, he thought. He kept turning that same thought over and over in his mind and must have said it aloud, because Paris says, yes, you should have, everyone was wondering, but not really, they figured it was the circumstances, but even so, you should have been there, I see that now, only I didn't then, but then we were beside ourselves, weren't we?

He doesn't answer her, and she goes back to the point of her being there. She's going to marry this guy, some yankee who lives in Chicago and is in banking and she will be moving to Illinois and can't take Josey's things and so does he want them? Otherwise, she'll send them to some charity, that's what Josey would have wanted, for some other little girl to have them; and if he didn't let her know within a week, that's what she will do. She'll be at her mother's until Thursday and after that in Chicago and she'll take care of Josey's things if he doesn't come by or call.

Then, they have another drink or two, he doesn't know how many, her talking and Jake half listening or not listening at all and then she turns to see his group setting up on the bandstand and he sees her shoulder where the dress falls away from it for a moment.

What's *that*, he says, and she says, what's what? at first, and then realizes what he has glimpsed, and says, Oh that, it's just a little bitty tattoo. Chuck and I had it done one night over in Algiers when we were drunk; he has one too; it's a black widow spider. Chuck being the Chicago banker she was going to marry.

She says, you know, it's been a long time since I've heard you play. Are you here every night?

After awhile she stands up and says she has to leave, since he has to get his horn and go play, and she offers him her hand to shake, which for some reason he does and then she is gone, out the door. For a minute or so, he thinks perhaps he has imagined it all, but no, there is her glass still part-way full of Anisette, he can smell it, and he can remember the paper-rustle of her laughter. And the tattoo. A black widow spider.

He goes up and tells Orlando he can't play tonight and Orlando says don't bother to come tomorrow neither and he says okay, that's cool, asshole, and he leaves.

He drives down to 4141 and watches the girls dancing in their designer originals and has some oysters. Why he's gone to 4141, he doesn't know, except he and Paris had gone there a lot in the old days. It was her kind of club, not his. He guesses he's gone there on the off chance Paris and her fiancée Chuck might be there. Paris and Chuck and their two black widow spiders.

And then, there they are. Paris in a different dress than the one she'd had on at the Mockingbird Cafe. The dress she'd worn there would have been out of place here. That one had sisters. This one was an only child. A rich, only child.

Chuck (he figured it was Chuck, perhaps not a safe assumption), was a short, burly guy, built along the lines of an interior lineman. Incongruously, his face has delicate, finely-chiseled features, a face that didn't match the trunk it sat upon, more like it had been sculpted in an airy study that caught the north light, by some purple-smocked artist who had then absent-mindedly stuck the head on this sturdy, peasant frame. He was also a full two inches shorter than Paris, and that made Jake laugh, which was not a good move as they had just come alongside him, and turned sharply at the sound of his chuckle. Paris is obviously surprised at seeing him here and her face registers fright, as well.

Jake, she says, with an exclamation. Exclamations are not her style, which make the words more dramatic. She recovers quickly, though, and begins to introduce the two men, when Chuck, whom she has introduced as "Charles" says, "Yeah, you're the asshole she used t' be married to. Listen, buster, keep outta our way. I know the whole story. Rape, my ass. He wasn't raping her and you know it. I told her she ought to come clean, but she's got this idea she's got to protect you, that it's her fault. Bullshit! You mighta fooled the sheriff, but I know the real story."

"Chuck," says Paris, in a still, small voice. Her eyes were wide and blinking, locked with Jake's. Chuck ignores her.

"You just keep outta my way. Fuck you and your sorry attitude. Your daughter'd still be alive if you weren't so nuts. You can call it an accident and Paris can call it an accident if she wants to be blind, but I know the truth. Not much of a hunter, are you, buddy? The first thing a hunter learns is to see everything he's shooting at. That includes what's *behind* his target as well. You're lucky I wasn't the law on that one pal, you'd still be in jail. Asshole. Who are you to have that cracker attitude anyway? You think everybody ought to get killed who screws someone else's old lady? Ha! Rape! You knew the score, all along. You mighta fooled Paris and the others but I see right through your little game. You're only sorry because you got your kid by accident. You make me want to puke. I'm telling you right now, man to man—I ever see you again near me or Paris and you're a dead man. You think you're the only one this affects? Take a look at her. Take a good long look, asshole. I hope your insides eat you alive. C'mon, Paris, let's get the hell out of here. All of a sudden, I feel the need for a long, hot bath and lots of soap."

Distracted by the suddenness and ferocity and just utter quiet *intensity* of the man's attack, Jake stands dazed as the couple walks off, Paris trying to look back at him as Chuck, gripping her arm, lifts and wrenches her along to the front entrance of the club where they disappear into the night.

At first, nothing registers. His mind is a blank. And then, a maelstrom of memories washes over him, mingled with the words of his ex-wife's fiancée, and he tries to fight it, tries to keep it out, but the thought, the *verity* keeps insisting, keeps forcing itself in, and he knows this was what he looked for each time he left his apartment; he knows this was the specter that always hovered around the edge of his consciousness, tried to penetrate his dreams; he knows this was the darkness he has been fleeing from all along. This was the thing that kept him from playing that C the way it needed to be played, the way he'd been able to play it at one time. His life, his *art*, his soul, his essence, was tainted, now and forever, and he can scarcely stand it, the guilt, the monstrous enormity as it comes bearing down on him with all the weight of an avalanche, and it is then that he begins to cry aloud and doesn't notice that he is sobbing uncontrollably or that men come and get him and lead him out the door, talking to each other while he shudders with the pain that is racking his heart, and is scarcely aware that he agrees to get into a cab and keep quiet, which promise he doesn't keep, weeps uncontrollably all the way home, the cab driver one of those implacable souls who does the honorable thing and takes him straight to his door and takes only out of Jake's proffered wallet, that which was due him for the fare and a proper gratuity.

He sits up all night in his one chair and stares out the window, red neon flashing at three-second intervals, but there are no more tears, all the moisture in his body is expended and used up, and all he can see is the face of the daughter he has killed, a face he knows now will never go away.

In the morning, he flags a cab and goes first to the Mockingbird Cafe where he retrieves the horn he has left with the bartender, and then he has the cab take him out to St. Louis Cemetery. He finds the grave right away. It is in the family plot. Paris's family.

He stands there for a long time and then he remembers the trumpet case in his hand and he opens it up and takes out the gleaming golden horn. Following some sort of internal, icy sang-froid that moves his arms and fingers, he slides the mouthpiece into the opening and raises it to his lips and *blows*, the warm, winter, New Orleans sun glinting off the bell, and from the mouthpiece into the horn's chamber he pours his moist, hot breath, around the coil, gaining momentum and force and energy, until it comes out that shining bell and he blows the goddamndest C that has ever been heard by man or beast, the C that Miles achieved in "'Round Midnight," only higher, more piercing, more *lucid*. It is pure and sweet and clear like a January wind off Lake Michigan, that wind they called the Hawk, mean, and low-down, and . . . and . . . *honest*. Caught up, out of control, weeping without benefit of tears, he hears it, a memory wisp at first and then more and then there it is, right in front of him, it's Miles, man; goddamn it's Miles himself, he isn't dead, he's right here, in St. Louis Cemetery, in fucking New Orleans, at the graveside of Jake's daughter and he is playing his horn as only Miles can play, as only the gods have ever allowed one man in this particular universe to play, and Jake can only go with him on this ride, this gig, play along, blow his brains out, and it is like one horn playing, the whole time the notes coming sweetly and effortlessly and achingly; up, up from the depths, a truth that is coming, a dark specter riding on the back of the music, and Jake can feel it, sense it, know it, know that *this* is what he has been hiding from, powerless, swept along, not knowing what it is he feels, afraid of the power and the force in the undulating, pulsing spasms he feels rising in his gut, all the forces there are, above and below, all the good and the bad and all that there ever were are behind them, he and Miles, somehow they are one, riffs of pushing and screaming and demented wild horses, driving, driving, driving, and then they hit that C together, the high one that those in the know claim made Miles's lip bleed when he'd hit it, and in that instant, in that burst, in that intense, throbbing, terrible, last blast of pent-up fury and frustration and guilt and anguish and loss and death, he, Jake, feels his own blood begin to trickle down his chin and the taste of salt explodes in his mouth and he tries to cry tries to cry tries to cry but he can't can't can't can't.

# The Bad Part of Town

He was so mean that wherever he was standing became the bad part of town.

At that moment, the bad part was State Street just past Maplecrest, in the Georgetown Shopping Plaza. Behind it, actually, back by the dumpsters behind the Cap 'N Cork.

Into one of which he was stuffing the body of his wife. Abner wished she had bled more. She would have weighed less, he figured. What's the human body contain, he wondered. Eight pints? That must weigh what, ten pounds or so? He had no idea what a pint of liquid registered on the scale. She seemed to weigh much more dead than she had alive, but he knew that couldn't be true. Years ago, he had read an article in some magazine that said there was a perceptible loss of weight at the moment of death. They had weighed people as they expired. In the article, some were of the opinion it was the soul leaving the body that accounted for the loss and if that was so, an average soul weighed about an eighth of an ounce. Hardly in proportion to the amount of thought that has been directed to the subject over the millennia, he figured, and laughed at the thought. And then, he thought about thought itself. *I wonder what ideas weigh*, was what went through his mind and another soft chuckle escaped his throat.

He got the top of the leaf bag up to the edge of the bin and paused to catch his breath, holding onto the top of the bag to keep it from falling back down on the pavement.

Ever since he'd read that article he'd wondered how they'd gotten permission from the dead person or their family. The article didn't mention that; only gave the results of the study. Would such a form be a standard kind of form, or would it require some new legal language? There'd be a lawyer involved, he bet, and money would change hands. How long would such a form have to be kept on file was another question he thought of. Tax forms have to be kept for seven years he'd heard. Something like that would have to be kept longer, most likely. Maybe fourteen years. And a day. They always liked to add a day, things like that. Made it sound Biblical or something.

Abner bent down, still keeping hold of the top of the bag, reached over with his other hand and grabbed the bottom of the bag. His hand went around something squishy and then he knew what it was. Her hair. Her hair was long, about three feet long, and since she was upside-down, it would be at the bottom where he'd grabbed.

I wonder how much three feet of brown hair weighs, he mused. Two pounds? Then he decided to forget about what things weighed and just get her into the dumpster. It took just about everything he had to hoist her up and push her over the edge, and when it was done he was perspiring. I hate it when I sweat, he thought, considering driving home and taking a shower, changing his clothes. It was somewhat chilly out and a light breeze was blowing so in a minute he was dry again and decided against going home just yet.

From the trunk he pulled a tarp, the kind painters use. Indeed, there was old paint splattered all over it. Off-white. From the time she'd painted the kitchen. He threw it on top of the leaf bag. He folded the top of the dumpster closed. It banged loudly.

※ ※ ※

Abner was halfway through his second beer when a man walked in the door, looked around, then with a grin on his face walked over and sat down.

"Hey," he said to Abner, and "Genuine Draft, please," to the bartender, a heavyset woman with a wedge haircut. "Glad I caught you here," the man said, after taking a long swig out of his beer. "I saw your truck outside, thought it was yours."

"I'm here," Abner said, without turning his head, just looking straight ahead at the pool table where two guys were playing.

"Yeah. So you are." He took out his handkerchief and wiped it across his forehead. "Man! I thought it would be cool enough to mow the lawn, but it's hot enough, all right!"

"Yeah. It's hot enough."

The man glanced at the side of Abner's face and then back at his beer, turning it in his hand to read the label. Satisfied with what he saw there, he lifted the bottle and took another long pull. That done, he turned and cleared his throat.

"Ah, Abner."

"Yeah."

"Abner, I wanted to talk to you about something."

"Yeah."

"It's not me, it's Beth. You know me, I hear a little racket, I can live with it, but Beth, well she is pregnant y' know, and she wanted me to say something. I know things been rough for you since the layoff and all—I don't know how you do it, you know, take care of Mary Elizabeth and all . . . " His voice trailed off and he tapped out a cigarette and lighted it.

"I mean, I know things're bad and all, but still. I got my own family to think of. You understand." He gave Abner a quick sideways glance and then took another pull on his beer.

Abner didn't respond, only crooked his finger at the bartender and laid two singles on the bar, pulling them out of his trouser pocket.

"The thing is, Abner, Beth needs her rest. That business last night kept her up all night. She didn't get a wink of sleep. She's sleeping now, in fact. Twelve o'clock on a Sunday! Can you beat that?"

"No," said Abner, sipping on his new beer. "I don't believe I can."

"The thing is, I hate to say anything, believe me, but I've got a pregnant wife here and she needs her sleep. What can we do about this?"

"Don't do nothing."

"What do you mean?"

For the first time, Abner turned his head and looked at the other man. Just stared at him until the other man turned away and picked up his beer.

"I mean, don't do nothin'. There won't be no more noise like last night. That's all over."

"Oh!" said the other man, startled-like. "Oh." He seemed to ponder that a minute and then picked up his beer and killed it. "Well then, I guess that's that. Well, thanks, Abner. Thanks a lot. I guess I'll go now. Yes. That's it. I'll get going. Put it in the wind."

"Yes," said Abner.

The man went back out the door, swabbing at his forehead again with his handkerchief. Abner picked up his change. He saw the glare the bartender gave him and just stared at her until she looked away. She walked down to the other end of the bar and began rubbing down the counter with short, furious strokes, her wedge bouncing in time with the towel.

He walked down to her end and stopped just in front of her. From his pocket he took two quarters, which he laid on the bar.

"How much you figure hair weighs?" he said to the woman.

"Huh?"

"Hair. I said, 'how much does hair weigh?'"

"What kind of hair?"

"Hair like this." He reached over the bar before she could react and wrapped his fingers around her wedge and pulled her toward him.

"Ow! Stop that, asshole! You crazy or somethin'? Let go of my hair!"

He saw the two men playing pool stop and look in their direction. One man took a step toward them and the other put his arm across his friend's chest. They stood and watched, waiting. It didn't matter to Abner, what they did.

"I'm just after some information," he said to the woman. He hadn't let go of her hair. She seemed to discover that if she didn't move it wouldn't hurt. "How much does hair weigh? Say, three feet of hair like yours. Brown hair."

"I dunno," she said, her voice sullen and low.

"Make a guess," he said, and squeezed, just a little.

"Ouch! Ow! Okay, okay. I'd say half a pound. Now, let me go."

"Just one more question." He watched the two men. One started walking over, the other behind him coming too, only a little slower. He noticed they'd both held onto their pool cues.

"How much you figure a soul weighs?"

He waited for her answer, squeezing his fingers together slowly, and he waited for the two men to get to them. He just watched and waited and squeezed his fingers together tighter and tighter and everything slowed down just the way he wanted it to.

# My Idea of a Nice Thing

S he woke up at three in the morning, like she'd been doing for more than a week now, and her brain was buzzing, all kinds of thoughts flying around in there, so she used the trick she'd come up with, of lying perfectly still and picturing a single goldfish swimming in a small fishbowl. The next thing she was conscious of was the alarm ringing in her ear and her mouth being dry and her head hurting. And she wanted a drink in the worst way.

**✖ ✖ ✖**

"It's why I drink," she said, the first time she stood up at A.A. "My job. I'm a hairdresser. See, you take on all of these other people's personalities and troubles and things, ten or twelve of 'em a day, and when the end of the day comes, you don't know who *you* are any more. It takes three drinks just to sort yourself out again, bring the real you up to the surface." That brought scattered laughter. Someone started a basket around for contributions.

"So I drink. I drink and try to figure out what it is I want. Once, I had a good job—manager of a good salon uptown, had a husband and a kid, had it all—and then, just like that, one day I got off the streetcar on the way to work over on St. Charles Avenue and there was this bar that looked so . . . so inviting, you know? Not that I'd ever been much of a drinker, I wasn't, a highball on my birthday, a beer at the beach, that was pretty much it. Only time I ever got drunk was the day I graduated from beauty school, when a bunch of us . . . well, that's not important.

"Well, anyway, I jumped off the streetcar and went into this bar— and didn't go home for three days. Somebody picked me up and we got a bottle and went to his apartment and it was like . . . like . . . I can't explain it. It was like the greatest thing that ever happened. And the worst. Then, a lot of stuff happened. I lost it all. Husband, little girl, job, *everything*, the whole bit. I sound like everybody else here, don't I?" She laughed self-consciously. "This is my first day without a drink in a long, long time. Actually, I want a drink right now in the worst way. Anyway, that's how it started and that's where I am. One day of sobriety. Not even a full day yet."

"You can do it, Raye." Someone in the back. "One day at a time. That's the secret." A chorus of yesses, like people amening in church.

"It's okay, Raye. Take your time. We're all friends here." It was Jim, the chairman of the meeting. She tried to smile, then she was aware that she was crying and that none of the people she was standing in front of were talking to one another, they were all looking at her, and so she giggled, took out a Kleenex from her purse and dabbed at her eyes, and said, "Well, check out the weepy babe. Sorry, folks."

Voices came from the audience.

"That's okay, Raye."

"We been there, Raye."

"We're with you, girl."

She had it together now. "So, I started drinking. That was a long time ago. Now, I can't seem to get it under control. I guess . . . I guess I've hit my bottom. That's why I'm here. To get help. That's all. Thank you."

Chants of "Raye, Raye" and she sat down and another woman strode up to the podium. "Hi, my name's JeriSue and I'm an alcoholic."

During the break, she found herself talking to three or four people, continuing the recital of her drinking history. Her voice was in a high register, and she was unable to stop the words tumbling out, in the back of her mind seeing a tumbler of vodka, glacially cold in her hand.

"I'd go in a bar, thinking I'd only have one, maybe a shooter or two, and then leave. I started playing my horn. I was first cornet in high school. I was going to make records then, fly in airplanes to New York, give interviews in *Down Beat*. I bought this trumpet. I'd always wanted to play the trumpet. I found I couldn't play it any more though. Correction. I couldn't play it sober. When I was drunk, that was a different story. I could kick some ass, then. I could kick off the traces, play some licks. So, I drank for that. That's what I told myself. That's when I lost my job. That meant I had more time to hit the bars. At first, I tried to be good, just have a short one, maybe meet somebody nice. I thought I had to have another husband, another baby. I'd tell the bartender, 'just let me have one, two at the most. I have to be somewhere.'"

All of the people gathered around her shook their heads knowingly. "We've been there, honey," said one of the women, patting her lightly on her shoulder.

"And then, well, then, you're just feeling so damned good and you don't want to lose the feeling, the high, so you just keep on ordering them. Black Russians. That's what I like. The European way. Here, they use Kahlua—in Europe they use dark crème de cocoa. A White Russian is with white crème de cocoa." It was at this point that the moderator of the meeting who had joined the group—"Hi, my name is Jim and I'm an alcoholic!"—interceded.

"Uh, Raye. Raye, I have to interrupt. One of the rules of this meeting is that we don't talk about the merits of alcohol here. It gets folks to thinking about drinking and . . . well, you see, don't you? Bad form, doll." He flashed his teeth and turned away, walking toward another group.

Later on, after the meeting, she let Jim take her out for more coffee—like they hadn't had enough, she felt like Juan Valdez for Christ's sake. She sat across from him in the booth wondering what she was doing there with someone who was already grating on her nerves, listening to him explain again the protocol of meetings. Knowing what was coming and lacking the energy or the willpower to stop it.

A quick bang is exactly the way she would have described the activity she and Jim engaged in next, and he apologized, telling her with a little laugh that when he drank he had the staying power of a

Brahma bull, and he almost felt like taking up the demon again, in times like these, and she knew instinctively that was a cue for her to say, oh, no, Jim, it was fine, really. Don't you know it's quality, not quantity that counts? It's the size of the fight in the dog, not the size of the dog in the fight. She actually said that, mixed it up like that, although it was true; not only was he quick, but he was a peewee, and all the way home after she left him, she kept laughing aloud, she couldn't help it, and as soon as she hit the door it was out with the vibrator, and it wasn't "Hi, I'm Jim and I'm an alcoholic!" she pictured as she lay there in bed, but Richard Gere.

✳ ✳ ✳

It was the third meeting this week—it had been a tough week—waking at three every morning. But it was this or vodka, and she just couldn't do that any more. It was plain, even to her, she had to quit. She'd lied the first time she stood up in the meeting and told the thing about taking on ten or twelve people's personalities—hell, that was a long time ago. She hadn't cut that many people's hair a day for a long time now. Her business stunk, too many lost days, incoherent days, days of cursing and boozy breath just under the mint odor of gum as she struggled with hair that wouldn't do anything, days of alternatively weeping and throwing things—hair brushes, curlers, shampoo bottles—in the back room, and days when she didn't even make the effort to get up, but lay in the sour-damp of her bed, a bottle of vodka her lover, the TV going but not quite loud enough to catch what the actors on the talk shows and the soaps were saying and her too exhausted to get out of bed and turn up the volume, dozing by fits and starts, and even peeing the bed because she just couldn't get up and make that trip to the bathroom, and besides, what did it matter? Ten or twelve clients a day was distant history, the situation now was that she had a good day if she saw two or three people, mostly those who had even bigger problems than she did, and she was down to a booth rental situation, the lowest professional status there was, her own shop long since closed and the government sending her regular letters for back taxes like any other dunning agency, so many she no longer felt the fear jump up in her gut when she received one of their envelops.

This was her bottom and she finally knew it, so here she was, but how much longer she could keep going this way she didn't know and didn't hold out much hope if this was the best chance she had.

When the urge hit (when didn't it hit . . . ) the meeting sounded great, a place of refuge, of salvation, but as soon as she got there, the optimism evaporated and looking around at the pale, pinched faces of the other alcoholics just made her crazy to go out and get *faced*. The places they met in all looked like cheap bars with the lights turned on, and the people there seemed like the people she'd seen in the one Fellini movie she'd ever attended and which she hadn't understood except that it depressed her. All the actors hollow-eyed and unshaven and wearing blank stares and speaking in long Italian monotone sentences the translator had reduced to a few short English words on the screen in Caligula letters. She felt she was missing something crucial that the other, obviously-better-educated people sitting around her—including her date—knew, and then she knew she was right when her date, whose hair she'd cut for the first time that afternoon, kept calling it a *film* instead of a *movie*, and right then she knew she'd have to give him a fantastic piece of ass, screw his silly, effete brains out, even though she didn't want to, and knew she'd never see him again, either, and that was the only good thing about it; the relief that gave her; get the fuck the fuck over with and get on with her life.

Here, the people had the same ghoulish patina about them, as if they'd just given blood and then slipped back into line again to earn a little extra, and it seemed everyone was a used car salesman or acted like it. Personality-plus, oozing out of their pores. The meetings, which had originally held out a promise for her, quickly turned into something like a glass of 7-Up left standing on the coffee table overnight.

"I wish they'd dim the lights," she found herself whispering to the person on her left.

"I know what you mean," said her neighbor, a lady on the far side of middle age, her cheeks rouge-red with broken capillaries. "What I hate is the coffee. You'd think they'd serve something better than this Maxwell House mud. I mean, we're in New Orleans. They could get something with flavor, Community or Café du Monde, couldn't they?"

Raye liked the woman.

"God, yes. Wouldn't it be nice if they served herbal tea? And put it in china, not these godawful Styrofoam cups. I keep biting these cups and it's like somebody's nails on a blackboard, only worse. You can *feel* it, not just hear it."

"I know just what you mean."

Those were things she hated about the meetings, but she was here again, at the gathering at the hospital, downstairs in one of those rooms painted no-thought institution green, and even though the heat was turned up high, it felt cold and damp and she kept her sweater on. She picked this meeting because it was close to the room she was renting, within walking distance. Raye's purse was full of little hand-drawn maps and addresses and even brochures of where meetings were held, and a copy of what she called "The Drunk's Prayer." At virtually any given time of day or night, there was a meeting going on somewhere, even in the French Quarter. Especially in the French Quarter. She'd had no accurate assessment of the extent of the problem until she'd begun to collect the cartography.

✄ ✄ ✄

"So. How long you been sober?"

She'd been standing in line for almost five minutes of the fifteen-minute break and just now reached the pot, the huge chrome kind they always had at these meetings. Large coffee pots and large green ash trays. Standard A.A. decor. From Alaska to Alabama, she bet. If you've ever been to more than one meeting, from then on, if someone were to lead you into a room, blindfolded, then take it off and ask you where you were, if you saw a large coffee pot and green ashtrays scattered about, you'd know. It was a place where you came to think hard about the thing you loved most so that you could find ways to avoid it.

❈ ❈ ❈

"My idea of a nice thing," he said, "would be a world where you could get drunk and it wouldn't harm you, physically, anyway."

"Raye," she said, turning and offering her hand. "My name is Raye."

"Hi, Raye. Emory. Like the board."

She didn't quite get it at first and then she did and smiled.

"I liked what you said that time, about sorting yourself out."

Again, she didn't get it at first, and then she realized he must have been at the meeting she'd first gotten up and spoken at.

"Well, yeah, it's kind of like that, but boy did I get in trouble saying that!"

"From Jim, right? 'You shouldn't talk about the joys of drink at a meeting or a place where that's all the people think about?' That Jim?" He grinned, and she saw he had great teeth, even and white, and what was nice was the way he smiled. Like he was unaware of how great his teeth really were, that he was smiling just because he was happy or had thought of something funny. "There's been talk of replacing ol' Jim. He gets his meetings mixed up, thinks this is Parents Without Partners."

There must have been something in her face that made him realize he'd said the wrong thing.

"Look, I'm sorry. Let's get out of here," he said. "Go get a drink."

They use the same pick-up lines here they do in bars, Raye thought.

"I don't mean a drink with liquor in it," he said. "I mean a Coke or something, but in a bar. This place feels like a hospital. It's depressing."

"This is a hospital . . . Emory," she added his name haltingly, knowing that once she'd said it she was going to leave with him.

**✖ ✖ ✖**

"What do you do?" she said, sipping her Perrier. The juke box was throbbing with an old Doc Pomus cut and it made her leg jump. Emory was sitting across from her drinking ginger ale.

He grinned and said, "I take human experience and distill it, add my own to it, and give it back to others."

"Oh, you're a writer," she said, pleased at her insight and surprised, as well. This was going to be a different conversation than the ones she usually had at work. When this conversation was over, she had a feeling she wouldn't be needing a drink to figure out who she was.

"No, but you're close. I play the trumpet. In a band. Not a band, actually. A group. We play Uptown. Off Magazine. You know, the Street of Dreams."

"Oh, where?"

"E Carté."

"Oh."

All of a sudden, she craved a drink. More than she ever had in her life, even more than in the middle of her first A.A. meeting.

"Are you any good?"

He laughed, teeth flashing. "I'm not Chet Baker, but then who is? Yeah, I'm not bad. I'm not greedy, either."

"Greedy?"

"I could make a lot more money if I played a different way. I used to do studio work. I did work for groups you've heard of."

The way he said that, she knew he was poking fun at her, possibly even sneering slightly, at what he assumed to be her ignorance of music. It made her mad, and also it made her almost forget her need for a drink.

"I play myself, Emory."

"Well . . . right! So you know jazz. I remember you said you played something in high school. The trombone, wasn't it? That's great. That's really great."

"It was the cornet. I play a little trumpet, too." She stopped and looked at him a minute as if deciding something, and then said, "Never mind. Order me another Perrier, will you?"

They didn't speak for awhile, just sat and sipped and looked around, and she tried not to think of obvious things like how drinkers always look awful to people who aren't in the same condition, and she was proud that even though she thought it, she didn't say it to the man across from her.

"Why do you drink?"

She was surprised she'd said that, and afraid for a minute that he would just get up and leave.

"I didn't feel any pressure."

"Excuse me?"

"When I'm on the wagon. Like now. I don't feel any pressure unless I drink. How do I explain that? There's no tension in my music, no pain. There's no pain now, none at all. I drink for the pressure. I can't explain it, Raye. When I drink, I feel pain and it's exquisite and it's beautiful and it's an *element*. As in *elemental*. It's something I need, for my music. Since I quit, got off the sauce, it's not there. The pain. The tension. Now . . . I don't know . . . I feel like . . . like—"

"This?" She picked up one of the cocktail napkins on the table, a plain white one.

"Yes," he said, staring at her, a grin that was not a grin, starting, teeth showing, more a grimace than a smile. "Yes, that's it. Like that." He reached over and took both the napkin and her hand in his and then he plucked the napkin away and crushed it in his fist and opened it, the napkin now a crumpled lump. He turned his hand slightly and it fell on the table.

"I think that's why I came here tonight. I think I'm going to have a drink tonight."

"You are?"

"Yes. I'm sorry. I wasn't clear about it until I got here, but now that we're here, I know I'm going to have a drink. And then another. And then a whole bunch more. I don't guess I'll be at any more of the meetings. As a matter of fact, maybe you'd better go. I'm really sorry— I didn't mean to bring you here for this. I was just after a little . . . you know . . . romance, or something. Now, I see that wasn't what I was after. I just wanted a witness."

"Oh, Emory." she didn't know what else to say. What *could* she say? "How long has it been?"

"Since I've had a drink? Three years. Close to three years. And I stink. My music. For close to three years it's stunk. Know what Ortega y Gasset said? He said, 'Man will even use sublimity to degrade himself.' Think about that."

Raye didn't have a clue what he was talking about, so she did the honest thing. She asked what it was he meant.

"I signed a contract last night to do a recording. Someone heard me play. A big shot. From Atlantic. He thought I was great, signed me up on the spot. Isn't that terrible?"

I must have missed something, she thought, and then she said so.

"This guy heard me play something technically good, but it was nothing. A nothing piece. Like I've been playing for three years. It was like practicing the scales, like playing classical music. He wanted me because I was perfect, not because I was good. Do you understand? Look at this."

He reached into his jacket pocket and brought out a piece of folded paper which he held up briefly and then put away. It was a check made out to Emory Duplessis, but she couldn't see the amount, and there was a logo, but he didn't hold it up long enough for her to make it out, see if it was really from Atlantic.

He did a surprising thing. He tore the check in half. Then, he turned and signaled the waitress, snapping his fingers, and when the woman came near, he told her he wanted a Jack and water, make the color dark, and Raye sat there a minute, wondering what to do, and then she decided, and got up. She held out her hand and he took it, not shaking it, just holding it, but not looking at her, just grinning, those great, perfect teeth shining, his eyes on some distant point. The drink hadn't even arrived and already he looked like the other drinkers in the place, disheveled and awful, just as a consequence of his decision, but he looked good, too, of a sudden embued with a quality those back at the A.A. meeting lacked—a look of purpose. That was what had been missing with those coffee-swilling wraiths at the meetings, that was what she had suspected in herself and even in Emory here, and was now dissipated, replaced with a firmness and tilt of his jaw. He's got his pain back, thought Raye, and it shows, and he's happy, too; that shows, and then she saw something in his eye as she lingered awkwardly there, standing and staring down at him, that the pain was there, and the joy too, but it was not real, the light in his eye was the light of a fever. She remembered the same light in her father's eye right before he spent his last breath swearing he had just seen God in one of his hallucinations and was now happy and could die, and it came to her that this man, this Emory, was only preparing to die, to commit suicide, and when that knowledge struck her brain, she dropped his hand and ran from him, gasping, bumping into someone who clutched at her then tearing from his grasp and rushing out the door and somehow finding a cab, or a cab found her, and she was riding through the wet-blackened streets of New Orleans and then home and in bed, clothes flung all around, and trembling so that she turned up the heat and pulled the covers over her.

She lay there, every muscle tensed until she had to jump out of bed and stand on the arch of her foot to relieve the cramp, and then she went to sleep and slept in frigid perspiration, soaking the sheets as if she'd peed herself.

She slept for maybe an hour, an hour and a half, and then she got up and adjusted the water in the shower until it steamed. For a long time after her shower, she stood naked in front of her closet, then pulled out her black cocktail dress, the one she called her "Come fuck me dress," and telephoned for a cab.

To the Absinthe House, she answered their question into the receiver; what the fuck do you care?

In the kitchen cupboard, right behind the scarlet bag of Community dark roast, was a jar with her booth rental money for the next week, and she took all of it and stuck it in her purse.

When the cab came, she saw its lights from the bedroom window, but went over and sat on the bed instead of going out. The driver honked and honked and finally came to the door downstairs and began banging away. She could hear him cursing. The landlady must have been away for no one answered, and after awhile, he went back to his cab, honked once or twice more and then left, screeching his tires.

She sat there for the longest time, just staring, and then dumped her purse on the bed. She hunted through the bits and scraps of papers, looking at each one until she got the one she wanted. It was the address of a meeting that met for the convenience of shift workers and it met in two more hours, at 5:00 A.M. It was close enough to walk to.

She went through the apartment hunting for cigarettes, ripping cushions off the sofa, finally finding part of a pack in a utility drawer in the kitchen. She put water on for coffee. She sparked a cigarette to life, drawing the smoke into her lungs sharply and audibly. She went over and tapped her fingers rapidly on the outside of the coffeepot, feeling its warmth. She turned the flame up higher. She hated that coffeepot. It took a fucking lifetime to reach a boil. She turned it as high as it would go.

This time she was going to stick to it. Fuck Emory and all the other Emorys in the world. They have their nerve. She started to cry, then forced herself to stop, wiping the tears angrily with her forearm. She got up and got the stool from the kitchen and brought it over to the bedroom closet. Way back in the corner, so far back she was afraid she might fall as she stretched for it, she felt the round, smooth bottle of Stoli. Taking it over to the bed she started to drink straight from the bottle.

"No," she said aloud. "Be a lady, Raye."

She got up and went to the kitchen cupboard and got down a glass that said "1984 World's Fair" on it and sat down at the table and poured it half full of clear liquid.

*This is it*, she said to herself. *I'll kill this one last bottle and then I'll go to the meeting and that will be the last time I will ever drink again.*

She gulped half the glass down, feeling the warmth spread from her fingers clear out to her fingers and toes. She finished the glass and poured another, this one full. That done, she got up and went back to the closet and picked up a weathered black case and took it back to the table. Opening it, she took out the horn that was inside, resting on a carpet of red velvet. Putting the mouthpiece in was a little tricky; her fingers fumbled a bit, but she got it in and put it to her lips.

And blew the sweetest, highest E imaginable. Blew and held it and played with it, letting it stagger and fall and rise again, higher and higher, and then she went through the scales, not the way a beginner does, but the way a magician does, going off into half-notes, quarter notes, sending impossible trills bouncing around the tiny apartment, off the bed, the walls, through the open window, and out into the street below and off into the distance, as far as sound could travel.

"Hey you in there!" Somebody on the other side of the wall pounded, a man's voice yelling, "We're trying to sleep. Cut that crap or I'm calling a cop!"

"Fuck you," she screamed, spittle erupting at the corners of her mouth. She brought the horn back up to her lips, shutting out the renewed thumping on the wall, whatever the man began shouting.

She sent pursed, razored waves of rage into the mouthpiece, a tune as old as violence and as new as sex . . . the notes flying about and tumbling into a raggedy-ass, mean, low-down, sweet-as-sin, organic *thing* that said, *There, motherfucker, that's soul, Emory-boy. That's what soul is, you poor, sad sonuvabitch.* And the goldfish from her dreams swam up from somewhere and circled her, rising and falling with the sound of the trumpet, and she played faster and faster and more and more maniacally . . . but always, reluctantly and helplessly, with one steady, unforgiving eye on the clock so she wouldn't be late for the meeting.

# Ten Cents a Dance

I'm not sure how I found this place. It's hidden over on Camp Street, a part of New Orleans I never frequent. It's a dance hall, the old-fashioned kind where you buy tickets and dance with "hostesses." It's certainly not a place I would have stumbled upon while Caroline and I were together.

There is a price sign hanging on the wall when I walk upstairs and enter the large ballroom and it has obviously been there a long time. The sign is a historian's find, a chronicle of inflation, and I eye it nervously as I dig down in my pocket. "Three bucks" is at the end of the list, the only virgin. I have the feeling the latest price could be raised any minute; the sign-changer is in the bathroom just now and will be out, Magic Marker in hand, revision his mission.

"Three dances," I say, sliding a twenty through the little window. The crone in the cage doesn't want to give me my change now that it is clutched in her blue-rivered hand, but I wait her out, staring until she releases her breath and my change, thrusting crumpled bills at me, damp and soft.

I move away, checking my armpits, pretending to scratch a difficult place on my back, and then head for the girls lined all in a row like clothespins on a Monday line. Tic-Tacs hide the Bushmills, four of them scrunched twixt my cheeks and gums, positioned for slow time-release.

It is just past noon on a weekday. Only three couples are out on the floor. I wish there were thirty; I need people to blend into. I feel on display. I am no John Travolta, but since I have gone this far, I go ahead and take the arm of the first girl in line, my eyes meeting hers for the obligatory second, and it is only when we are out on the floor moving in circles that I sneak a better look at her.

"Pumpkin," she says, and it takes me a minute to understand she's giving me her name.

"Evan," I say, completing the social trade. And, "I'm sort of between jobs—I'm on kind of a sabbatical," to answer the question that follows.

"Me, too," she says, and giggles and her teeth flash, very white and a little crooked, on the bottom, a cute little gap between the top two.

She is blonde except for about an inch of orangish-brown at the front hairline, and carries well what I estimate to be an extra fifteen pounds; she appears attractive enough in her blue dress and matching pumps. It is what I always think of as a "sundress," and I don't know if that's the correct name, but it's the one that pops into mind. The kind where the bottom flares out when the girl twirls and you can see her panties.

It is just such a dress Caroline wore the last time we were together. It only seems like six weeks, but next week it will be two years. A lot of time spent answering "What's yours, pal?" and running black and white movies in my head in solitary moments while attempting to achieve a state of waking coma.

I saw her one day, coming out of a hotel on Canal with a man who looked familiar. I'd played football against him, in fact. Sam something. I'd forgotten his last name. He was a starter, a tight end, well-known. All-City, that kind of thing. I was just a scrub on the sideline when he set a record with a ninety-nine-yard touchdown run against us. He ran right by me, passing by less than twelve inches away. He was making this tremendous run, and he had this dreamy look on his face, like he didn't even know where he was. Unconscious. That's what somebody standing behind me said. "That fucker runs like he's unconscious." Somebody else said, "Fucker's on drugs."

I guess I recognized him because that was the look on his face the day I saw him with Caroline. Dreamy, like he was in another world. Arbutux 12. Maybe he was on drugs. He looked the way my mirror said I did when I'd gotten a speedball inside me, that period of my life.

They didn't see me; I was just part of the general street scene, but it didn't much matter.

It was odd I hadn't run into her before that. New Orleans is good-sized, but not that big. Come to think of it, she had never liked the Quarter much and that was where I pretty much stayed. She was more partial to Uptown, places like 4141 on St. Charles, with the long lines of Jags and Porsches and limos, or Que Séra, or Flagons over on Magazine, the "real" Uptown. Commander's Palace for Oysters Bienville, that sort of thing.

She was an Uptown girl, down to her styled "unstyled" hair and raw silk blouses, and even though we had lived in Metairie for several years, she never forgot where she came from and who she was, and would leave a party at the first hint of a "yat" accent. She had never considered so much as a cab ride through East New Orleans. Algiers, across the river, might as well have been in Pakistan. Those were the sort of places only missionaries would be interested in. New Orleans to Caroline was a small fiefdom, the Quarter only a sometime excursion, mostly for the sport of laughing at the tourists. Certainly not to eat. Arnaud's was the only restaurant that had ever seen her gold card.

I see the sundress on the girl I am dancing with, and that is the movie that plays, and it makes her a real person, and my stomach skitters a little like it did way back in high school when a pretty girl said "hi" in the hall. I realize this is the first woman I have been this close to in almost two years; at least the first one upon whom I have conferred possibilities. I am embarrassed by my hands, and the more I am aware of them the worse they perspire.

"Sorry," I mumble.

"Just get out of jail?" she says and then laughs.

There is no logic for my sudden shyness. It makes no sense at all, the girl I am dancing with is obviously a prostitute, poorly-educated, and while her looks aren't all that bad, she isn't in Caroline's league. It has to be the dress, which is silly if I think about it, which of course

I do, trying to figure out why my chemistry is reacting this way and why I am desperately considering with a seized-up brain what to say to this person.

We dance twice more, using up all my tickets and then I start to leave, having no plan.

"Thank you," I say. "Here." I thrust a five-dollar bill at her and she gives me her name and tells me to ask for her next time. I find my nerve when she says this. "Well, I guess I don't have to leave right this second," I tell her, and buy five more dances, two of which I spend on her before a man in a blue business suit comes up and says her name and she goes over in a corner with him. She returns and stands before me.

"I have to take a break."

We had gone through all the dancing stages until we were cheek to cheek, metabolizing our movements. Now that I have the rhythm, I consider using the rest of my tickets with one of the other girls, but then I go out to the street instead, where the tourists with their go-cups are walking in pairs and even-numbered groups. When I get to my apartment, I toss the unused tickets on top of the dresser, where they began talking to me as soon as I laid down on the bed and closed my eyes.

"She gave you enough hints, man."

I was surprised to hear them speak. For a moment, I thought someone else was in the room.

"I think you're mistaken."

"Mistaken? Hell, man, we work for her. How could we be mistaken? You like her, you should do something about it. How do you think *we* feel? We should be at work, doing our job. You know that guy she left you for? You really think that was a *break* she went on?"

"Leave me alone," I said. As soon as I opened my eyes, they became cardboard tickets again. I threw them in the waste basket in the kitchen and went out to find a bar.

This was all several weeks ago. I am here for my tenth visit to-day; which makes it an "anniversary." I tell her that and that I have a surprise for her.

"Jeezum," she says, confirmation that she had an Irish Channel childhood. After nine visits I know it is her professional name which is Pumpkin, and her given name is Gwendolyn. "Pumpkin is my stage name," she'd said, while Patsy Cline was singing "Faded Love." For some reason, which she refused to divulge, we had to sit that song out whenever they played it. We were sitting on the wooden folding chairs along the side of the dance floor, watching others take their dancing pleasure.

"My agent said I needed a name to catch the eye of casting direc-tors," she said. "Whaddya think?"

I agree. I say it would catch my eye if I was a casting director. I am not anything remotely that interesting. I am only an heir, having inherited from parents who died in a car accident. I omitted saying that "Gwendolyn" would do the same if I was a casting director and glancing down lists of names. Gwendolyn is not a name I have wit-nessed outside of fiction.

I have resisted asking why she did not take a Greyhound to New York, or Amtrak to Los Angeles for her dream, and am glad that I have. She tells me on her own on the second or third visit that she has already had a part in a Clint Eastwood movie two years ago, and that the New Orleans Film Association has her on file, and to move to either coast would cause her to lose the name she has built up here. She would lose valuable momentum by leaving.

The part she got in the Eastwood flick was brilliant typecasting, I think when she describes it. She said they even let her make up her own dialogue, *two lines*.

"What's this surprise?" she says, to my announcement. "Dia-monds or something?"

There is a smile in her voice, but I can see she is serious, under. I am way ahead of her. I pull out her present. It is a roll of squash-yellow tickets, Saturday's color. Seventy-five dollars worth. I resisted saying "hi" to them. I have all her dances for the evening. We wouldn't even have to dance all of them. None of them if she wanted. It was her choice. I explained it all to her. I didn't tell her that I'd made reservations at L'il Cajun Cuisine. That was another surprise. It would be like a date and the beauty of it was, I wouldn't be taking up her work time, costing her wages. I could have just given her the money, but I thought her pride would prevent her from taking it.

"Oh fuck," she says. "I gotta talk wit' th' manager, him."

She leaves me standing in the middle of the dance floor with Barry Manilow's vocal stylings and six or seven couples, mostly sailors and older businessmen. I stand there a minute, like a misplaced semicolon, and then go sideways through the dancers, through armpit odors and fruity perfume. I go to the far side of the hall and lean up against the handrail, avoiding the mirror that reflects everything. I can see Pumpkin. She is talking to the boss, a man with the body shape of a duck, a man who combs his hair on his birthday, which is also when he must wash it. The money he saves on shampoo cannot possibly be used on clothing, for each time I have seen him, he has on the same green-banana leisure suit with the stitching showing like the outline of a skeleton, so I guess that somewhere there is a mattress stuffed with bills.

There is a lot of arm-waving between them, and then she points to the spot where we'd been dancing. Her finger strikes out there and she moves it in an arc until it lights on me, freeze-framing for a minute. Somehow, I think of Caroline. She would never point in the direction of a human being. Uptown girls never point. I see something else that has escaped my notice until now. Pumpkin is wearing the blue sundress she had on the first time. I look away and out the window high on the opposite side of the hall. Tree tops are bending and the sky is the color of bullets. We are going to have a blow, I think. A norther.

"I got your money back."

It is Pumpkin. I had daydreamed for a minute and she crept up on the edge of it and walked in. I watch my daydream fall to the floor and shatter into crystallized dust.

"Why would you do that?"

She has fire in her eye, and I think maybe I need to teach her fat boss the proper way to talk to a lady. I look around for him, but he has vanished.

"You stupid creep—I don't make squat from tickets. Tips and extra services is what fills my sock."

"I'm sorry, Pumpkin." What was I to say? "I didn't know."

"Here." She thrust a wad of bills into my hand and grabbed the roll of tickets from the other. I saw they looked depressed.

"Go bother somebody else. Less you want an extra service." She stood staring at me for a moment, eyebrows raised, and I realized I was supposed to say something, but what? I knew what "extra services" meant, but I didn't want to think of her in that way.

She walked away from me and right up to a portly sailor who'd just come in. She linked her arm with his and pulled him over to the ticket cage. I saw him reach into the little pocket in front where the swabbies keep their wallets and pull out green bills. She took up one of them and handed it to the cashier and tore off a ticket from the roll she'd taken from me and gave it to him, handing the rest back through the window. I could see my yellow ticket in his hand, a smiley face materializing. It still felt like it belonged to me, but then I saw the bills in my hand and realized that was not so.

She walked onto the floor with the Porky Pig sailor and Frank Sinatra sang "My Way" for them. We had danced to it before. Four times.

I watched for awhile, a non-erasable smile that didn't reflect my state of mind but I couldn't get off. Then I left. On the way out, Pumpkin looked over at me. Piranhas swam from her to me. They swam along the paths of her eye-rays. I lowered my head and looked away and they dropped to the floor, flopping and writhing about in the poisonous oxygen. Just a short; not an entire movie.

I went downstairs, edging sideways past a drunk who'd misplaced his razor, sitting halfway down, nursing a paper bag. He thought his bottle of Ripple to be gold and me Jesse James by the look I got. I nodded to him and passed by, and went out into the street. I wandered about for awhile, ending up on St. Peter Street, and then a red neon sign begged me to enter the building that supplied its juice. Symbiotic relationship, I deduced, wondering if there were any other kinds. The sign spoke in a blue-collar voice and whispered seductively: BEER.

I had a Bushmill's and soda and thought about the hole in the ozone layer for awhile. Then I thought about God, but it was too big a subject for one drink, so I went poking about in the corners of my mind for something smaller, maybe a souvenir from a past trip. The hole in the ozone layer kept niggling me back, so I played for awhile with it and then snuck up on a small gray box wedged under a rafter in my attic. I opened it with trepidation and fingers that trembled slightly, and found a cabin in Wyoming, in the Grand Tetons, where I hunted elk and rabbits and wrote poetry and stories like Rick Bass, and came home to a yellow-haired woman who called me "Slim" and wore no bra under her gingham dress. Pretty soon, though, that nice little image got away from me and it swelled up as big as the hole in the ozone and nearly as big as God. I put it away and ordered another drink.

"Double, please." I put down twice as much money.

"Wife, girlfriend, or your dog Spot just die?"

I looked around. I was the only customer, so he was talking to me.

"No."

"Girlfriend, eh?"

Bartenders, presidential candidates, fathers and people in barbershops. They see everything, know everything.

"Maybe."

"Well, I say try booze. If that doesn't work, try drugs. If that doesn't work, sometimes you just have to plain kill yourself."

I listened to him laugh. He was quite the psychiatrist. I looked away, toward the back where a pool game was going on.

"Well, shit happens, bud. Just trying t' make you laugh, get your mind off your troubles. No harm, no foul, eh?"

He went back up the bar, polishing things with his bar rag.

I had another double, and then another, and then I had to go to the bathroom. I left my change on the bar. If you couldn't trust bartenders, civilization was over. Thinking about the trust of bartenders gave me a warm feeling. Bartenders and drunks. The brotherhood of man. I pictured a t-shirt: *We're All Buds on the Apple Tree of Life.* Red letters on a blue background with a little apple tree below it.

I took the shirt with me to the bathroom where it accidentally fell in the stool while I was pissing. I had to flush it and hoped it wouldn't stop up the plumbing.

I must have been in the bathroom a long time. Maybe I was sick.

When I came out there were two other people on barstools and a different bartender. This one looked at me like I was Pancho Villa and he came down to my end and stopped in front of me.

"What's yours?" he asked, his eyes mean and suspicious. I noticed the money I'd left behind was gone.

I said, "Bushmill's and soda, please."

Ten Cents A Dance

I see the sign in my head, like credits rolling. I see lines through the numbers and words and I wonder if the current owner was the one who drew them or if he bought a defaced sign on purpose, along with the rest of the business. He's the one that did it, I decided. He's the type.

※ ※ ※

It is later that evening and I am at the dance hall again. In the alley where she comes out each night. In my nostrils is the sickly-sweet odor of spoiled oysters and boiled shrimp and stale beer in the bottoms of garbage cans. I am trying to think of something witty and urbane to say, but all I can manage is to remember part of a joke. Just the punch line. "She wouldn't shut up so I married her."

Canada has sent us the weather they're tired of and I wish for a warm coat, or better, a pint bottle.

I am waiting for Pumpkin. To clear up this little misunderstanding. When I left this afternoon, I didn't know what to say to her. Now I do—Bushmill's has given me another language—the language of lovers. I am Rudolph Valentino, Richard Gere.

I know what to say to Pumpkin now—the magic is in me. She will laugh at my poetry, throw her arms around me and whisper in my ear—"take me away, jazz me, marry me, make love to me, suck on my toes and use my bath towel when it is still wet from my shower." We will laugh, our music mingling, and I will know exactly how many angels fit on the head of a pin, but I won't tell anyone, just her, and she will smile at me, a soft gaze, respectful, and she will be amazed, awe-struck at my knowledge.

The alley is dark and shadowy but with distinct lines around even the fuzziest of shadows, like one of my black and white movie settings. I am at the far end. I have waited for what seems hours and my body would like another drink. The word "need" jumps around in my mind. Suddenly, the door swings wide and yellow light pours out, What will I say to her? It was so clear just a moment ago. I start to panic.

Hold on, bud, I tell myself. Just remember we're all buds on the tree of life. You know what to say. I move toward the door, knees creaking, needing oil. I've stood too long in one place.

"Hi," I start to say and then I see that she is not alone. Someone follows her out of the building, poured out with the yellow light and Pumpkin. They stumble as they both hit the pavement, and the other person grabs her and steadies her. He has a sailor suit on. He danced with her with my ticket. It had my fingerprints on it. It was still warm with the heat of my hand when he held it. The cashier had it, then I, then Pumpkin, then the sailor, and now the cashier has it back again, torn in two, I imagine. What stories those tickets could tell, what conversations they have overheard. There is a book in those tickets. They are experienced travelers.

Pumpkin and the sailor have not seen me. I am too far back and it is too cold to see or hear. Eyes dance at this temperature, and try to hide in upturned collars. Ears shut down, pay attention to only what is near. I have myself stopped and stand there, forty feet from them. We are playing "Statues" and I am "it."

They seem to argue. Arms are waving, there are gestures, and I catch a word or two, not enough to matter. It seems to be about money. I am trying to think of her in another way. I am trying to justify her behavior by inventing a miserable childhood, a drunken mother, an abusive father who is absent much. I am in a storyboard meeting with myself and we throw around ideas that will provide the proper motivation for her character. We end up agreeing with the one about the abusive father, and for a different spin, a sexually abusive older brother and a mother who is plugged into the Old Testament God and not aware of outside stimuli, like her family.

They turn and walk my way. I panic. I don't know why I panic; I have as much right to the alley as they do. But they only go a few feet, past some garbage cans, and they stop. I am invisible to them.

He begins to unbutton the front flap of his trousers. Thirteen buttons.

Please, I think, but I do not move from my oily blackness. He would not obey anyway. Perhaps if we had known each other for years and years, he might feel guilty enough to stop, but since we are strangers, my appearance would only anger him, so I lay back in my pool of darkness and wish I had come here later. I shut out the soft moans and whistle a happy tune, but only to myself, in my head. I try to remember the words to a song I learned as a child. It helps to concentrate. By and by, he is buttoning up his trousers and she has risen, wiping her mouth with the black sleeve of her coat. I imagine I see a silvery trail, but that is ridiculous. I am much too far away.

He turns, and she reaches out and grabs his arm. Even from where I am, back among the trash cans, I hear his raspy laugh. He takes her arm and flings it from him like a snake that has attacked him. He turns again and she reaches into her purse for something and cries out. The word bastard! hangs in the air; he turns and she swipes at him with something glittery. It catches on the bluish-black sleeve of his pea coat and opens it up. I have begun walking toward them, but not too fast. I walk as if I am late to church and have to walk clear up front to the only empty pew.

She raises her arm again and as she comes down, he reaches to meet her arm and I see the two arms continue together in a perfect arc, stopping at his knee, which he has brought up. The knife clatters away on crushed oyster shells. He curses her with a low voice and then walks off, holding his injured arm with his other hand, cradling it. He half-runs, half-walks, to the alleyway entrance, turns, and disappears.

I am in front of her and do not remember walking there.

"Are you hurt?" I say.

She looks up and what strikes me is the absence of surprise in her eyes, as if she expected me, although that is impossible.

"No," she says. "But that bastard is. I got him good."

"What was—"

"He wouldn't pay me," she goes, turning around and looking first to one side and then the other. "Do you see my knife?"

I walk in the direction I saw it go and there it is.

"Here," I say, handing it to her. There is something on the blade. Wet and black. No; red.

We stand there, not saying anything. There is something. I have to ask her this, even though I am afraid of what she will say.

"Thanks," she goes. "I have to get back inside. This means overtime tonight. Goddammit all to hell!"

"Wait," I say. How to say this? Did I really want to know?

"Well? What is it? I've got to go. The rent don't get paid, if I stand here socializing."

"I just want to know . . . if I . . . if you and I . . . if I refused to pay you . . . would you do the same thing to me?"

"You bet your ass!" she says, and laughs gaily. "You, your brother Bill, your friend Jim, your cousin Boudreau. Screw me, I'll cut your ass in a New York second! Just don't try it, see?—and we'll get along just fine. Look, you seem like a nice enough guy. Business ain't personal. It's just business, is all. We make a deal, you don't keep your end, I gotta do something about it. Listen, come on up sometime, dance with me. You been there before, ain'tcha? You look familiar. Yeah, I remember. Listen, just ask for Pumpkin. You know the score. You gotta go in the front, though. Up the steps. This door's just for employees."

Then, I don't know, we say good-bye or something; she opens the door behind her and slips back in and I am out in the alley, alone.

Alone and . . . *okay*. Yes, that's the word. Okay. *Trés* okay. Something has happened and I realize my body has changed, rearranged itself in its proper molecular order. It has been all mixed up before now and I haven't known it. My bones lose their softness, I feel my heart pumping right where it should be, kidneys, lungs coming back from wherever they've been and plugging into the right places. My eyesight clears and is keen, gifted with the power of hunting tigers.

I've been alone all along. It's suddenly clear. And it's all right. Being alone doesn't kill you, not unless you let it. It's a kind of power. The knowledge that yes, you can allow others to become part of your life, can transfer to them those feelings we call love, affection, whatever, but you can do it on your terms and that is the real root of happiness. When you bend your emotions to alien worlds you've sentenced yourself to misery. And when your terms and the other person's terms are in harmony . . . well, that's the best of it for both of you. That's a love that reciprocates, grows daily stronger.

I leave the alley, begin to walk back to my apartment. There are crowds of midwesterners shoving by me, taxis edging through them, grifters grabbing my arm, selling me the goods inside the strip clubs they stand before, grease smells from the Takee Outee's, fist fights down the street, black kids breakdancing on sheets of cardboard, a drunken sax player, haunched down on his knees, his upside-down hat in front of him—there is all this and more, a New Orleans Saturday night and I don't see it, any more than I see the air in front of me. I am two feet off the ground, weightless.

I see a pay phone. I put my quarter in, begin to dial, then realize I have forgotten the number. I recognize that as a good sign. So good that I hang up, save my quarter. If I can't remember her number, then it is obvious I have nothing important to say to her. I've been mistaken about thinking I had, for so long. So I hold a conversation in my head, save the fourth part of a buck.

*Well, then, good-bye, Caroline. It's been nice talking to you.*

I walk up the street and turn and there is Pat O'Brien's. All my life I have lived in New Orleans and I have never gone inside its most famous club. I do now. I go all the way to the back, where it opens into a patio and I sit at one of the little wrought-iron tables. There is a girl at the table on my right. She is pretty and I'd guess about my age.

When I get my drink, she catches my eye, sees me staring at her. I lift my glass. She hesitates, then lifts hers and smiles and we both raise liquor to our lips. She has no wedding band on her finger and no tan line there either and she is still smiling, so I get up and take that first delicious step into the future.

# Dream Flyer

They *never* bust cock fights—least-ways I never heard of it before—hell, half the spectators is always cops—but here I was, in the Orleans Parish Jail, and here I would sit my butt another ten days. Twenty down, ten to go.

I'm not one to bellyache, but it just ain't fair, this roust. I was just there, as a sort of observer of the human melodramaticus, not betting or nothing, and the judge sentenced me anyway. I might have had five lousy bucks or so down, but that was it. A hundred, tops. Hell, some'a these players light their Cubans with a C-note!

I even brought up my college education to the honorable barrister, but that didn't cut no grass.

"Your Honorable," I says, "I've got nearly a full semester in right here at our own Delgado J. C. and woulda finished up pret near the top'a my class, only there was that ruckus at the Saints' game you mighta read about, landed me in the clink right before mid-terms and that washed my higher edification right down the spigot. And," I tacked on, "I only made a general comment about our famous quarterback, which I might add, half the town agrees with, having witnessed with their own two eyeballs ol' Junebug Taylor out and about the party trail powdering his nose over to Pat O'Brien's before the home games, and besides, I never laid a glove on the other guy as he had me down and tromping about on my rib crate before I knew which end was sideways, and it wasn't my fault twenty or thirty other hotheads jumped in and began mixing it up and got the security guys involved in stuff that wasn't none'a their bidness."

I figured he would see the logic of my calculations when I further explained that since I was bum-rapped on that litigious, I figured the state owed me one, but not this bailiff, no, he just raps his little hammer down and says, "Mr. Thierry, you've been before me four times in the last year and a half and you still don't get it, do you? Thirty days! Call the next case. By the way," he leaned over as they were leading me away, "it's water down the *drain*, you nitwit, and my report shows you were flunking both your classes. How do you flunk fizz-ed, lessen you're in an iron lung?"

So much for the value of an education these days.

And then, they had the effrippery to put me into the same cell as the "Dream Flyer." That's what I called him, right from the gitgo—you probly read about him in the *Times-Picayune* and thought some reporter give him that name—but it was my oneself that named him, not no booze-hound with a typewriter. What happened, one of the other inmates let it out that's what I called him, and that's how he got his brand.

His real name, which you might not know, seeing as how the papers always call him the "Dream Flyer" now, was Karol Block, with a K, not a C, but which don't matter nohow, since nobody re-members his real handle no more. It was in all the papers, even up north. Nobody likes a kid molester, but everybody sure likes to read about the skunks!

I probly know more about him than his own mother, who he didn't much cotton to t' begin with, bein's she usta crank him over the head with the cast iron fryer when she was in a mood, and so never did any serious confiding in, like he done with me. Being cellmates makes you closer than Siamese kittens, and what I don't know about Karol wouldn't take three minutes to foretell.

"I'm gonna beat the rap," he says, first day I checked in, and I only half-heard him 'cause everybody in here's gonna beat that same rap. "I raped her, sure, but I didn't kill her. I wasn't even close to her, being knocked out and disambulatory. She killed herself. Got up and run into a tree branch, knocked her inta the river which she pro-ceeded t' swalla half of, not having taken the caution of closing her trap like anyone with any sense woulda done." He was talking about the twelve-year-old moppet he was in jail for rendering extinct in a particularly gross way.

I shook my head in sympathy cause that's what you do in jail, you agree like you was up for reelection, specially if you're in the same cell as a mad-dog killer. Not agreeing with folks makes 'em mad, and jail is no place to get somebody PO'd at you, specially a ice-cube cold rape-killer like Karol. You can't just walk away and climb on a bus, happen they take exception to something you say. So I agreed with him most of the time, even at his craziest, which was generally all the time, maybe arguing on some minor point just to show him I was no pushover, but a tough tomato, same as him.

"I got a plan," he says, meaning to beat the rap, and proceeds to let me in on the scam. It seems laying around in jail gets him to re-membering about when he was a juvie and he comes up with this idea that when he was around seven or eight, he could fly. The story he gives me is that he could get out of his body, like a pearl-diver shucks his wet suit, and float around and buzz around into other rooms to check if his parents was playing bedsheet tag or what-not, and one thing leads to another, and pretty soon he figures out how to fly while still in his body, by holding his breath and suspending his molecules and some other tricks and deceits of the trade. First time, he finds this out accidental, when he was nine, when he jumps off a little hill and finds he can stay in the air longer than other kids of his same general weight and height classification, and then, by a lot of practice, he gets to where he could take off from a flat spot and go clear up into the clouds, dodging aircraft and flocks of robins and spy satellites and other such artifices. Kind of a nine-year-old Super-man, 'cept he didn't have any x-ray vision or incredible strength or work on the *Daily Planet*. He could just fly. Then, he claims he got older and interested in girls and lost the art.

"You shoulda kept flyin'," I says, cracking wise. "Girls is what got you into this fix," but when he doesn't laugh, I drop the subject like a match burned down to the tender part of the fingers.

I asked for another cellmate, but they said no, they was over-crowded. I can help fix that problem, I come back; give me my walking papers, but Whitey the guard only walked away giggling and shaking his head, like he thought I wasn't serious.

After giving me this look that makes my blood turn to Kool-Aid, Karol tells me that he remembers all this flying business from his youth again, under the stress of the predicament he's in, and not only that, he's been practicing every night and has regained his powers. He's been in the slammer almost six months before, working out with the aeronautics, so he's up to the point of loop-de-loops and fer-de-lances, or so he says. Since I only been here twenty days, I can't attest to this, but I think one night I seen him raise up off the floor a couple two or three inches, but then it might have just been a mirage-a-twa, since I seen my ex-wife Dixie at the same time, sitting over in the corner on the stool, doin her regular occupation which was boffing her nails, and besides, I had drunk a half-pint of apple-jack I got for two packs of Camel regulars, maybe an hour before I dozed off which mighta had something to do with what I was visualizing.

Dying don't bother him none, Karol says, but getting exterminated for something he didn't do, gets his dander up. He done the rape, sure, but it warn't his fault she run into a tree and kilt herself, is his take on the deal.

Weird, huh? I had to stay in there, across the bunk from him and pretend the puzzle that was his brain had all the pieces.

His genius plan is to wait till his big day up at Angola, when they take him to the little room where they pop the needle into you, and just up and fly away from 'em. Then, he'll come back and let 'em give him his shot. This will prove his innocence, he says, and also show them that dying don't mean a hoot in a pile of owlshit in the mote of his eye, and he can die joyous.

Well, there is some squirrely folks in jail, and I've met a couple of 'em, but the Dream Flyer, he's an original-diginal if I ever come across one, with both cheeks fulla walnuts and pecans.

Least he was. Yesterday was the day they was supposed to extinguish him, and they even let me go to a conference room and listen on the radio for when it happened. All the stations had remotes there since it was such a big deal and one of those days the governor hadn't accepted a bribe—slow news day is what they call it—and I guess the turnkey thought me'n Dream Cookie was bosom sidekicks since we celled together awhile, and so I got to go up and listen with Whitey and the other moron guards. Beats laying around in your six-by-ten, winking at your trouser worm and teaching it to sit up.

Well, believe it or not, he never made it to the death room. Course you know that unless you've been living out in Houma or the Okefenokee, cause that's all that's been on the tube since.

He fell and broke his neck, is what it said in the *Picayune*, but they wasn't real clear about what went on, only that he fell three tiers and squashed himself like a Halloween pumpkin off the overpass. Neck-breaking was the official cause of death, but the way it sounded, there wasn't a bone left in one piece. He went from Dream Flyer to Dream Whip.

Now, all this has got me to putting my thinking cap on. The way I figure it, there's just the skootch of a chance that the Dream Flyer was onto something. I even disremember something way back when I was in short pants myself, a time when I used to get out of my body and float around the trailer. Thing is, I can't tell if I really remember something like that, or if talking to the Dream Flyer makes me *think* I remember it. But the more I cogitate on it, the more I'm sure I done it.

Starting tonight, I'm gonna start practicing. See if maybe I can get out of my body a little bit, for a few minutes or so, maybe fly over to the cafeteria and get hold of one of those steaks the cooks save back for themselves, cop a piece of that sweet tater pie they claimed they was out of. If it works, then I guess it's possible to fly. I remember everything the Dream Flyer told me about suspending the molecules and such, and if it's possible, I guess I can do it as well as he could. *Better*, I hope.

If it's possible, think of the feasibilivities! I mean, there's not a jail built that could ever hold me! I'd like to see that judge's face, next time I stand up there for some cockamamie crap like gambling. I'd fly up to the ceiling and wave at him right before I shoot out the window.

"Hey, judge," I'll yell, "I believe I'll do those thirty days over on the Redneck Riviera over to Panama City."

That's the kind of *statement* I'll be making.

Let's see, Karol said you suspend your molecules and do something with your breath . . . Damn! This is gonna be easy! See how the justice system likes it, playing on an even field.

Color my ass *gone*.

# Rubber Band

Plainfield, Indiana is where I picked up the thing about rubber bands. That was a long time ago.

Twenty-two months I spent there. I would have been out in eighteen months, but there was another boy killed, under suspicious circumstances, so I had to stay longer. In the end, four months was deemed an appropriate punishment for the unsolved crime. The second one, not the first.

The first was for my father, but, hey, I was just a kid that time.

As for the second, nothing was ever proved. I was ten when I went in, almost thirteen when I walked out, on a drizzly spring day that smelled like the underside of a board in a vacant lot. That wet socks smell. I had a bus ticket in my hand and I sat down and waited for the 11:45 Trailways, sitting on a cardboard suitcase less than a hundred yards from the Indiana Boy's School. I had a ninety-mile ride before me.

My mother didn't drive, therefore the bus ticket. We had no relatives to request transportation from and I don't think she had any friends she wanted to share a one-hundred-and-eighty-mile trip with. Especially since I would be along for half of it.

I measure my life from that point. It was my Vietnam, my bar mitzvah. I'm not Jewish. The ten years previous are a mist, condensed into a single dream. I connect whatever present I am in to that bus ride, the weeks, months and years since, a rubber band that keeps stretching and getting thinner. Someday it will break and that will be that. My mother's rubber band broke when I was eighteen, and I have no idea what hers was connected to. I broke my father's for him, when I stabbed him with a large knife my mother liked to use for chopping onions. I stabbed him eight times before my mother took the knife away from me, her eyes sad and brown, only her voice hysterical. I have a feeling that was what her rubber band was connected to. If so, it was a pretty good rubber band. It lasted eight years before it snapped.

Sometimes, when I'm walking down the street I can see everybody's rubber band, all at once. It's a pretty amazing thing to see.

I had the figure thirty-three in mind when I started putting holes in my father, and ever since I have the feeling of something unfinished. I have no idea why that number, but, hey—who can figure kids? The boy stabbed in Boy's School and with whom I was linked in "suspicious circumstances," was stabbed thirty-three times with a laundry pin. A laundry pin looks exactly like a giant safety pin, one of Baby Huey's, and if you bend them out, they look quite lethal, and are, actually. It wasn't the first time someone's rubber band had been snapped that way for them at Boy's School. It was the favorite shank for most of us, second favorite being a soup spoon filed down on the concrete of a cell floor. Another popular version was a double-bladed razor blade melted into the end of a toothbrush, except you really had to chew at a person's neck to get deep enough, and most times you didn't have that kind of time.

Anyway, I don't know what my father's rubber band was connected to. Maybe he didn't have one, except the day he was born. I know when I'm drinking I don't seem to have one, and since that was his normal state, maybe he didn't see his.

What Boy's School did was teach me what people wanted to hear and how to fashion a shank from practically anything. It also taught me to distrust people who looked like choirboys, since the choirboys at Boy's School were the rapists and murderers, and the fiercest-looking ones usually turned out to be petty burglars, snatch-and-run artists. I also learned how to tell when someone is trying to sell you a bill of goods, what we called a wolf ticket.

I had a weekly session with a psychologist that I testified had "helped me a lot" when I went up for my parole hearing. It helped; I was given a release date of December twenty-fourth so I could be

home for Christmas, an idea which made the parole board feel good.
Only a boy died, thirty-three laundry pin stab wounds scattered about
his body in various places, and I didn't catch my bus until April 12,
long after the Christmas tree had been recycled. Some of the board
were convinced it was me, even though I had an ironclad alibi (I was
at the Saturday morning movie and had six witnesses). The reason
they thought it was me was that on my sheet was a notation of an
altercation between the deceased and me when I'd first arrived.

No other proof ever came forth, so the board reconvened and
again decided, in its infinite wisdom, that I was "socially and men-
tally rehabilitated," and they ordered the state to pop for a bus ticket
for yours truly, one way, home.

The psychologist did help a lot. I had a half-hour with him on
Friday mornings. We had a set routine. He would lock the door, and
then pull out a bottle of Jack Daniels and pour both of us a slug in a
paper cup. He would drink his neat and I got a Coke for mine. Then,
he would try and bugger me. He had various methods. Sometimes
he would try to con me into it; once, he just whipped it out and
showed me, as if that would be enough to send me into a sexual
frenzy. Mostly, I'd laugh at him. He was harmless enough. Somehow, I always knew he'd never try any rough stuff or anything, and
sure enough he never did. I always wondered how many of the other
boys he was successful with. Jimmy DeAngelo, for sure.

But, even though he never jumped my hump, he seemed to like
me. He wrote glowing reports about my "progress," and it was because of those reports that I eventually got my parole. I still send
him Christmas cards even though he is out of the prison system now
and has a small private practice here in the same city, specializing in
helping men with impotency problems. I would like to be a fly on
the wall, those sessions!

He helped me with my dreams. Even before I was sent there,
while I was in city lockup awaiting trial, I'd started having the same
dream. It was always about my parents.

"Bucko," he'd say. "When you're in your dream the next time, remember you have the power to end it."

I didn't answer, being ten and up against an adult. We had just talked about my dream, where I always wake up with my father coming home. Drunk.

"It's his penis you're afraid of," he said. "Classic. It looks formidable to you. Makes you feel inadequate. Like you'll never measure up. You have to resolve this."

How? I ask silently, and he reads my mind.

"By cutting it off. Then, your nightmare will end."

Sound advice. I am ten so what do I know? I follow the Jack Daniels-inspired advice of this reform school psychologist-pederast and, next time my father enters the house in my dream, I whack his thing with a broadsword. I feel great/bad about it and awaken with a hard-on of my own. The next night I have the dream again and it continues the rest of my life. It doesn't end as the psychologist has promised, and for this I am angry, but not angry enough to quit sending him a Christmas card every year. He has increased my nightmare, but he has also given me Jack Daniels and a place to go when my nightmare has too much yeast in it and gets too big.

The psychologist had problems of his own. He must have forgotten I was just a kid, some of the things he told me.

Like his becoming a psychologist was his second attempt at understanding why he was here. By "here," I mean *here*, alive; on the planet earth. Originally, he had been a writer. He even had a book he'd written, stuck way up high on the bookshelf in his office. I saw it one day, and said, "Is *that* Maxwell Donne related to you?" I tried to read it, but it was way over my head. It wasn't that the words were too big, they were just arranged in a way that gave me a headache, trying to understand what they meant.

He had quit being a writer the day his book was published. All his life (he said), he had believed the written word to be magic, to hold secrets that would explain things. He devoured books, searching for the revelation that would explain the mystery of life. It was in there, if not in one particular book, then in an accumulation of books. If he just read enough, everything would be clear and make sense.

But it never did, he said.

We were drinking Jack and Cokes when he was telling me all this, and I remember staring at the patch of sunlight on the floor. It had lines in it, from the bars on the window. He only talked about it that one time. We really got drunk, I recall, so much that he had to walk me back over to the dorm, tell my supervisor I was sick, to excuse me the rest of the day. Rest, he told him. This boy needs some rest.

He walked down to the bookstore to see his book, he said. He was real excited, in a feverish, agitated way. There it was, in the front window. Next to it, was a new edition of John Donne's poetry. He wondered at that, and then thought maybe the bookstore manager was trying to make the public think there was a connection between the two Donne's.

He said that was when it hit him. There his book was, next to one of the masters of literature, one of those who he had always believed to possess the mystery of what life was all about, and in that instant, he knew there was no answer to any of it. Because he didn't have a clue. He knew no more then than he did when he first began to search, but he had a book, one of those places where others would search for meanings, just as he had.

That's when I knew it was all bullshit, he said, knocking back his drink which was mostly all Jack and just a tinge of Coke, and laughing, only it was the kind of laugh that you knew wasn't based on any kind of good feeling. That's when I knew life was utterly meaningless, he said. There are no answers because there are no questions, just some crap we make up to keep our minds engaged. Our minds are a useless appendage we would do better without. Like your appendix. Maybe, at some time they were useful, but not any longer. Now they just got in the way.

He said he knew this was the basic building stuff of existentialism, but that was bull too; existentialism was just another excuse to ask more questions to be answered in another way that was just as nonsensical.

That was when he decided to study psychology, he said, only he knew it was just another useless mental exercise to divert people from arriving at the truth, the truth being that there is no truth, there is no magic, there are no answers, and there are no questions, and that the human animal is a totally useless life form, worth less than a termite, and that if he had any grace at all about him, the best thing would be to just commit suicide, get out of this misery, but he was cursed in that regard because he had been told about God at too early an age, an age when it made an impression, and even though he knew in his mind that there was no God, he couldn't bring himself to take a chance he might be wrong. All he could do at this point, he said, was just to go on and on and on, and thank God or someone that there was Jack Daniels and some other things to keep that useless appendage—his mind—at bay, or at least occupied with other things.

I can't help you, son, he told me. If you killed that boy, then I guess you killed him. If that helps you out, makes life less painful, then I think it's a worthwhile thing and I'll do what I can do to get you out of here. If that's what you want. You let me know.

I think about the psychologist now and I thought about him as I sat on my cardboard suitcase, waiting for a bus to come along and take me to a place called "home." And my dream. I think about my dream now, just as I did then.

In my dream, the rest of it, I hear my mother scream and my eyes fly open. I am in her arms and my mouth is around her nipple and I can taste the coppery taste of blood. Her blood. I have bitten her nipple neatly off, with my small, white teeth. I am six years old in this part of the dream, and I have a body that is firm, almost no baby fat. I do not know how I am six, but there is no doubt that I am. I know, too, that this is the last time my mother will breast-feed me. I am free. No more will I come home from school and have to climb into her lap. I am about to fix that, in my dream. I will not have to hide the fact that my mother has never stopped breast-feeding me and I do not know that if I would only tell an adult, they would get her for child abuse. None of that has ever been explained to me, and, of course, back then we didn't have Oprah or the Donahue shows.

She screams again, and this time succeeds in disengaging me from her torn breast. Blood spurts and I smile and coo. Now that I think about it, a six-year-old cooing is pretty disgusting. I am supremely happy.

Even in her pain, she takes care not to drop me. Instead, she hurries me gently into the bedroom and lays me down in my crib. Yes, I still have a crib, with bars on the side, and I am in the first year of school. I detest it. This will be my last night in this bed. I know this too, but I cannot say how it is I know. This is a dream.

My mother hurries into the other room, clutching her wounded breast in both hands. The blood seeps over her fingers and I hum a happy tune with no words. I can speak, even read; but I coo like I am six weeks old and not six years. I am so pleased. If I were a Cocker Spaniel, I would wag my tail.

As soon as she leaves the room, I climb out of my crib. I am adept at this, having done so hundreds of times. I go into the living room and my mother is nowhere in sight.

Then, the front door swings open and my father appears in his khakis and stinking of booze. I can smell him from where I hide beside the couch. He does not see me. He bellows out my mother's name and she answers him back. She is in the bathroom, seeing to her breast, making little puppy sounds. He stumbles in that direction and I hear voices, muffled like they are talking underwater.

My father emerges from the bathroom. He is shouting and I hear my mother's noise behind him. He commands me to appear, his voice a rusty iron door opening in a hollow room. I get palsy and hide my face in wet hands. He finds me, or, his foot finds me, and he plays soccer.

This is when I want to stop the dream but cannot. All I hear are my own screams and those of my mother. She does nothing to help me though. Her answer to this man and what he does, always, is to suffocate me with a blanket, after, and stick her breast in my mouth. This is her answer to my life.

The only sounds my father makes as he goes about his work are short grunts and the solid thump of his work boot as it skids across my ribs, the one sound punctuating the other.

I don't want to dream any longer; I sob and my face is filthy with snot and blood and he keeps kicking me with his boot. My heart is breaking; this my father whom I adore, my daddy, and he is hurting me and I beg him to stop, my voice weak and despicable, and yet he continues, kicking and kicking, and I start to scream for he is killing me and it is one long piercing sound that springs up and grows from where I do not know; it comes not from me it seems, but it does, from some center I don't know about, and the sound goes on and on, frozen eternally and, at the very apex, something clicks so softly I almost don't hear it, and the pain is gone, even though he has not stopped, no; it has not gone, it is there, but it feels good, *welcome*, and I feel my mouth begin a huge, *huge* grin, and each thump of his foot feels better and better and *better*, and now I am a man and I want to hurt him and I have a knife in my hand, no, a broadsword, a Prince Valiant broadsword, and I am cutting his prick off, the penis he has just brought out, hard and swollen and monstrous, and then he is nowhere, gone, and I wake up, and that is about it.

I thought about my dream sitting on my cardboard suitcase and I think about it now. In the distance, I saw the silver gleam of the

Trailways, and stood up, putting on my Boy's School swagger, and that was the beginning of my rubber band. It began stretching from that point.

I think it is stretched fairly thin now.

# A Shortness of Breath

All events prior to John Sykes's father's funeral were useless prologue, unessential except for comparisons, and few remained who cared to expend time in such pursuits. What was there to say? That John Sykes was a young man with active hormones, quick to show strong white teeth to the young ladies, first on the dance floor, first to head for the back row of cars with a giggling girl in tow? That he was like any twenty-year-old Louisiana country boy who enjoyed snagging a six-pound largemouth, shining for frogs, pushing a pirogue through a bayou in a gator hunt?

It was the funeral that brought the change in John and made this story.

Adam Sykes fell dead of a stroke, not a newsworthy event in itself even though he was only forty-seven, but remarkable when it was noted that was the same age his own father and grandfather and that man's father before him had died as well. It was whispered about that the Sykes men had *all* died at that inopportune age, back farther than memory, perhaps forever, even to the time of the original Adam, but that may have only been rumor.

That this story happened to transpire in Placquemine, Louisiana, a bayou settlement where cos cos and voodoo still had their adherents even then in the 1950s, and where phrases like "the seventh son of a seventh son" were taken seriously, Adam Sykes's passing had more consequence than it would have just about anywhere else.

Tongues ceased, eyes averted, the day of the wake when John wandered through the kitchen of his home where the older women had settled in. Fell silent that is, except for one old matriarch sitting with her back to the rest of the room, warming herself at the stove, saying to no one in particular, "Poor John. He's what? Nineteen? Twenty? Only twenty-seven years before he goes too." And then someone, one of the other women with warning eyes reached to touch her shoulder and the blood crept up to show through her papery skin but it was too late.

It was John's best friend Dell O'Dell, who found him sitting in his dad's old brown rocking chair upstairs, chin in hand, eyes on the floor.

"John," Dell said, his hand on his friend's shoulder. "I've been looking for you all over. The minister's leaving and wants to talk to you." He paused. "Don't listen to those old biddies," he said. "You okay?"

John said something, rose and went downstairs, where the preacher held one of his hands in both of his and murmured to him, after which he patted him on the back, picked up his hat from the hall tree and made his departure. The rest of the house emptied soon after.

✖ ✖ ✖

"So, John," said Dell, a week or so after the funeral. "What's wrong? Is it your father still? That's on your mind, isn't it?"

"Yeah," he answered. "This thing has got me all worked up. Do you realize I'm already twenty? My life's half gone!"

"Hell," Dell said, laughing. "I wouldn't worry so much, horse. It's just a coincidence. One of them funny things in life. Look at your grandma. She's seventy-something. And your great-grandma! Wasn't she close to ninety-six last year when she passed? Who says you won't take after them instead? C'mon, let's go get us some catfish."

John shook his head side to side, slowly. "I'm just not up to it right now Dell. Maybe tomorrow."

Dell stared down at the floor, silent, and then he glanced up and said, "Say John, I know what you ought to do. You ought to go see Rosalie."

Rosalie was an ancient shaggy-haired crone who lived just outside Placquemine in a rough-hewn shotgun house that had been there from when the Cajuns came down from Nova Scotia. She was the town's mystery, rumored to be a gypsy, perhaps of Spanish or African blood or both, and she raised strange-smelling plants and herbs in a tiny plot out back. She read fortunes, sold love charms, gris-gris, things like that. Folks used her but they usually came at night so they wouldn't be seen by their neighbors.

"Rosalie?"

"Sure. Rosalie. She can tell you when you're gonna die. She's got powers."

"No way!" said John at first and the two men argued for awhile.

"All right, all right! I'll go! Anything to shut you up! That old hag can't predict the future any more than you can be King of England, but I'll go. Then will you leave me alone?"

They even went in the daytime. Dell wanted to wait until the sun went down but John said no, you want me to go let's go right now, and so they did.

"What you boys want!"

She stood inside the doorway dressed in a man's gray work trousers and a drab green shirt. Her hair hung loose and tangled, bits of dead grass in it, and the color was impossible, red as the fires of Hell. One of her eyes was blue, the other the brownish-black of coal tar. Neither John nor Dell had ever seen her up this close. She didn't have any eyebrows.

"Well? What you want? I ain't got all day."

"Sorry," said John, stepping down from the stoop. "This was a mistake. We don't want nothing."

"Don't want nothing! You look like you don't want nothing!" mimicked the woman. "You want your fortune told don't you?"

John turned to leave and Dell stepped after him and grabbed his arm. "Yes'm. That's what we want. Not me. Him. He wants to know when he's gonna die."

The old woman said nothing, only shoved her unpainted door wide, taking a step back inside the darkness. There was nothing to do but go in.

There was barely enough light to see. Even though the sun was bright outside, in the house it seemed to die. As the two young men followed their hostess they kept bumping into objects in the darkness.

"I hope that's furniture," whispered Dell, poking John in the back with his finger as they followed Rosalie. John jumped and flashed his friend a dirty look.

"Sit," she commanded when they reached her kitchen, which was a bit brighter—enough to see each other's features. She indicated two chairs on one side of a massive oak table the color of leather. She took the lone chair on the opposite side.

"I won't tell you when you're going to die," she wheezed, showing tiny white, perfect teeth. "I won't do that."

"You said you won't," John said, leaning forward. "Does that mean you know? Can you really tell things like that?"

She got up and went to her stove. The kettle began to whistle at that exact moment. They hadn't seen her put it on and they hadn't seen her pull any cups out of her cupboard, but there were three cups sitting on the sideboard. She poured water into each of the cups and sprinkled something into them from a packet she brought from her apron pocket. She brought the cups over, first John's and Dell's and then hers.

"Tea," she said. "It's a special blend."

Both boys picked up their cups at the same time and pretended to sip.

"This is good," lied Dell. He hadn't tasted enough to tell.

"I won't tell you," she said. "I will do something for you though."

"What?" John asked.

"You're the Sykes boy."

The whites of John's eyes shone. "You know who I am?"

"You look like a Sykes. I knew your father and grandfather. Abraham's dog! I knew your grandfather's father. I expect you've come because your father's died."

John didn't speak, just sat up ruler-straight.

Rosalie drank deeply from her cup and exhaled her breath. It smelt of milkweed.

"Forty-seven. That's what's on your mind."

"Yes," said John.

"Nine generations. That's how many Sykes men have gone at forty-seven. That's as far as I remember."

Her breath drifted to them, smelling now of almonds. She got up and refilled her cup from the kettle, adding more of the powder from her pocket.

"I won't tell you when you'll die young Sykes," she said. "I won't do that. I will tell you one thing, though."

She kept her eyes on John but raised a long thin finger and pointed it at Dell. "You leave. This is for him."

When the front door closed she walked over and sat down in the chair Dell had been sitting in. This close, John smelled mushrooms and dark earth.

"This is what you want to know. This is all I will tell you. What you do with this is up to you. . . . There is an *allotment*."

"Allotment?"

"So many breaths. Each of us has so many breaths. In a lifetime. It can be one breath or it can be a billion. Or more. Or less. Some never get even the first one. And the Sykes men!" There was a sound like glass breaking and John realized it was her laughter.

"What the Sykes men have is exactly the same amount. That's the secret. You don't get forty-seven years. You get the same number of breaths."

"Yes, but how—"

"You're not the first Sykes to sit in that chair. Are you sure you want to know?" The look she gave him was as cold as old blue ice.

"Why did they die at the same age?"

"They didn't have to. None of them knew for sure they would. Each of them tried saving their breaths. At first. When they found out. And then time went on and they forgot, got caught up in life. And then they got close to forty-seven and they remembered their history. They would take to their chairs then, sit perfectly still, try to measure them out slowly, make all the air in their lungs go as far as it could, sit as still as petrified wood. I wasn't there, not there in their house, but I saw them."

She was right. John remembered his dad sitting, hour after hour, not moving, flashing pained looks whenever someone asked a question, requested a favor, his face red and contorted. He was strong, vigorous, in his youth, everyone said so, but John only remembered a frail, wizened old man, a perpetual shudder upon him, a father who never played with his son, took him hunting or fishing. He began to understand. He asked,

"How many?"

Rosalie shrugged. "I warned you. You can't say I didn't warn you. Come closer."

He leaned forward until his ear was near her mouth. Her smell changed again to the odor of a baby's milk-breath. She put her mouth to his ear and whispered something and then she told him to leave.

Dell was waiting for him outside.

※　※　※

That day they had gone to Rosalie's, Dell came back to John's house with him and watched as John did a strange thing. He went straight to the chiffonier in the living room and took pen and paper from a drawer and went over and sat in his father's Morris and began writing, shielding what it was with his hand.

The transformation was immediate, overnight. Dell would come around, ask John to go fishing, look for girls, but the air between them had changed. Each time Dell came by John would say: no thanks, I can't shoot squirrels today, I have some things to do. It got further between visits. One hot day Dell stopped by to say, "That yellow-haired gal you like so much is in town visiting Emily Vincent.

You know them Baton Rouge girls. Come on, let's go buy them a beer."

No, said John, all bundled up with a flannel shirt. There's a chill in the air and I might catch a summer cold. Nothing worse than a summer cold. You get a fever and just pant like a wolf. I guess I'll just stay home this time.

After that Dell came by less and less and finally he stopped coming by at all. Six months later he joined the navy, but he stopped by John's house the day before he was to leave.

"Goin into the navy, John," he said. "I go to boot camp tomorrow. Just wanted to see if you wanted to go out, tie one on like old times." He tried not to be shocked at his friend's appearance. John looked ten years older and had lost at least twenty pounds. His skin was yellow and drawn.

No, said John. I've got a touch of the flu. I guess I'd better stay in till it goes away.

✹ ✹ ✹

A year later, at his station in San Salvador, Dell got a letter from his mother saying among other news that John's mother had choked to death on a chicken bone. He couldn't come back for the funeral since it wasn't a relative and he'd used up all his leave on a trip to Las Vegas. In the letter, his mother told him all the news of the town and then about John. It seems John's mother had most of his father's insurance money in a shoe box beneath her bed, so he would never have to worry about getting a job. Good thing, his mother said; he sure didn't look like he was ever going to leave that house. The minister even quit going by. All that ever happened was that kids would run up and knock on the door and make "the funny man come out and chase them." Nobody ever saw him any more she said, except every two weeks when he would go down to Hatcher's and buy groceries.

Dell wrote him a letter but never got back a reply and after a time he forgot about his old friend, being too busy with the navy and life in general. From time to time his friend's face would come into his mind but those times became fewer and fewer and eventually disappeared. His own parents moved to New Orleans and the years passed. He stayed in the navy, making a career as a radioman and cryptographer. He saw duty in Spain, Bermuda, and Italy, and spent several years on mostly destroyers except one tour aboard the *Enterprise*, the new nuclear flattop.

Twenty years flew by. He passed his physical and they let him stay in. On his forty-seventh birthday he was in a bar in Hawaii having a drink with a WAVE and she mentioned something about "old friends" that made him pause and think for a minute about his old friend John. His birthday was coming up too. An important one. He wondered if John had made it this far.

The operator told him she had no listing for any Sykes. He tried to think of someone else in town he might call and was surprised to discover he couldn't remember a single name from his youth.

Hell, he thought. I'll go home, see the old homestead.

Two days later he was swinging down from a bus step and walking around a large black dog that lay in front of him refusing to move. He was dressed like a city slicker in a charcoal suit and one of the new wide ties, also blue. He walked over to a building that used to be Hatcher's Grocery and now bore the name "Cornucopia" and walked through the electronic door.

"This where Hatcher's used to be?" he asked a young boy operating a push broom in aisle two.

"Who knows," said the acned teenager, scowling, pushing debris just inches from Dell's spit-shined black wingtips.

"Hey!" An older man came up and stood in front of the boy. "If you can't be more civil to folks you might not have a long future here." The boy didn't say anything, just took his broom and pushed it along farther up the aisle.

"I'm the manager, sir," he said, beaming. "May I help you?"

"Yessir. You know a fella named Sykes? John Sykes?"

The man thought for a minute, his brow wrinkling, and then he shined the smile again. "Shoot yes. Crazy Sykes! We send his groceries out once a month. Old coot eats nothing but beans, bread, and peanut butter. No sugar! No sir! Nothing sweet for that nut. Makes his heart beat too fast or something. Oh . . . say, I'm sorry. He a relative of yours?"

"No," Dell said and walked out of the store.

It took fifteen minutes to walk it and then he was standing in front of the Sykes's house. It looked as if a good hard push could collapse it. It was years from a good paint job, weathered, soft wood that sounded like mush beneath his knuckles when he knocked. Termites, he thought. Weeds, waist-high in the yard.

"Looks like Rosalie's house," he muttered to himself, waiting.

He knocked again louder, and thought he detected a slight movement inside, although the pane was so dirty it was hard to tell. "John? John Sykes?" he said, his voice sounding loud and alien in his own ears like laughter in a graveyard.

"It's open." The voice was low and gravelly and came from somewhere in the house. It was dark but by pushing his nose almost up to the pane, Dell could just make out a figure in a chair. Opening the door and jumping at the loud creak, he entered the house.

"John? Is that you? It's me, Delbert O'Dell."

"Delbert . . . who?"

"Dell. Dell O'Dell."

Now, he could just make out faint objects in the darkened room. And smell. It smelled like the underside of an old board that had lain for months and years in a vacant lot. It gagged him slightly and he swallowed.

A step forward and now he could see the features of the man in the chair. It wasn't John. It was John's father. No, hell, it was his grandfather!

"Is that you John? My God, your hair's white!"

There was no answer from the man in the chair.

"John, this is your old friend Dell." My God, this was horrible. This creature was John, had to be. An old, old man, hair white and hoary and hanging down past his shoulders, eyebrows grizzled and flaked with dandruff . . . and his skin! His skin was creased more than a man twice his age.

Tremulous and brittle, a voice came out of the hole in the man's face, but Dell didn't see any lips, only a slight movement of the whiskers.

"Dell? . . . That you? . . . I'm sorry, Dell. . . . I can't . . . go fishing. Maybe tomorrow. . . . I feel a little . . . down today. Have to . . . conserve my energy . . . so I don't . . . get sick . . . you know." The voice trailed off into a silvery wheeze.

"John, I didn't come to go fishing. I came to see you. Good God man, it's been twenty-seven years. What's happened? Are you sick?"

The man crooked an emaciated finger and motioned at him to come closer. Dell bent forward. "Yes, John? What is it?"

"Mustn't . . . talk . . . Dell. Uses . . . air. Not . . . much left. . . . There. Over there. . . . Get me . . . that paper . . . pencil." He jabbed his finger across the room to the chiffonier.

Dell brought back the notepad and pencil and placed it in John's lap. The old man picked up the pencil, licked the end, once, twice, and began scrawling in tiny, wavery letters.

*Dell,* he wrote, his visitor going behind him and watching the words form. *Can't talk much. Takes too much breath. Have to conserve. You understand.*

Even the act of writing seemed to exhaust him. Dell walked back around the chair, found a smaller one near the front door and brought it back, straddling it to face his friend. He felt flushed, feverish, from the miasma of the house, finding it difficult to draw breath, the air pushing down on him. He began to chatter, a flood of words gushing. He was animated, excited, a pain somewhere near his lungs.

"John, John. It's been so long. Almost thirty years. I'm in the navy, you know. Been everywhere. Around the world at least twice. Been married that many times. I'll tell you about Bermuda, you'll get a kick. Damn. Never thought I'd see Placquemine again. Know why I came back, doncha?"

He saw the old man's head quiver and took it for a no.

"*You*! I came to see *you*! My old friend John Sykes." He felt like bawling. "I remembered it was your birthday, John. Today. You know how old you are?" His voice was bright, cheery, but the tears were running down his cheeks and John's face was hard to see.

The man in the chair shook his head. He smiled, opening his mouth enough for Dell to see he was toothless. He bent over and wrote on his pad. Dell craned his head to see. *48* it said and then John made a huge sprawling exclamation point on the paper.

"That's right, John! Forty-eight! You made it! You got past forty-seven!" He grinned from ear to ear but the tears kept on rolling down his cheeks. Outside, he was aware of the sound of children laughing and talking as they neared the house and then there was quiet and a few seconds later he heard them on the other side going away. The pain in his chest grew more acute.

"Tell me John," he said, his voice husky. "What was it Rosalie said to you that day?"

"She told me . . . " The voice halted, barely a whisper, "how many . . . breaths . . . the Sykes men . . . were allotted. . . . Not how many . . . I had left. . . . Just allotted."

The memory of the day rushed back to Dell. How the first thing John had done was to grab some paper and begin writing. Ciphering, that's what he'd been doing!

"Oh, John," he said, his voice nearly a sob. "Poor, poor John." His own voice sank to a whisper mirroring John's. His chest was on fire.

"Was it worth it John? Was it worth giving up fishing and hunting? Women?" He put his head in his hands, unable to look upon his friend, and his voice became louder, the words coming faster. "Was it worth not going dancing, getting drunk on Saturday night, playing a pickup game of basketball? Kids. Was it worth not having any children?" His chest was hurting and there was another pain down lower in his belly, the spot where his ulcer had been. He heard the rustle of pencil on paper. He slid down off the chair onto his knees, closer to his friend John, trying not to see the snowy hair, the rheumy eyes, the deep, leathery crevasses in the skin, the smell of rot and piss and shit that came from the form in the chair. His stomach rolled and burned as he read what his friend had written, the longest stretch of words yet.

He stared at the paper, afraid at first to read what John had written, and then he took a deep breath and focused his eyes.

It read: *Dell, I can't go fishing. Have to conserve. Scared. Help me. Lost. Don't know how many breaths are left. Lost count when I went to sleep. Forgot to count the breaths when I slept. Never thought of that all these years, til yesterday. Oh God. Find Rosalie. Find Rosalie for me. She knows. Rosalie will tell me how many I have left. Please help me, my friend. Dear God please help me.*

※　※　※

It was a boy and his younger sister, on their way to school, who found the man lying alongside the road and ran to the nearest house to relay their discovery. When the ambulance arrived, the driver saw that the man had suffered an obvious heart attack but was still breathing. The tips of the man's fingers were blue.

On the ride to the hospital, one of the two attendants in the back turned suddenly and said to the other, "Did he just say something?" The other man, engaged in untangling hoses from a portable oxygen tank, nodded.

"Sounded like 'breath,' I think."

"Breath?"

"Yeah. Look, help me get this hooked up. He's losing color. And tell Charlie he better go faster."

※　※　※

The old man sat in the chair and waited. The hours crept by as the shadows snaked inch by inch toward the other side of the room and for awhile it was all shadow for a period until the moon began to provide a dull luminosity. Still he sat there. He didn't move, except for the slight rise and fall of his chest as he breathed slowly and deliberately, the beat of each breath exactly three and a half seconds long, a long pause at the end of each exhalation and then another three seconds expelling the used oxygen, a machine of breath control. Once, he felt the need to urinate, but he sat where he was, letting the hot liquid seep down the inside of his leg, puddle in the seat of the chair. Only when the dead-whitish glow of predawn began to fill the room did he so much as look up, and when he did he gave a shake of his head, a small one, and another, more violent, as if he were waking from the deepest of sleeps, unsure of where he was.

He stood up sharply, his legs protesting at the unexpected movement, staggered and then found his balance. He began to walk hesitantly toward the front door but with a speed of movement not accomplished since he was a young man. By the time he reached the door he was into what could only be called a run, albeit a stutter of a run, the ambling, awkward gait of a toddler.

Bursting from the house, door slamming behind him, he stopped momentarily, throwing up his arm as the morning sun—just rising over the tops of the houses across the street from his—smote his eyes. He began to run again, southward on the road before his house. As he ran, new vigor seemed to overtake him and he ran faster and faster. His breath came in gasps, and of all things he began to sing at the top of his lungs and to windmill his arms like some child who has been loosed from the prison of school for summer vacation.

He ran like this, singing his song, while people emerging from their houses looked on in amazement. Only a few knew it was Crazy Sykes, but all who observed the running, shrieking man shrank back in their doorways, wrapped their arms around themselves, opened wide their eyes.

*Forty-eight, forty-eight, I made forty-eight,* he sang, pumping his legs, swinging his arms, leaping straight up in the air every few feet, clouds of dust flying every time his feet struck down until he got to where he was going. Stopping in the middle of the road he bent over, his atrophied lungs sucking in air in buckets, making such a racket just by his breathing that Rosalie came out to stand on her porch.

I made it, you old witch, he screamed when he saw her, his back bent, hands on knees, head lifted at an angle. *I made forty-eight. See?*

He laid himself down in the dusty road and stretched his limbs out to their fullest, his hands palm down, sifting through the red dust, picking up handfuls and letting the grains trickle out. He stared up at the clouds and began to laugh, first a chuckle, then another and then he was putting forth a full-fledged belly laugh that contained no promise of ending. He didn't think once about counting his breaths, only began beating his fists on the road and kept on laughing and laughing and laughing and gasping for air and his lungs began to fill and expand so that he thought he would burst his ribs and a joy began to spread through his entire body until he thought he would die with the ecstasy and wonder of it all.

# Monday's Meal

BARROW

# The Last Fan

It wasn't something he set out to do. It was more like something that was happening and all of a sudden he was in it, a player in a drama, but a drama he could have ended by simply walking away. The drama would have been over had he done just that, put one foot in front of the other and just left the stadium. The woman would have kept her record and her dignity and her reason for existing.

But he hadn't.

How many situations like that had there been in his life that he had failed to recognize, or worse, *had* recognized at least on a visceral level and had removed himself from? There is another kind of failure, he thought, a failure of deficiency, of neglect, not the failure of nonperformance.

This was something he wanted to say to her but he didn't know how, so he said nothing. Another failure of deficiency he thought, feeling like a man standing in an open field watching a tornado hurtling toward him and unable to move even his eyes to seek out a safe ditch.

❌ ❌ ❌

Always, she sat at one end of the kitchen table and he at the opposite. She liked the end nearest the stove. It had been her seat so long that if she was absent, say shopping with her mother, he would still sit in the chair at his end of the table, even if it was inconvenient.

It wouldn't be, of course. Inconvenient, that is. He wouldn't have anything on the stove that required watching. It was just one of those things that had become a habit and was just the sort of thing he supposed she was talking about right now.

"Robert," she said. "It's over. You know it and I know it. And this is just a good example of why."

"Janey, I sit here for consideration of you. That's your spot. You earned it. Just like I earned the brown chair in the living room. By

151

bringing home the bacon. You earned yours by frying it up." He laughed at his small joke, a small, brittle sound with no warmth in it.

"See? That's why this has to end. Why it has ended. There's nothing serious between us any more. The more I think about it the more I realize there has never been anything serious between us. I don't really care why you always sit in that same goddamned chair. Not really. That's not it at all. I'm sorry Robert. You're a sweet man. You're a sweet man." She repeated the last sentence like she wanted to give him something more, but that was all she could come up with, that saying it again could give it a value that she didn't really believe was there.

Robert looked down at his hands curled around the coffee cup. He lifted his head and glanced at her but she was staring out the window at the back yard. Leaves were swirling at the bottom of the hill by the storage shed. Oddly, he was reminded of a day long ago, nothing like this day. Janey was running along the sand at the beach, Lake Ponchartrain, when she slipped and fell, cutting her knee on a piece of driftwood. He had raised up from where he was lying on the towel and looked at her. He hesitated a moment then pushed himself up and ran to her, the hot sand searing the bottoms of his feet. They went to the hospital, East Jefferson Hospital, and he remained in the waiting room while they stitched up her cut. They hadn't allowed him to go in the room with her. If they'd been married they would have had to most likely. If that had happened yesterday they'd have had to allow him to stay with her, he guessed.

Later that same day they'd gone to Fitzgerald's and had boiled jumbo shrimp with hot sauce and he asked her to marry him.

They got married almost three months to the day before the baby was delivered still-born. A year later they got pregnant again and the same thing happened. They didn't try any more, started using the Pill instead.

The leaves settled down on the lawn and he noticed the yellow heads of dandelions, a big patch near the shed. Later, he'd boil some water and pour on them. She'd asked him to a week before.

"Get rid of those damned dandelions," she'd said. "They ruin the way the lawn looks. If you don't get rid of them they'll keep growing all over the goddamned place. They're like a cancer. Cut them out before they spread. We might want to sell this place you know. What do you suppose a buyer will think if he sees dandelions all over the yard? Get rid of them."

She had just lately taken up cursing. It disturbed him but he knew better than to say anything unless he wanted to hear even more.

※ ※ ※

There were leaves swirling and dandelions too, that other time at the stadium back in high school, the time he kept thinking about and wanted to bring up but couldn't seem to fit it into the conversation. Those dandelions weren't green though, they were hoary-headed and fluffy. It was later in the year. Fall. Football weather. LSU versus Tulane. Tulane Stadium. The Greenies against the . . . well, it was goddamned LSU nationally ranked as was usual then. They'd fallen on leaner recruiting times these days but back then was the era of the awesome Bengal Tigers, monster teams.

The game itself wasn't what was important. Just another Tulane loss, people leaving, grumbling, swearing, snarling, although some were high-spirited, even some of the Greenie fans. It was after all a football game played under the lights on a southern Saturday night and what could be more fitting to the order of life as it is properly supposed to be?

Usually he would be somewhere in the throng making his way past green-clad pockets of people, an occasional purple-and-gold island of Bengal rooters grinning at the expected good fortune of their team, but on this night for some reason he had stayed in his seat up forty-odd rows on the ten-yard line. He was in the midst of some reverie, enjoying the breeze that seemed to spring up as the others were leaving, smelling the pungent odor of barbecue and garlic from outdoor grills and oleanders from Audubon Park.

Maybe he was daydreaming about the history exam he'd flunked that day, another disappointment in a long list, or perhaps he was thinking about one unobtainable girl or another, but suddenly he noticed the stadium was bereft of all humans save himself.

Well, almost; there was one person, down below him, over by the tunnel to the locker rooms, a woman it looked like, and she appeared to be making her way toward him in a zigzag way, lifting her leg up on one tier and then walking down the concrete aisle, then climbing another and repeating, like she was making some huge graph. It became clear she was coming for him, so when she got to within a few rows he stood up.

*What're you doing?* she asked, and he said, *Nothing, just sitting. Well, you'll have to leave*, she said, politely enough and at first he thought of doing just that, thinking her to be some sort of official connected with the university or the stadium, and then something made him ask her why and she said *because I said so.* That got his dander up, no reason, and he said: *I've got to have a better reason.*

*Because I'm always the last to leave*, she said, and he said, *So, what's that* and one thing led to another and before he quite knew what was happening she was screeching and cursing at him, telling him he had to leave, he was messing with something here, she was a season ticket holder and had been the last fan to leave at every home game since nineteen hundred and fifty-four and *this is what I do, everyone knows me by this, what else do I have, I never married or even had a career, please don't take this away from me, I'm begging you* and at this last he said, *Okay, then, I guess I'll go in that case.*

⁂

"I'm serious. I was just making a small joke that's all. I still love you."

"I know." He could feel her eyes on his but he continued to keep his gaze on the dandelions. The best way to get rid of them was with boiling water, rush it out and pour it on them when it was still bubbling in the pan. Copper held the heat the best.

"I love you too. That's not the problem Robert. This has nothing to do with love. Love has nothing to do with love. What the fuck is love, anyway? It doesn't exist."

"Well then, what's the problem?"

"The problem is there *is* no problem. We've just simply used each other up. And you don't excite me. You never did. You never *do* anything. You're so fucking . . . so fucking . . . boring! That's it. You're boring. If you'd only just once done something exciting for me, something unusual, something memorable. But you never have."

He couldn't think of anything to say so he sipped his coffee and stared out the window like he was thinking, but there was nothing going on in his head in that way. There was nothing in his head at all, only a general kind of sweet sadness that was gentle and *genteel*, not very deep but just kind of there like it was what should be there, what was needed to get him through this part of his life.

He watched the wind picking up, swirling the leaves around faster down there at the bottom of the hill and he started to mention something about the rain that was coming when she spoke instead.

"I'm going to class now. I think tomorrow I'll go to Mother's until we can figure out what's best."

She picked up the dishes and stacked them in the sink. It was his job to rinse them and run the dishwasher. She liked him to do it without waiting too long because of the roaches. *New Orleans roaches aren't very patient* she said. *They're like me.* He was still sitting there when she went out the front door with her book bag.

After she left he poured himself another cup of coffee. He rinsed out the small saucepan the lima beans had been cooked in and poured in some milk and placed that on the stove, turning up the gas jet. When it began to churn and bubble against the sides of the pan he poured some of the coffee out of the cup and replaced it with boiling milk and then spooned in a large spoonful of sugar. Café au lait the way his mother made it except she used milk that hadn't been homogenized yet, milk from their own cows. This was all right though.

✖ ✖ ✖

He didn't leave the stadium like he had promised the woman. He only pretended to, and when he reached the end of the stands and walked below, out of her line of sight, he ducked behind a stanchion and sure enough, here she came, by and by, and went out of the gate no more than ten yards from where he was hiding. She was whistling "Popeye the Sailor Man" and sounded positively cheery. He almost didn't announce his presence she sounded so happy but then he did because she did sound so happy.

*Hoo, hoo,* he goes, *Here I am; I'm still in the stadium and you're outside and now your streak is over* and the woman sees him and comprehends what has happened and begins to cry something awful and begins beating herself on her chest with her forearms and she tries to walk back in and halfway there must have realized it was futile and turns and goes back out still wailing toward the parking lot and how he's scared 'cause this isn't funny any more, it's scary the way the woman is carrying on and he just stands there, the sound of her crying getting farther and farther away and then it's quiet, real quiet and he goes home.

✖ ✖ ✖

And this is what he must tell Janey; when he does she'll see him in a new light and things will be different. She will have misjudged him and will realize her great error and there will be denial, sure, and recriminations of course, but that is just because of her embarrassment and he will show her that there is no need to be embarrassed, she has just erred in her appraisal of him, she has just done a normal human thing and how can he blame her for that? Something happened to me back there Janey, he'll say, what it was I can't say exactly but I did something that was wrong and bad and took me in a different direction from then on, and she'll already know that. She'll say, "I know that, I can see that in you, I guess I've always known something like that must have happened," and as soon as he thought that he knew she wouldn't say anything like that at all but say something like, "This is all a bunch of crap Robert. What are you telling me this crap for? You think your pathetic little incident was some kind of earth-shaking experience or something? You think it's something like those zombies down at the VA hospital went through in Vietnam or something? You're a pathetic little worm Robert. It's no wonder I'm leaving you."

✖ ✖ ✖

There was a knock at the door when he'd drunk about half the café au lait and he went and answered it. It was a man delivering a pizza. He told the man he hadn't ordered it and the man argued and then he said, *Aren't you supposed to call back to confirm orders?* and the man left talking under his breath. The pizza man wasn't a man actually; it was a young boy of about seventeen or eighteen with bad acne on his forehead under the pizza store hat. He squealed the tires when he left.

When he got back to the kitchen table the coffee was too cold to drink so he poured it into the sink and put the cup on top of the other dishes. He opened up the dishwasher and stood there for a minute peering inside and then closed it up again. He went over to where his wife kept the pots and pans and got out a large copper pan and filled it with cold water. His mother always said that cold water boiled quicker than hot and even though that had never made sense to him he had never dared use hot water.

When the water began to froth he picked up the pan and took it out to the back yard to the dandelions. It took six trips and killed the better part of an hour to pour water on all the weeds and by then the sun was starting to set.

After awhile his wife came home and went into the room that used to be the spare bedroom that lately she had been referring to as her study, to deposit her books he supposed. That was where she kept all of her schoolbooks and supplies, notepads and items like that. There was a typewriter, rarely used any longer since he'd bought her the word processor she'd asked for last Christmas. He had the TV on, some show about Africa and the veldt, zebras, lions and gazelles, all eating each other, only they would cut to the next scene before much carnage was shown. He had the volume so low you could barely hear it.

"There was a man delivering pizza," he said. He was sitting in his brown chair in the living room. "Someone played a trick or he just got the wrong address. I told him to hit the road. I thought it might get nasty for a while there. Get physical maybe."

"Why aren't the dishes washed?" she said, removing her sweater and crossing over to the closet to hang it up. "Get physical? Robert don't do this. Don't start."

He looked at her, considering.

"I did something once you don't know about," he said, slumping down in the chair.

"Oh? What's that?"

"Something unusual."

"Well?" She had plumped down on her chair, the beige one. She kicked off her shoes and ran her fingers through her new haircut. He'd liked her hair longer and there was nothing he could see wrong with the original color, the gray she claimed she saw was all in her mind he thought but he was getting used to the way it looked now he guessed.

"When I was in high school."

"Oh yeah. High school. I've read your yearbook Robert. 'To a nice boy who will go a long way. To the nicest boy in the entire Senior Class?' Wow. I had to go and get married to the 'nicest boy in the entire Senior Class.' What do you suppose I did to deserve that?"

He was going to say something but she went on.

"You know I hope to God I never again meet a man who was the 'nicest boy in the Senior Class.' That's one of two things I never hope to hear. You know what the other is?"

He just stared.

"I never want to live in a place where the people say it's a nice place to raise kids. I lived in a town like that once. Bor-ring!"

Neither said anything for a minute or two.

"Well?"

"Well, what?"

"Well, what was this terrific thing you did in high school? Now that you brought it up I suppose we have to hear about it. What'd you do, feel some girl up in the movie theater?"

"No. I didn't say it was a terrific thing I did. I said it was a *mean* thing. Don't you ever listen?" He surprised himself by the testiness of his answer but he noticed her eyes widened and she didn't come back with a wisecrack.

"It was a mean and unusual thing. I was the last fan."

"The last fan?"

"Yes. Haven't you ever wondered who the last fan out of the ball game is? The last person to leave a concert? A play? Someone has to be the last fan. Haven't you ever wondered what such a person is like? I don't mean the person that is the last one out *occasionally* because they're old and in a walker or they know the conductor of the symphony and want to talk to him or something like that. I mean the kind of person that has to be the last person out *all the time*."

"There's no such person. That would be the biggest weirdo of all time. What are you talking about? What is your point?"

"I'm talking about LSU vs Tulane. I'm talking about a woman who had been the last fan out for dozens and dozens of games. Hundreds of games maybe. I'm talking about a woman who had something precious to her, something I destroyed. It wasn't a big, flashy thing I did but definitely an unusual one. And mean. I don't know why I did it and I'm not particularly proud of it but it just proves I'm capable of something out of the ordinary. Don't judge this book by the cover. That's the point."

Janey laughed. She actually laughed! Of all the reactions he'd expected this wasn't one he'd considered. She began to laugh softly, just a little at first and then more and pretty soon she was in convulsions, bent over, her arms folded at her waist, face red as a boiled crab.

"You old faker! What are you telling me this hooey for? That wasn't you—that was J. T. Winslow! You're talking about the old lady who used to be the last fan out of the stadium aren't you? That wasn't you that tricked her and broke her record. That was J. T.! I've heard that story a hundred times! A million times! I don't even know if that was J. T.'s story. I've been hearing that story every since I came to New Orleans. My God, that's an awful, pitiful little pissant of a story! I can't believe you appropriated it for your own. It's not even a good story! Christ, if you were going to steal a story to impress me with, couldn't you at least steal a good one? You are a genuinely pathetic human being."

She got up and walked over to his chair, looking down at him.

"That's it Robert. I'm going to go in and take a nap. I've got a date in an hour. I wasn't going to tell you but . . . fuck it. I was going to just leave tomorrow but I guess I'll just go tonight. I'll have Steve drop me off at Mother's later. It's over Robert. I can't live with a worm like you any longer. I'm sorry. The last fan! I can't believe it! Steal J. T. Winslow's story. That's sad. That's very, very sad, Robert."

She walked away, went into their bedroom, closed the door. He lit a cigarette and picked up the remote control and pushed the button for volume. The sound from the set went dead although the picture remained. It was on ESPN, some ball game, they were interviewing somebody in a baseball uniform and the fans were leaving but he was looking at the closed bedroom door and not at the screen.

It was J. T. Winslow's story. God, it really was. Now he remembered when J. T. had told it to him down at the Café du Monde in the French Quarter years and years ago. Why had he thought it was *his* story? *When* had he started to think it was his story? It *was* his story, even now when he knew it wasn't. It had been his story too long. He knew it better than J. T. Winslow. He had lived it more often more intensely than J. T. ever could. No, at one time it was J. T.'s story but not now. Now it was his. He would wake Janey up after awhile, tell her this, make her understand.

He began thinking again about being the last fan at the Tulane game. He had never known a single other human being who had been the last fan at any event sporting or otherwise. Except that woman of course. It was the damnedest thing. He could see now why it was so important to her. He'd been too young then to appreciate it. He hoped the woman hadn't done anything foolish. He'd just been young, he told himself. Youth's folly.

He went out into the back yard and down the hill to where the dandelions were. First he turned on the outside light. He put his hand down on the ground around one of the dandelions and felt it and then he felt the ground a few inches away from it. Both spots felt the same, cold, the early dew wetting his hand, the place where he'd poured the boiling water and the place he hadn't. He could tell the boiling water had done the trick. They'd be withered by the morning and gone in a day. Janey would be happy they were gone and the lawn would look better. He'd bring her out to see. She'd see he knew how to take care of dandelions.

He felt the ground around the dandelions a last time but couldn't tell if the moisture was dew or something else.

He wished he knew why he had told that particular story to his wife. He could have told her another story but that simply hadn't occurred to him at the time and besides what other story did he have? He could have told her about almost going with J. T. to New Zealand but he wasn't sure right now if that had actually happened or not.

He could have talked to her about the two children they'd buried but that hadn't occurred to him then either. Maybe he should have. He considered and then brushed it all out of his mind, determined to think about it no more, only walked back to the house and to the kitchen where he got out the largest of the copper pots and started filling it with cold water from the tap. He held his finger under the water as it ran and when it finally filled his finger was numb. This ought to heat up really fast he thought, as cold as it is. If his mother was right that is. He waited, sitting in his wife's chair. It felt odd to be sitting in that spot.

He went to the bedroom door and opened it carefully. Inside he could just see the form of his wife on the bed and hear her light snoring. She had her red dress draped over the chair, the one she called her "dancin' momma dress."

When the water was at a throaty, grinding, vicious boil, he went to pick up the pot but the handle was hot. He found the heat mitts where she always kept them in the first drawer. He was very careful not to spill any, walking slowly all the way to the bedroom.

"I fixed those dandelions for you dear," he said, just as he began to pour. "The yard will look wonderful tomorrow." He smiled gently as her eyes and mouth came open and widened at him through the steam. "You see my darling, I can do something unusual. I can do *anything* for you. I just never knew that's what you wanted."

He smiled as he poured, her screams of joy nearly bringing him to his own tears of delight.

"Your happiness is my happiness," he whispered, and when he was done, and she had drifted off to sleep, he leaned over and kissed her lips and was surprised at their warmth.

# The Mockingbird Cafe

S aturday nights, Lucious Tremaine went to the Mockingbird Cafe in New Orleans. He came always by himself and seldom talked to anyone save the bartender and that just to order another drink. The bartender, Fathima, knew more about him than anyone else who frequented the place, not because of any confidences exchanged, but because of two neatly folded-together newspaper clippings from a Michigan paper that had once fallen from Lucious's pocket and were found later by Fathima when he swept up. One clipping was a report of a shooting and a death and a trial and a jail sentence meted out; the other about a convict who had escaped from an Ann Arbor hospital after an operation and a massive transfusion for wounds gotten in a dustup at Jackson Prison. The man had somehow removed catheters and needles from his body and removed his body from the hospital, walking out sometime after midnight, somehow unseen past the guard posted outside. The writer of the second article seemed amazed that such a thing could be done, considering the deleterious physical state the patient was in. There was a brief human-interest mention of the man's family—a wife on welfare, and a daughter on a dialysis machine, in Detroit. The subject of both articles was a man named Lee Atwater, and there was no photograph, but the bartender had no doubt they were about the man he knew as Lucious. Fathima kept what he read to himself. He knew lots of secrets. He had a few of his own.

Lucious favored cheap wine and shots of Seagram's 7, which was just fine with the bartender, since that was his stock in trade. You could tell that by the stale air, soon as you stepped inside. If the smell wasn't enough, if you were a heavy smoker or had sinus trouble, then a glance at the backbar at the six or seven bottles there would let you know this was a boozer's kind of establishment, and didn't pretend to be anything else.

The Mockingbird Cafe wasn't really that anymore. A cafe, that is. At one time, yes, you could get a burger, fries, and even a malt that had real malting in it, and a waitress with piled-high hair who called everyone "Hon" and suggested the "red beans and rice—it's real good today," but no more.

There was another Mockingbird Cafe in New Orleans, not far from this one, and that one was famous and was pointed out to tourists in buses by uniformed guides. That one had rows and rows of bottles on the backbar, all different colors, with heads of shiny stainless steel shot measures, and brisk waitresses and polite college-age bartenders in forest green shirts with tiny white and black birds on the breast pocket. Tourist buses were careful to avoid the street the other Mockingbird was on.

Originally, it had been called "The Sweet Shop," and then the founder and owner, Miz LaFouchette, renamed it after her favorite bird, on the occasion of adding beer and hard alcohol to the fare, because when she was barely a teenaged girl, a boy who sat in front of her in algebra class told her one day she reminded him of a "cute li'l ol' mockin'bird." Then Miz LaFouchette passed away and Ike Washington had it fifteen years, and then there were six other owners in rapid succession within the following decade while it completed its transmogrification into its adult stage, a honky-tonk.

You had to step to your left halfway back to the bathroom to avoid a hunk of ripped linoleum. You didn't know if the rust stain on the wall above the lone urinal was water damage or blood. It could have been a legitimate source of speculation in the Mockingbird Cafe, if anyone had cared.

That was how Lucious Tremaine found it and it seemed to suit him.

※ ※ ※

In the fifth decade of his life, Lucious Tremaine sat always on the same stool at the far end of the bar, leaving only one possible seat beside him and making it plain with the pitch of his head and the incline of his spine that he wasn't open to socializing. The regulars, wise to this breed of man, kept their distance, omitting him from conversations about the heat or how the ponies were running out at Jefferson Downs, and even the worst of the derelicts bypassed him when sponging drinks. Now and again, a yankee tourist wiping sweat from his brow might stop in by accident, a stray from the tourist paths, and plunk down next to Lucious, and such a person might ask him where the best place for shrimp or girlie-shows was, but Lucious would stare straight ahead and growl in a low, don't-mess-with-me voice, "I look like a fuckin' cabby?" and the tourist would slug down his drink or not, and get out, leaving a too-large tip behind.

Where he lived or got his money to drink on, no one knew. Fathima figured he worked in one of the shipyards over in East New Orleans, from a few chance remarks Lucious had made, and what he deducted were burn marks from a welding rod he'd seen on his forearm once. Some of the smaller shops were fairly casual about background checks, especially if the applicant agreed to less than union wages. His clothes were faded and worn but clean, and he fancied a New Orleans Saints baseball-style cap. He didn't smoke and he kept dollar bills in a wad in his sock, inside the left work boot. Whenever he put a new bill on the bartop, Fathima would pick it up gingerly with thumb and forefinger, a delicate move for someone who weighed three hundred and fifty pounds and had killed another kid during a high school football game. The cross-body block he threw which killed the kid was legend even beyond the Irish Channel where Fathima was from, but as mean and respected as Fathima was, he never said a word to Lucious as to the sanitary condition of his currency; he might have thought of doing so at one time, but not after he read those clippings; he just put those bills aside in a separate part of the cash drawer and gave them back in change to people he didn't particularly like.

Sometimes Lucious would stare back at the group of men shooting pool as if he wanted to walk back and pick up a cue, but he never did, and no one ever asked him to join them.

❈ ❈ ❈

It was of a Saturday evening, one of those hot and steamy New Orleans nights when the knives and guns came out a little quicker than usual and Charity Hospital's emergency room looked like a MASH unit, that two tourists stepped through the doors of the Mockingbird. A man and woman, she pretty and dressed in something smart, black and expensive; he small and snarly-looking and black-tied and tuxedoed and the both of them white people. They walked the empty length of the bar and picked the two stools next to Lucious. The cacophony of the bar dissolved and the sound of the last click of balls at the pool table hung in the air for a long, pregnant second as all movement paused and then started up again at a higher intensity.

"VO and ginger for me," said the man, "and a daiquiri for the lady." He pulled out a bunch of crumpled bills and dropped them on the bar, picking them up one by one and snapping them straight.

"No blender," Fathima said, his weight shifting back on his heels, "and no VO," and the man didn't get it for a minute and then smiled and came with, "Well, then she'll just have a Jack and ginger and the same for me." He settled for Wild Turkey and 7-Up for the both of them, and they had a grin over that, and then they asked Fathima to turn on the TV, as the Miss America pageant was about to begin and there was no way in the world they were going to be able to get back to their hotel in time for it, which is why they had stopped at this fine establishment, the man explaining all this in a loud voice. You could see Fathima considering the request, but then he shrugged and turned and switched on the set and flipped through the channels until he found a crowd of girls in evening gowns. That done, he went down to the other end of the bar and picked up the sports section of the *Times-Picayune*.

"Miss Mississippi." It was the tourist lady.

"No way. Miss North Carolina. She's a brunette. Mississippi's a blonde. Brunettes always win."

"No they don't. There's been plenty of blondes. Besides, Miss Mississippi's much prettier. She's got more talent, too."

The man and his companion were having a friendly argument. The woman decided to ask Lucious for the tie-breaking vote.

"Which one do you like, sir?"

At first, he didn't realize they were talking to him and he ignored them, but then the woman patted his arm and asked him the question again.

"Don't matter none to me," he said, not looking at her, both elbows on the dark wood of the bar, eyes fixed on a point in front of him.

"Oh, come on sir. Which one you think's the prettiest?"

It was the man, leaning around, mouth grinning and eyes shining.

"Or most talented." The lady, chipping in.

"Look alla same t' me. Look like white folks business t' me."

The noise level in the Mockingbird lowered several decibels. Even those who hadn't heard him, could sense something was about to happen.

What, what? someone said, back by the pool table.

*It's Lucious, man,* someone else said. *He's talkin' t' them white folks.*

"Excuse me, sir?" It was the white man. He leaned forward farther and peered around the girl, his mouth still smiling, his eyes bright.

"It's a joke, Sam." Between the two men, the girl smiled, turning first to beam at Lucious and then at the man she had called Sam.

"A joke?"

"You know how some people think black people all look the same. The gentleman's saying all white people look the same." She kept smiling at both men, back and forth.

Lucious didn't answer, just sat staring ahead, his hand on his drink.

"Is that it?"

It was the white man, Sam. He was twisted sideways in his seat, his whole arm on the bar, head in hand, looking around the girl at Lucious.

"Is that it, sir?"

"Wasn't no joke." Lucious didn't turn his head, just stared straight ahead. Up at the front of the bar, Fathima folded his newspaper with exaggerated, noisy motions, then laid it aside, staying where he was, but pointedly staring down the length of the bar at the trio on the other end.

"You think we all look alike?"

"Don't matter what I think."

"That's right, podner. It 'don't matter' what you think."

"Sam." It was the girl. Her voice was small, scared. "Sam, let's go."

Sam stood up, looking hard at Lucious, never taking his eyes off him, even though his words were for the woman.

"Shut up. Go outside and get us a cab."

He spoke to Lucious.

"You know what I am?"

Lucious turned his head for the first time, in the man's direction, but didn't make eye contact and then turned back.

"I know what you are."

"And what would that be?"

"You're a cop."

"Yeah." The man laughed. "Yeah, I'm a cop. I kinda figured you knew. You been in the joint, ain'tcha?"

Lucious stood up, picked up his drink and walked around the couple, up toward the front of the bar, and sat down on the farthest stool. He pushed his glass at Fathima. Fathima picked it up and turned around for a bottle. Lucious reached down and took out a small wad of bills from his sock, extracted one and put the rest back in the sock. Fathima took the dollar bill between his forefinger and thumb and took it down to the register and put it in the special drawer. He asked the white couple if they wanted a refill.

When the white man got his drink, he picked it up and walked up to where Lucious was sitting. The girl put her hand on his arm as he got up, but he ignored her. Her face was pale. She remained on her stool.

"My name's Sam," said the man when he got to Lucious. He put his hand out and Lucious just stared ahead, at the row of bottles behind the bar. Sam stood there, hand outstretched, then turned his palm up, looked at it, wiped it on his trousers as if it had somehow gotten dirty. He laughed and pulled out the stool next to Lucious and sat down, swinging around so that he faced the black man.

"You're not real sociable, are you?"

"Leave me be."

"No, sir, not too sociable," the white man went on, as if he hadn't heard him. "Now, why would that be? Let's see, you're a big one, look like you could handle yourself. I'm a white guy, in a black bar, kind of gettin' up in your face, if you want to look at it that way . . . but you, well, you don't do nothin' about it. Ain't that just about the strangest thing you ever heard of? Now, it could be you just naturally respect the law, but somehow I don't think that's it. You know what I think?"

Lucious took a swig of his wine, looked dead ahead, jaw muscles working, but not a word to say to even acknowledge the man was there.

"I think there's paper on you. There's a warrant on you, ain't there? You done somethin' real bad, ain't you, ol' son? Now, I ain't from around here, I'm Tennessee law, but I bet I could find me a police around here like t' talk t' y'all."

Again, Lucious lifted his glass, took a swallow, stared at the backbar in front of him. The other man slugged down the rest of his drink and slammed the empty glass down on the bar, hard, and got up, swinging his leg wide to clear the stool, like a cowboy getting off his horse. Not an ear in the place heard their exchange, but not an eye had missed it.

The white man walked halfway back to where his girl was still sitting and told Fathima in a loud voice, "How 'bout another one, pal, and give my friend here one, too." He winked at the bartender and inclined his head toward where Lucious was sitting.

Lucious got up, drink in hand, and walked around the man and then the girl and back to the rear of the bar, where the pool table was. He sat down on the bench where the kibitzers sat. Even though he sat apart from the couple of men who were already there, they scootched down even farther away from him.

The man called Sam came walking back with a drink in each hand, and sat one of the glasses, a wine highball, down on the ledge just behind Lucious's head.

"Here's your drink, boy," he said, and somewhere there was a sharp intake of breath, and for the first time Lucious looked directly at the man.

Before anything could happen, a huge shadow slid between the two men.

"Leave it alone," Fathima said to the white man, standing between the two, his back to Lucious. A look, not of fear exactly, more of surprise, passed over the white man's face and then something else, and then it was gone, and he was too, with a loud, strained snort, back to the bar where his woman sat on her stool, twisting a strand of her hair nervously between her fingers.

Fathima waited until the man had reached his companion and then he turned and eyed Lucious, who held his gaze for the briefest of seconds, then looked down and away.

"Some things is worse'n the joint," Fathima said.

"Yes," replied Lucious, in a thick voice. "Maybe."

"That was a piece of trash."

Lucious kept his head down and went over and sat back down on the kibitzer's bench. Fathima watched him for a minute. Then, he shook his head slowly from side to side and went back up to the front. The white man started to say something to him as he went by and then must have thought better of it and turned to the woman instead, uttering a laugh that was cut short when Fathima's head whipped around.

※　※　※

About ten minutes later the white couple left, laughing, the man's arm around the woman's waist. Soon after that, Fathima came walking, white towel in hand, making his rounds. Stopping in front of Lucious, he looked down at the man and said, "You want another drink?"

Lucious just stared ahead at the pool table, at the balls caroming. The balls stopped moving, but the man who had the next shot waited. Everyone was watching Lucious.

"No thank you," he said. He didn't look at Fathima, or at anyone else, just kept staring at the pool table.

"Well, man, you got to buy a drink here or you got to git. Don't want no loafers here."

Lucious seemed to consider that for a moment. Then he stood up and put his empty glass on one of the little wall holders behind him. He turned and faced Fathima. Surprisingly, he seemed to be about the same size as the bartender, though more muscular and not so fat. He drew his shoulders back, expanding his chest until it seemed the buttons would pop clear off and the sleeves seemed to tighten around his upper arms. His eyes were wide and there was red in the whites and for a moment the two men stood there, and a collective breath was held as everyone in the bar sensed the tension, and then it was over, and Lucious seemed to sink into the floor a little, and he said, in a small, still voice.

"Well, then, I guess I'll go."

"I know what you did," Fathima said as Lucious moved away, and the words seemed to strike the man in the back physically, almost like a blow. He slowed a step, hesitated, and then commenced to walk once again.

"Lucious!" The name was spat out with force and fury, hurled like a fireball, the sound filling every speck of space in the room.

This time Lucious stopped.

And turned.

"I know what you did, Lucious. It still ain't right. You got a powerful stink about you, man. That man shit on you, Lucious."

Lucious stared at Fathima for a space that seemed long, and then said, "I'm not you, nigger," and he was saying it to only one person, and the way he said the word *nigger* was not hard or vicious or mean-spirited but in a voice that had everything of what could be called a *human* quality. He turned and walked toward the front. Halfway there, he turned around as if he were about to say something else. Fathima looked up and said, "Yeah?" Lucious started to speak and then must have changed his mind. He put his head down and turned and walked out the front door.

There was a split second when the only sound in the Mockingbird was that of Bert Parks on the TV.

"Therrre she is, Miss Ahh—" and then the hubbub started up again, balls clicking on the pool table, glasses clinking, the buzz of voices, laughter. Fathima walked up to the front and turned the TV off, twisted the knob so savagely it broke in his hand. He looked at the piece of plastic for a moment and then hurled it from him with the suddenness of a pitcher picking off a base runner who's leaned a little too much toward second at just the wrong time.

# Telemarketing

There was this big ol' yellow dog they were chasing out in the parking lot when I first noticed them. The girl I'd seen before, but the man was a stranger. Back and forth they ran after the mutt and then a stray comes from around our building and the fight was on.

"Jim," I said, "come and see."

That's when the man steps in between both dogs and grabs each by the scruff of the neck and throws them apart, drop-kicking the stray in the slats. It was some athletic feat I can't begin to describe, like Bruce Lee or something. Jim watched for about thirty seconds and then wiped his hands on his apron and went back to the grill. I stayed glued to the spot until they got a collar on the yellow dog and led him back to their shop.

"Andrea's Dog Grooming Salon," that's what the name on the building said, a converted two-car garage painted Bic-lighter yellow, Tweety Bird yellow. Some kind of ugly. I even said so more than once to Andrea herself, (that's the owner), and she'd grin, but I noticed she never raced out and painted it a nice blue.

"Why you call it a salon," I asked once, and she said something in her la-te-da voice, I disremember. A salon! Like we were in Dallas or Paree. I never heard of such nonsense. People even brought in their cats. Their cats! To a dog groomer!

Why would anyone take their cat to a dog groomer, I asked Jim, but he couldn't be serious, as usual. "To get a sex change," he said. And then, "Why worry about it, Rose?"

I worry because that's the nature I was born with. I worry about a lot of things, Russia, the President, little kids who aren't buckled into their seat belts, things like that. Everything. I worry about everything. I felt like telling him it's my worrying keeps this diner afloat, but I didn't. Like he would have heard me anyway—Mr. Calm and Collected with his nose buried in the sports pages.

Ever since our own baby died . . . It was like all the bones went out of Jim's body and since then I've tried—Lord knows how I've tried!—but Jim's gone somewhere else in his mind, seems like. I loved our little boy as much as he did, but a person has to go on. Some of us have the strength, others don't. I wanted to try and have another baby, but Jim says you can't replace a child like you do a puppy. That isn't what I meant, I told him, but he's still all tore up over Jimmy, Jr. One of these days.

The girl over at the groomers, her I had the scoop on. Not from any great conversations she and I had, no, you could barely get a hello out of her, even though I made a special point to take our bank deposit down to the branch the same time she did, hoping to strike up a little girl-talk. No, the mailman, Charley, clued me in. For some reason she told him all kinds of things. Or maybe he just looked at her mail. I've always suspected he does that. I don't know where Andrea found her.

Charley said she told him she moved here to Freeport to get away from some old boyfriend she was dearly in love with. According to Charley, this guy wouldn't marry her, so she left New Orleans to put some distance between them and get over things.

Why *Freeport*, I asked Charley, but he hadn't thought to ask that. It was strange. Nobody moves to Freeport unless they're going to work for Dow Chemical or they've got kin here. You sure don't move here to manage a dog grooming place unless you've got a Swiss Cheese skull. Can you imagine living in Freeport after New Orleans? If she wanted to move to Texas, why not Houston or Dallas?

Five weeks she's been here, and I've had barely a hi-de-ho from her, and then this young fella shows up—it's obvious he's the old boyfriend—don't ask me how I know, a woman just knows these things—and here they come, across the parking lot and into the diner.

They pick our best booth, the one with the picture of the Alamo on the wall with all the cute little schoolkids looking at their teacher near the spot where Jim Bowie got shot.

"Caught that dog, I guess," I say, and give them a big Texas smile. I had my waitress pad out and doodled a little smiley face on it while I waited for them to order. I always put a smiley face on my tickets. I get bigger tips doing that. It's just an example of our Texas hospitality, I tell Jim, and he laughs at me. One day, for an experiment, I didn't put any smiley faces on my tickets and I didn't end up with half what I usually do. If Jim didn't think of it personally, it's not a good idea.

"Yes, ma'am," says the boy, and I can see right off he's a charmer. "We're your neighbors over to the groomers. I'm Terry and this is Cheryl." He has this accent that's pure New Orleans, like a Brooklyn accent, and so does she, turns out. In five minutes we're practically family, and I've got the whole lowdown. From Terry, mainly; he likes to chin, and it turns out Cheryl's no Chatty Cathy, in fact I suspect she's got a speech impediment for a while until she says something or other and turns out she talks just fine. Just a bit shy, I'm thinking. Jim even came over and got introduced and had a Dr Pepper and talked to Terry. Turns out Terry's a barber and Jim wants to know what causes that little bald spot on the top of his head. "Grass doesn't grow on a busy street," Terry says, and we all laugh, even though we've all heard that one a million times; it's the way Terry says it, makes it funny, like we never heard it before; it's a way he seems to have.

He's waiting to get his Texas license, says Terry, and I was right; he is the boyfriend from New Orleans she can't get over. His version is he was having a ball being the playful bachelor with dozens of girl friends and Cheryl can't take it any more so she lights out for Texas. Once she's here, she's been burning up the phone lines, calling him, and vice versa, and he comes to realize she's the one for him after all, and comes after her. You can tell she's embarrassed the whole time he's telling this, but she likes to hear it, too; she slides her hand over and puts it on top of his.

Texas and Louisiana have reciprocity, he says, which means he can get his barbering license okay, but it was going to take time to cut through the red tape. Isn't that the same all over, I put in. Bureaucrats! We had inspectors for this and inspectors for that, coming out of our ears in the restaurant business, and a license for this and a license for that. I said this to Cheryl, trying to draw her into the conversation, but all I got for my trouble was a smile. She didn't look you in the eyes, neither. Picked out a spot just above your nose and stared at that. I didn't catch it at first and then I saw what she's doing and it starts driving me nuts. I had a teacher that did that, back in high school.

Secretly, I came to the conclusion Terry could have done better in the girlfriend department. That wasn't any reflection on Cheryl; just an observation. Which didn't really matter. If you go around trying to figure out why people are with each other, you'll end up jumping in front of a Greyhound bus in about one week. Long as they were happy with each other that's what counts, I say.

After that, they began to come in on a regular basis and we got to be about as friendly as chipmunks. They were living in Cheryl's little efficiency apartment over on Brazos Street, and there was some other odds and ends I picked up about them, like the fact Terry'd left a really good job, cutting hair in the Fairmont Hotel, to come here. That's the hotel they wrote the book *Hotel* about, and he knew a lot of famous people, cut some of their hair. He'd seen Paul Newman once and the country singer Freddie Fender. Now he was eating cheeseburgers in a dinky Texas town and I'd find myself staring at Cheryl trying to figure out why. See? If I don't watch it, I'll be out there myself, waiting for a speeding bus to run me over! You just can't figure other people's tastes.

✹ ✹ ✹

It was in the late afternoon and Jim waves me over in the back room. There's no one out front, so I go on back.

"Your friends haven't been here in awhile, have they?"

They hadn't, not for over a week, but I didn't think he'd noticed. "Know why?"

"I guess 'cause they been busy."

"Naw. That's not it. They're broke."

"Broke?"

He's chopping up onions and *I'm* the one starts to sneeze.

"What do you mean, broke?"

"I mean broke, as in no money."

"I don't understand." It had been bothering me, their not coming over. I'd thought of every possible reason except for that one. It never occurred to me they couldn't afford to.

"Max told me he caught the guy, Terry, going through our garbage cans." Max was the man who had the trash pickup service we used. He comes in every Friday for S.O.S. and biscuits and he and Jim talk about Vietnam.

"I've been putting out a couple of sandwiches at night. On top of the cans, in a paper bag. It's always gone in the morning."

"Maybe it's raccoons," I said, but I wasn't really thinking about what Jim was saying. I was trying to decide if I should go over and talk to them, let them know we knew, see if they'd take any help. I went back out to the front, and all I could think of was—*those poor kids*. Especially Terry. I know Jim thought the same as I did about him. Reminded me in a lot of ways of our own little boy. I think that's why Jim cottoned to him so soon. My heart was all twisted up inside. I wanted to do something to help, but I didn't see how I could without embarrassing them. Maybe we could put a couple of dollars in with Jim's sandwiches was all I could come up with, but that night I didn't. It made me feel bad, but I think I would have felt just as bad if I would've done that, put dollar bills in a bag with sandwiches. They'd know who did it and how would that make them feel? Pretty low, I imagine. Not that the sandwiches probably didn't have the same effect, but money was different.

Almost a month of this went by, and not a peep or hardly a sight of them in all that time. Once I was outside just as Terry was coming around the corner of the groomers, and he couldn't very well ignore me, so he waved and I waved and he smiled and then went on inside the shop.

A week later, he came in holding his left arm kind of funny, with his hand propped up under the elbow, and asked for a take-out, french fries, and I asked him if his arm was hurt, starting up a conversation like we had just finished one the day before.

"Yes ma'am. Pinched nerve. I just need some fries to go."

"Oh my," I said. "Those hurt terrible. My Aunt Bernie used to get those. She had an operation."

"Yes ma'am," he said. "I don't know how I'm gonna work. Can't even get t' sleep, it hurts so bad. I guess it don't matter—they ain't sent my license yet, anyways."

I told him about Doctor Carrothers, down on Broad Street.

"He's a chiropractor. They know how to fix a pinched nerve. I told Aunt Bernie to go to him, but she didn't listen, and got an operation instead. Worst mistake she ever made in her life. She might as well be paralyzed, way that operation messed her up. You go see Doctor Carrothers. You don't want to end up paralyzed."

"Yes ma'am," he said and that was it. I knew he wasn't about to take my advice. He smiled, but it was a stiff kind of smile, the kind salesmen have when they're telling you about their life insurance policy, the one that looks like it's been practiced in front of the mirror. Later on that same day, he surprised me. Jim had already gone home since we were slow. I'd said I'd stick around and close up, to go ahead and go. I had some end-of-the-month bookwork to do as well. I had just finished up and was going out the door, key in my hand, when here came Terry across the parking lot, like he had been watching for me.

"Can I talk to you, Rose?"

"Sure," I said, and pushed the door back open. "Come on in. No sense standing around out here. How about a Dr Pepper? On the house."

Things were bad. No, they weren't bad; they were *terrible*. They'd lost Cheryl's apartment and were sleeping on the cement floor at the groomers. They didn't have a dime. He didn't have his license yet and it didn't matter cause he couldn't work with his pinched nerve anyway. The dog grooming business was in a slump and Cheryl hadn't cleared twenty a week in a month, with her commission. There was more, but that was the gist of it.

There was good news too.

Cheryl had found out about a job over in Galveston from a friend of hers that lived there, someone she'd known in New Orleans. Terry didn't seem to care much for this friend; it was evident in the way he talked about her, and when I asked him why, he just said the girl was kind of wild and he'd never cared much for her. But, he said, she did call Cheryl about this job that sounded heaven-sent, so that was something in her favor.

It was some kind of telemarketing job, where you sold stuff over the phone to housewives and such. He didn't know much about it, what it was they sold or anything, but it paid well and she could work weekends and still keep her job here.

"Why don't you just move to Galveston?" I asked, but he said Andrea had told them she'd sell them the business at a good price, just payments, and they thought they could make a go of it, once they had some capital to work on.

The problem was, and the reason he wanted to talk to me, was that Cheryl could start work that very weekend, but they didn't have enough for her bus fare and for a motel room for her to stay Saturday night. He was wondering if maybe I could make him a loan.

You could tell it was worse than having a tooth pulled for him to ask for money. Myself, I was just plain delighted I could help them out. A hundred bucks I gave him, even though he said he only needed about sixty, and I'd have it back with the interest Monday morning, thanking me so much it was making me blush.

"No interest," I said. "I'll be insulted if you try to pay me any interest. What are friends for?"

I watched him go back across the parking lot and he was walking with a different step now, a spring in his stride.

Then here comes Cheryl.

"Hi, girl," I said, once again my key out, ready to lock up.

"Hey, Rose." She didn't say anything for a second, just looked down at the ground, and then she said, "Rose that's a wonderful thing you're doing for us. I just wanted to thank you personally and promise you you'll get it back first thing Monday."

"Just glad to help, child," I said, and turned the key in the lock. Instead of going back to the groomers, she just sort of stood there, staring at me. "Well," I said, "I guess it's time to go on home. Good luck in Galveston."

"Rose," she said, and I noticed she was looking into my eyes directly, not at the bridge of my nose like she usually did.

"Rose, can I ask you a question?"

I just nodded.

"Rose, you and Jim been married a long time, haven't you." It wasn't really a question.

"Lord yes, Cheryl! More than twenty years. Ask him though, he'll say a hundred and twenty!"

"Rose, if Jim was in a bad way, say he was hurt or needed an operation or got hit by a truck or something, what would you do to help him out?" Before I could answer, she went on. "What if Jim needed a kidney operation? What if he needed a kidney and yours didn't work, wouldn't match up or whatever, and the hospital had to buy one for him or else he'd die. What if it cost a hundred thousand or half a million and you didn't have it. What would you do?"

"I guess I'd go rob a bank," I laughed, but the conversation was making me nervous. "Does Terry need a kidney operation?"

"What? Oh. No. It's just a pretend question. I was just curious, that's all. Terry? Not Terry! Terry's strong as an ox, believe me!" Her face got dreamy-like, far away. "It's not about Terry, I promise you. It's just a, whaddya call it? A hypothetical question. That's it. A hypothetical question."

I stood there a minute, wondering if she was done. She didn't say anything, but she didn't leave neither. The seconds wore on and it began to feel embarrassing. I cleared my throat, deciding to say good night and go, and then she said the most curious thing. "It's about love." She was staring back at the grooming shop. "How far do you go when you love someone? What won't you do? Where do you draw the line?" The words weren't for me—if they were, she wasn't expecting an answer—she just turned and walked toward the groomers. I had a strong urge to say something, call after her, have her come inside and have a cup of coffee with me, talk to me, something, but I didn't. I watched her walk away and then I shrugged my shoulders and started toward my car. I had my hand on the door handle when I heard her yell, "Rose!" I looked up. She was standing by the door of the groomers. "Thanks again for the loan! See you Monday." I couldn't tell from the distance, but it looked like she was smiling. Just then, Terry came to the screen and opened it and waved and I waved back, got in my car and drove home.

Monday morning, Terry was waiting for me when we pulled up at the diner, and he handed me an envelop.

"Thanks, Rose," he said.

I had some explaining to do to Jim, but he took it just fine.

"Good kids," he said later. "I hope everything works out for them."

Six weeks like that go by. They come in sometimes and eat, but Terry explains that they need to save as much money as they can so they can buy the groomers. Things are much improved, he says. Cheryl seems different, more subdued, if that were possible. She flashes into good nature at times, but then seems to withdraw into herself, as if something is on her mind. Terry doesn't seem to notice. He's too busy being happy about their reversal of fortune. His arm still hurts, but he's decided to try and find work he can do in spite of it, until he can get some health insurance and get it fixed. There doesn't appear to be a lot of jobs in that category, he says, but his spirits seem to remain high. The weeks pass, and I hear about the bank account they've started. We have an upswing in our own business and Jim and I talk about hiring a part-time waitress. I've had a secret concern about varicose veins which I finally tell him about and he surprises me by not laughing, but suggests we get some extra help so I don't have to be on my feet as much.

He's a peach, he is. 'Cept when he's moping. He seems to be doing a lot less of that, with Terry around. Maybe we can start thinking about having another baby soon.

✖ ✖ ✖

One Saturday evening, early, still light out, in came Terry, and he looks like a magazine model.

"I'm off to catch a bus," he said. "How do I look?"

"Just fine," I said, and Jim came out from behind the counter and whistled. "Well, ain't you the dude!"

"It's a surprise for Cheryl," he said. "I just got a job today. I'm gonna be a salesman. For the Lone Star Barber Supply Company. I get a van and a route and everything. And guess what else!" He was like a puppy with a new rubber ball. "I'm gonna ask Cheryl to marry me. I'm going to Galveston right now and ask her. We're gonna get married. I want y'all t' stand up for us!"

I ran over and bear-hugged him and Jim shook his hand, and then, being the practical one, asked him if he knew how to get to where Cheryl worked or to the motel she stayed at, and he said, sure, the address was on her check stubs and she always stayed at the same Motel 6. Even though Galveston was a big town, he shouldn't have any trouble finding either. He should get there in time to walk her home from work. The telemarketing firm was only two blocks from the motel. He worried she might get upset since he'd taken money out of the account for new clothes and for the bus ticket, but I told him no woman is going to even think about expenses when she's on the receiving end of a marriage proposal.

᙮ ᙮ ᙮

That was Saturday. Monday morning came and I should have noticed something was odd when we opened up, but I missed it. It wasn't until almost noon, when a lady carrying a Pom in her arms came in the diner and asked if I knew why the grooming salon wasn't open, that I realized it wasn't.

Celebrating, I told myself, and Jim said I was probably right, but the sight of the darkened window across the lot gave me a queasy feeling all day long. And the next. They still hadn't returned. I checked the paper to see if there had been any bus accidents, but there was nothing like that in there, and they wouldn't put the names of anybody mugged or murdered in Galveston in the Freeport paper, not unless they were prominent citizens, which, of course, they weren't.

The shop stood dark the next day and the day after that. People came and went and some came over and asked why it was closed but I couldn't answer them. Try back later, I kept telling them.

Wednesday morning, I saw the light on when we pulled up.

"You go ahead and open," I told Jim. I walked over, not knowing who to expect, Cheryl or Andrea. It wasn't either. It was Terry. He was walking out, a paper bag in his hand.

"Just picking up some odds and ends," he said, not looking me in the eye, but above, like Cheryl used to do.

I stood there watching as he locked the door.

He still had on his new clothes, only they were rumpled and stained and there was a shirt button missing and a small rip in the front pocket and who knows what had happened to his tie. And he smelled. I could detect booze and it was evident he hadn't been up close to any soap and water in awhile.

"Well," he said, turning and smiling as if he'd just now noticed I was standing there. He said "well" in the most charming way, the same way he had when we first met. "It's happy trails for me, Rose. If you're ever in New Orleans, look me up. Say hey to ol' Jim for me, eh?" And he was gone. He was gone so quick, I wasn't sure for a minute if he'd even been there. And then he was back and handing me something which I took, and still I hadn't opened my mouth. "Do me a favor, will you? See that Mrs. Graves gets this." Mrs. Graves was Andrea and what he handed me was the key and then he was gone again and I'd missed another chance to say something, just stood there with my mouth open and my brain in Australia or someplace.

I don't know why I did what I did next. I unlocked the door and went into the groomers. I guess I was looking for clues to what was going on. Whether that's why I went in or not, I don't know, but that's what I found. In the back, on a counter, was one of Cheryl's check stubs. Parker Telemarketing Services, it said. It had her gross earnings and the withholding items.

I locked the door and went over to the diner. Jim was hard at it, getting ready for the breakfast trade, but I didn't care, even when he yelled and asked what the hell I was doing. I went on back to the office and closed the door.

When information answered I asked for the listing for Parker Telemarketing.

A man answered on the first ring, like he'd been waiting for my call.

"A friend recommended me," I said. "I'd like a job." Don't ask why I said that or what I was trying to prove, I just said it. A hunch.

"Sure," said the man's voice. "You ever do phone sex before? Say, who was it recommended you?"

❊ ❊ ❊

That was all that happened, except that of course I drove poor Jim crazy talking about it and wondering where Cheryl was. It seemed pretty clear what had happened. I might have some of the details wrong but the main part is clear. The thought crossed my mind at first that maybe Terry had hurt her or maybe even killed her, but there was nothing in the paper or on the TV, so I guess they just had a fight and he split for other parts, back home to New Orleans. I wondered if she guessed the same and went there to try and find him. At first, I wanted to go to New Orleans myself and look him up, see what happened, maybe give him my opinion, sort of a woman's point of view, but Jim said don't even hint at it, it's none of your business, just stay out of it, and I guess he's right. I didn't argue, not the way he started to get after Terry left. Bury his nose in the paper for hours at a time, won't hardly carry on a conversation any more.

I keep wishing I'd thought of something to say when Terry was standing right there. Maybe if I'd just gotten him to talk, it would have come out and I could've said the right thing.

Sometimes I'd look at Jim and he'd have his head bent a funny way, maybe while he was working on the grill, and I'll wonder what I'd do if somehow we lost the diner and were down to our last dime, maybe so poor we were eating stuff out of garbage cans. I wonder what I'd do.

It must have been hard for her. For him, too. He was so excited when he left that Saturday.

There's a jewelry store now where the groomers used to be and they seem quite busy. Every now and then I look over and almost expect to see Cheryl and Terry coming out, on their way over for a cheeseburger. It's not going to happen, but it'd sure be nice if it did. They were such nice kids, and too young for such troubles.

Jim and I split up temporarily. The place is all mine now, and it's too much. I've got to hire some help, a cook at least. I hate to even get into that. You're lucky to keep somebody two weeks before they go on a bender and you've got to start all over.

It's my fault, I suppose. I just kept thinking about what Jim said when I asked him what had been on my mind, and he said, hey, there's always unemployment. He'd never eat out of no garbage cans, is what he said. I'm sure he doesn't even know why I asked for a separation, and what was funny was that he didn't even argue. It was like he'd been expecting it and was relieved when it came. I think he thinks this separation is my mid-life crisis. Maybe it is. It wasn't even the knowledge we were never going to try to have another baby.

Or maybe it was.

Life sure isn't what you think it's going to be when you graduate from high school, is it? They should warn people.

# The Tourist

*. . . she was cool . . . yeah, tits out to . . .* He walked all the way into the bar, the screen door slamming behind him, and made the first seat at the bar his, the seat nearest the front door, pictures of big-busted women with white blouses and too-red lips flashing on his mind's Sony, that channel punched in by a snatch of conversation between the two men in the corner booth as he walked by.

They were drinking Budweiser; is that why he ordered one too? Usually it was Heineken or St. Pauli Girl, not that he hadn't ever had a Budweiser, but maybe subliminal suggestion had helped him choose. Out of one corner of his eye he saw the two talkers were the kind of men he made fun of and admired, tough, t-shirted, three-buck haircut types.

He ran his fingers through his own thirty-five dollar style, knowing it was perfect, unmussable, and compensated for his inadequacies by asking the barkeep for a shot of Bushmill's. Another mistake, he realized, even as he placed the order; it should have been Wild Turkey or something like that, but it was before him now, and amber-colored, and only the guy who poured it for him knew which bottle it had come from. There had been dust on the bottle and the bartender was wiping his hand on his apron after replacing it on the shelf. He looked away, but it was no use; he could feel the bartender's contemptuous eyes on him.

He was surprised to even be here. Just out for a drive, he'd told his wife, get the car looked at, see what that noise was. He hadn't planned this at all, but the sight of the bar just naturally pulled him in. He'd have one and go. He knew the real reason he'd pulled in. Estelle's smugness.

*Yeah, sure you're going to get the car fixed, Harold. You just be back in an hour. I want to eat at that place we saw last night.*

Fuck her, he thought. I'm still in charge of myself, no matter what she thinks. I'm Harold Weintraub and I still run this show.

The shot and beer sat before him; no one saw him slug it down, and then someone else came in and perched two stools from him, a big-titted, white-bloused blonde who could have blown down from one of the posters on the wall, about three dollars and ninety-eight cents worth of Sherwin-Williams rollered on her cheeks and lips. He threw the shot down and kept it there, even though he had to count silently backwards from one hundred while his eyes watered and the fiery liquid tried to find its way back up, once, twice, and even a third time, and he was forced to wipe his cheek with his coat sleeve.

Buy you one, he said, once recovered, and remembered not to smile, Texan-style, and she looked over at him and said, sure, why not, sailor, but don't get any ideas, I'm meeting my boyfriend, he gets off in an hour and he'll waste your fat ass, you get fresh. I'm off duty now, she said, and Dusty thinks my social time is his. The bastard, she added, smiling.

What, me worry? he shot back, grinning and then he waved at the bartender who ignored him.

A drink for the lady, he said, and wished he hadn't spoken quite so loudly, as the two men in the corner booth quit talking and the bartender looked up from whatever he was looking at or reading, cutting him a look like he was the pup he shouldn't have kept, but then he came and asked the woman what was her pizen. He said it like that too—"pizen"—and then he gave her the shot of Wild Turkey from a near-dead bottle and took the five the man handed him.

Name's Harold, he said, and she took a sip from the shot glass with her little finger extended, like she was taking tea with Prince Andrew, and said, pleased t'meetcha, I'm Starr with two r's, and she slugged down the rest of the drink the way the Sultan of Swat probably did, after a four-homer day.

Comin' t'meetcha, she said, and moved over to the stool beside him, her perfume getting there way ahead. He heard the two in the booth snicker, but didn't turn around. He ordered another W.T. for the lady and the same for himself, wondering at the time how he was going to choke it down without embarrassing himself. He wanted water with it, in the worst way, but didn't relay that to the bartender, who took the ten spot he passed to him, and brought back his change, placing it squarely on top of the wet ring his beer can had made on the bartop. From behind him, one of the pair in the booth ordered another round of Buds and then one of them said, give me one of them Bushmill's, maybe my luck'll change, and they both chortled.

This time, he felt his face redden and he took a healthy sip of his drink for camouflage, and said, you on lunch from work, to which she replied she didn't work till night, and bet you can't guess what I do. No, he said, unless you are a telemarketer, and she said, sometimes, but usually I just meet 'em on the street and he wasn't sure he knew what she meant but he thought he got it.

You're not from N'awlins, she said, and he said, how can you tell, and she said, nobody from N'awlins dressed like he did came into a place like this, he looked more like he should be over in the Quarters 'stead of out here in some dive on Airline Highway, and was he out here on account of the preacher who'd been on TV, the one from Baton Rouge, and he said he didn't know what she meant, and she said, oh, come on, you been in Ethiopia or somethin'? Then he confessed, said, he guessed he'd heard this was where that preacher used to go, that there were hookers here and he wanted to see what the places looked like, he was from Fort Wayne, that was up in Indiana, and they didn't have nothing like that up there, and was this a place he could see some at?

As a curiosity, he added, not that he'd ever consider using a hooker, he was happily married, with three lovely kids that were all on the swim team back home, the girls too, no, he was just curious what places like this looked like.

You crazy? she said. What you think I am, Barbara Bush? You don't see a hooker in here, you gotta be carryin' a cane with red on the end, what you expect?

Oh, I'm so sorry, he said, I thought perhaps you were just a customer come in here to hear the band.

Yeah, I hit here at noon just so's I get a good seat, they so fucking popular. Listen, Jack, don't pull my coat, I got things to do, you interested or what?

Well, maybe, he said, the booze starting to work. Depends. He glanced at the door and then at the woman and turned in his stool to where he couldn't see outside. This time he just crooked his finger at the bartender and there were two fresh drinks in front of them for which she omitted to thank him, and he said did you ever see this famous preacher yourself, and she said, sure, why not, most of what we get in here is preachers, dressed like you, and he said, but I'm not a preacher, I sell electrical supplies and components back home in Indiana, and she said, that's a song, isn't it, "Back Home in Indiana," and he laughed and took a slug out of the glass and got it down the wrong pipe and required emergency attention which she neglected to perform, having more pressing matters diverting her attention, such as a touch-up job on her lipstick. He got through it on his own, while the two in the booth were wheezing until their eyes were red and wet and even the bartender was smiling.

Wrong tube, Harold said, his voice husky in a way he wished he could keep, sounding like Nick Nolte. How 'bout going over to that table in back and talk, he said.

Fine with me, she said, sliding off the stool with a little ploppy sound in her shoes. "Fraid your wife'll come in? At which he laughed, naturally, but still gave a little glance over at the door.

It ended up they went outside where there's a junkyard of sorts, two or three old cars rusting away on flat tires, weeds all over, and a busted-up sink half-sunk in mud, cracks rust-orange, and he got it unzipped and bent her over a car fender only it wouldn't go in very much, being half-soft and all, and so she did the first part of the half and half, which didn't require a lot of choking, and that's when the booze hit and he threw up.

He had to go back through the bar to get to his car and the two at the front booth were slumped down in their seats, baseball caps pulled low over their faces, hands over their mouths, shaking like they had the palsy. He pretended not to see them.

At the hotel, Estelle pestered him to death about where he'd been, but he gave her the story that he got lost coming back from the garage where he went to get the car looked at and she bought the dodge even though she said, I hope you can't get AIDs at this here garage, at which he laughed but then couldn't get the word unstuck from his mind.

AIDs.

AIDs.

※ ※ ※

Not a week later, "Back Home in Indiana," he goes into the bathroom one day to take a quick one and breaks off the toilet paper holder which he's grabbed when the pain hit.

They tell him, yes, you have gonorrhea, when he sees the nurse down at the free VD clinic, and we need a list of all the people you've had sex with in the last six months. He makes up two or three names to make himself look good and promises to contact them himself, and she says, okay Mister Schmidt, take these pills, since he's told her he's maybe allergic to penicillin, and is terrified she's going to ask him for some identification, a driver's license that doesn't say Mister Schmidt on it, but she doesn't and he beats it out of there.

Well, he's up against it now, is what goes through his thought processes. Here goes my lovely marriage and three kids on the swim team and Estelle, well she's gonna take him for the house, the car, the change in the couch, and Friday poker nights are not going to be what they used to be, since the money he's going to be playing on won't buy any pots, and he goes to this bar down on State Street, the Acme, and ties one on, even knowing the nurse told him not to as the pain of unloading the extra beer his body doesn't need is going to leave him cross-eyed.

Finally, he asks the bartender for a sheet of paper and a pen and he writes a letter to Estelle in which he says he's got a dose and in all probability so does she since they had sex a couple of days ago, and that he's very sorry but he loves her and he's going to let her read this letter while he goes and has a beer and when he comes back she can be gone if she wants while he collects his gear, or she can do what she wants, but he really does love her. With all his heart, which is how he signs it.

He goes home, gives her the letter, all folded up like the notes she used to pass him at Northside High School, and tells her to read this and he'll be back in an hour. When he leaves he considers driving the car until it runs out of gas and finding a job and staying wherever that is, but he knows he won't do that.

Two and a half hours later, he walks back in the house and there sits Estelle, on the couch, arms folded and mascara war-painted on her cheeks, but she's done crying.

Well? he says, and she looks at him with Charles Manson eyes, and says to him, I'm only going to say one thing—you got caught this time and I'm going to forgive you—I won't forget it—but it better not ever happen again. At which he breaks down and blubbers but knows better than to go over and hug her, but tells her the rest of the news, which is that she has to hie herself down to the free clinic and get tested herself.

She does, the next morning, and uses her real name, which is Mrs. Harold Weintraub, and when she comes home she's madder than a trucker with two flat tires. Seems she has no allergies and so they gave her a huge shot of penicillin in the nether area and she rants and raves all day about why she's got to get a shot which she hates and he only has to take some pills.

After a few days they begin to talk again, as she's shopped pretty extensively, maxing out all the credit cards she can find in her purse, and he feels like Henry Kissinger, having to practice diplomacy at all times, and she has already brought up the possibility they might have

AIDs, for which the clinic says they have to come back in six months to check on. But, at least they're talking again, only not long, drawn-out dialogues.

In the fall, his oldest, the boy, gets kicked off the swim team for going into a teammate's locker and borrowing his watch and a Guns and Roses tape, and his middle daughter gets notes sent home from school that say she's having trouble with first-year algebra.

At Thanksgiving, Estelle announces she's not going to cook the dinner but says they're going to a restaurant. She makes the reservations. Last year, they did the turkey bit at home even though Estelle pouted for a week when he wouldn't take them out. This year, it's not even a contest. Not since New Orleans.

Estelle and the two oldest order prime rib, he gets the turkey special, and the youngest girl has a deluxe hamburger and a Kiddie Kocktail. He leaves a ten for the tip, two fives, just over fifteen percent, and when they get up to go, Estelle stays behind and pockets one of the bills. He sees this and starts to say something but there's a new look in her eye and he goes on out to the car with his family. He makes sure he opens Estelle's door for her and he doesn't say a word when she says she wants to drop by her mother's house.

He can't.

# Toothache

We were having beans this meal. That's not news—when we *don't* have beans, that's news. My main concern was not biting down on a rock. There are rocks all the time in the beans. If I looked around, I would see everyone else eating the way I was. Carefully, so as not to bite down on a rock. As if I cared.

There are long rows of inmates, just shy of five hundred of us when we eat. Twenty to a table, ten on each side. Five rows of tables, five tables to a row. There are no tablecloths on the tables, just the metal, painted gray, gloss finish. They feed us in shifts. We do almost everything in shifts. They don't want us all together. That could lead to trouble.

Not every table is full. Here and there is an empty seat for the ones who didn't feel like beans tonight or the ones who stayed in their cell for another reason. I see a few spots where there are two vacant seats right next to each other and I can guess why they skipped supper. There are more absent than usual but that is because it is payday—when the state issues you your monthly pay—and everybody has been to the commissary, buying bags of cookies and Pall Malls. Because of their length. More for the money. If I hadn't owed all my money out, I'd be back in the cell myself, eating Oreos and not worrying if I was going to bust a tooth with these beans.

The man across from me said, "Hey, look at that." Then he kicked me under the table.

I looked where he was looking and saw one of the inmate cooks walking fast and he had a meat cleaver in his hand, held down, blade up. He was walking like a man with a mission, in a straight line. He walked with even, precise steps, each stride the same length as the previous and at the same speed. Not slow, not fast, just the same. He walked in a line that could have been marked off with a carpenter's plumb line chalked on the concrete, up to the head table. His last three steps were like this: On one, the hand with the cleaver went

194

back, like a pendulum; it swung forward in an underhand arc on two; sank into this inmate's blue denim belly on three. It was as smooth a thing as I ever saw. The man whose belly had received the cleaver cooperated, as if they'd practiced their little dance together for hours. He stiffened in awareness on the first (of those last three steps), began to rise on the second and was fully risen on the third, in perfect position.

There was a general hubbub of noise like what you'd expect. I forgot to check the spoonful of beans I had just put in my mouth and bit down hard on a rock. I was almost done with the meal and I did that. Stupido!

⌗ ⌗ ⌗

They were locking us down. I went in first, when we were all in front of our cells. What was the point in staying out on the tier walk for just a few extra seconds? We were going to be in all night anyway. Some people just like to torture themselves for a tiny bit of freedom.

My cellmate was awake. He was holding a magazine and pretending to read it. I knew why he had skipped supper. He didn't like waiting until I went to sleep to masturbate. "Look," I'd said, plenty of times. "Go ahead and whack your willie. It's none of my business. Just don't get any ideas." But he was from a small town. I guess that's the reason. Shy, you see?

"What happened at the chow hall?"

"What? Oh . . . I don't know. Somebody got whacked."

"I heard. Franklin told me." Franklin was the hack downstairs who put us in for the night. He would sit down at the desk all night and read those *True Police Story* magazines and pick his teeth with a folded-up gum wrapper. You could see him wince when the aluminum hit a filling. You'd think he'd learn, get a regular toothpick.

"Franklin said it was a guy from K-Dorm. He said Susie did it."

He was right. It was Susie. I could see that, the part I happened to pay attention to.

He went on, "Susie! That guy's a mountain! One big sissy!"

"Doesn't matter how big you are, you got a meat cleaver, you're the biggest guy around regardless your size."

"Yeah." He laughed. "Franklin said the guy ran out the chow hall with the cleaver sticking out of his stomach. He said he was holding it in with his hands."

I didn't say anything. What could I add to that?

"He said he ran all the way across the grinder to the hospital. He said he got halfway up the steps before he died. He said he fell, halfway up the steps and all his guts just popped out. God!"

I had the idea I was supposed to say something, but what?

"Is that what happened? Where were you?"

I saw what he wanted. He wanted details. Franklin must not have seen it himself. Well, of course not. He was here, in J Block. One of the other hacks must have come by, filled him in. They kept us over at the chow hall a half hour longer, brought in some extra guards, blew the whistle, all that stuff. They didn't want trouble. A thing like that . . .

"I guess that's about right. I didn't see that, but it sounds about right."

"Didn't you see it? Goddamn, A. J., you were right there! What happened?"

I looked at him.

"I don't know. I guess that's what happened. I wasn't paying attention. It was just some grudge thing. I bit a rock."

"A rock?"

"Yes. In the beans. I guess I'll have to go to the dentist tomorrow. I'm not too thrilled about that."

He just shook his head and picked up his magazine. He turned over, his back to me and began turning the pages. I could tell he was disgusted that I didn't have any juicy details. I just hadn't paid that much attention after breaking my tooth. He turned the pages faster and faster, making a lot of noise.

My tooth was starting to really hurt now. I could feel pieces of filling or maybe the tooth itself. That rock had done a job, probably cracked the actual enamel. I got up and went over and tried to look inside my mouth in the mirror but the mirror was metal, not glass, and it's hard to see something like that in a metal finish. After awhile I gave it up and went back and climbed up on my bunk. I tried to think about other things, keep my mind off my tooth. It was throbbing at a pretty good clip now. I wondered if I yelled down to Franklin would he get me an aspirin.

In a little while, I began to doze off. Almost.

"A. J."

I said, "Huh?"

"You got three weeks, huh."

He was talking about my parole hearing.

"That's right."

"You'll be back A. J. I can guarantee it."

Everybody always says that. It's jealousy, that's all it is.

"You remember Melrose, A. J.?"

Melrose was a black guy in the cell next to us, a long time ago. He was slow-walking somebody for a carton of cigarettes and the guy came by and threw acid in his face. He lay in his cell and screamed all night. The hack downstairs just kept on reading his magazine. It wasn't Franklin; it was somebody else, but he read the same kinds of magazines, *True Crime*, stuff like that. In the morning, after we went out for chow, they came and got Melrose, who was down to a little occasional whimper by then. None of us heard anything, we said when they asked. When Melrose got out of the hospital, he had pink blotches all over his face. Permanent blotches. Also, he lost an eye. That happened on my very first night in the population right after I got out of quarantine. Three years ago.

"You cried at Melrose. I heard you."

"I was new. It was a shock. I was probably scared. So what?"

"You yelled at the guard. I told you to shut up, you'd get us both in trouble."

Damn, that tooth was acting up!

"So what?"

"So what, is a guy gets whacked now and you don't even care. You got a problem, A. J. You don't fit out there on the bricks anymore. I should be the guy getting cut loose, not you. It's a waste of a parole. I hope when you come back they don't put you back in here with me. You're a scary dude. You used to be all right. You used to mind this place. You don't even care you're getting a parole, do you? Was it when you got that letter from your wife? That's when it was. I'm right, aren't I? Yeah. I know I'm right. Hey, when you go in and talk to them, tell them to give *me* your parole. Tell them they're wasting it on you. Tell them you're too far gone, you're institutionalized. Your heart is hard, man."

My tooth really began to throb now. I swung my feet over the edge, leaned over and grabbed the bars and brought my face up to them.

"Hey! Franklin! I need an aspirin! In twenty-two. A. J. Mayes."

I watched the fat guard say something, either to himself or up to me, and saw him toss his magazine over on his desk. He got up slowly and jiggled the keys on his chain. He bent over and unlocked a desk drawer and began moving things in there around, looking for my aspirin I hoped. They even kept the aspirin under lock and key. The druggies, they'd shoot up anything, even Bayer. Once, I was supposed to go with two other guys who'd gotten hold of some embalming fluid. It was supposed to give you the ultimate high. Only I got caught in a lockdown, somebody got sloppy, let them find his shank at the after-work shakedown and the whole cellblock was restricted to the cellhouse after chow even though it was our day to go to the yard or gym. The two guys, they were from another cellblock, went ahead without me. It was the ultimate high all right. They both died.

Dolores. I hadn't thought about Dolores in almost two years. There was a guy over in I.D., used to play pinochle with us out in the yard, said something right about that time, bunch of us were talking, nipping on some applejack. He wasn't talking about me, he was talking about somebody else, but what he said made sense. Think of them screwing other guys, he said. That gets you mad at them and then you're halfway home. Once you get past mad, then you can move into hate. Now, you're three-quarters there. From hate just naturally comes indifference and that's where you want to be. See, the opposite of love isn't hate. Not really. The ultimate opposite of love is indifference. Get there and you're home free.

An image of Susie burying the cleaver in that guy came up in my mind and I couldn't remember what the other guy looked like, who he was, even though I vaguely remembered seeing him around the yard. I could feel that tooth though. It was throbbing like nobody's business. I couldn't keep my tongue off it. You know how it is when you got a tooth hurting like that. You can't keep your tongue away from it. You have to keep worrying it. That's what I did. I kept worrying that tooth.

# Phone Call

Remembering that afternoon at the cafe, Grandma, Inez, Billy Watson the sheriff, me sucking on a Dr Pepper, all sitting at a back booth with the poster of Lone Star Beer, crackling, loose, yellow-dried gum showing from the corners where it was working free. Remembering Inez, black and huge, opening my Dr Pepper with her teeth, the cap thunking off, her wiping the bottle lip on her white apron and handing it across to me and Grandma saying for the thousandth time, Don't do that, Inez. You'll have that boy doing that.

And Billy, the sheriff, laughing and saying, Oh, hell, Nance, he's probly still just got his baby teeth, and Nance—Nancy, Grandma—going harumph or something like that, a snort, and me saying, Oh no these are my real teeth all of 'em but don't worry I won't try it I just like to see Inez do it, and them all laughing, even Grandma.

The memory of the pay phone ringing and Inez getting up, a chore for three hundred pounds of brown flesh even motivated by the requirement of her job and us talking, them asking me about school, how was classes, did you learn anything today, and then Inez, speaking from the booth and saying, Mr. Watson, it's for you, James at the sheriff's office. Me, not paying attention, adult business, phone calls for sheriffs, and telling them, Grandma and Inez who'd come back, about what we did in school that day, fractions or something, maybe a book we'd read, and not paying attention, not really until this very minute, when at last I can sit down and try to write this. Help me remember, you know?

Oh, they are? he was saying, over the report I was delivering, in that high skinny voice Billy Watson had, the voice that always sounded strange coming from the body that was almost as big as Inez's, but fat, not solid like hers. Fat is fat, and three hundred pounds of human meat is fat except on the tallest of men, but it was most definitely fat on Billy, even though he was four inches or so taller than Inez, but on her it wasn't in rolls like Billy's, but firm and round the way it most probably was even when she was a child or even before. I better get right out there, stop that, Billy's high skinny voice said, and there was a break in our conversation. This sounded like police business and when wasn't that interesting?

I believe I'll have another piece of that sweet tater pie, he said to my Grandma, coming back over and sitting down but of course it was Inez who got up to fetch it over from behind the counter, behind the stainless steel coolers that held all the kinds of beer people wanted. Pop, too. Dr Pepper, Coca-Cola, Nehi. Orange and grape. And a glass of milk, he said, I believe I'd like another glass of milk Inez.

Remembering watching Billy eat that pie, not the kind I liked I'll tell you, sweet potatoes naturally made me gag, and thinking it funny he took such little bites, not his normal four bites and out but little dinkybites, and little tiny sips of his milk. With an ice cube in it. Billy liked an ice cube in his glass of milk and so did I for a long time but not now.

Us looking at him, watching him eat that pie and drink that milk taking the longest time to do so, eat and drink, and then he picked up his hat on the floor beside him and stood up and hitched up his belt—he didn't lay down any money of course, he never did—and cleared his throat and said I gotta get out to Bryan Beach quick. That's what he said, his exact words I remember them like it was an hour ago. I gotta get out to Bryan Beach quick they're beating some nigger out there, bunch of white boys. He walked to the front door with I remember baby steps, little steps that looked awkward for a big man such as he was, and we could see him get in his car with the bubble on top and back away from the curb but slow, real slow.

Well Inez, my Grandma said after a couple of minutes and after Billy had gone and none of us had said anything, Well you better clean this up. And I saw Inez give my Grandma a look and Grandma said, Well Inez, Bryan Beach is a white beach you know that child, and Inez kept looking at her not picking up the dishes like Grandma had told her and Grandma didn't say any more, just fetched her pack of Pall Malls from the table before her and stuck one in the holder that was fastened around her neck on a chain and lighted it. I didn't say a word, just sat there like a kid is supposed to and wondered about all of it, only didn't have enough adult in me then to see what was going on for sure. Now—yes, of course, but then, well I was just a kid. See?

It was on the news that night some black man from Houston was killed by "unknown assailants" on Bryan Beach, struck with heavy objects, probably bats or pipes said the man on the news, and there were no leads according to the sheriff who was Billy Watson and they showed him and even talked to him, the man on the news shoving a microphone under his lip and asking him that—Do you have any leads Sheriff.

Not yet, Billy said, but we'll get 'em, don't worry about that. It don't matter what color a man is gets killed in Brazoria County he said, his face all grim and serious—We don't tolerate murder in this county.

That made me feel a little better but not much as it wasn't the first time I'd seen a grownup lie, but it was almost the first. The first was my uncle but that's another thing and a different circumstance.

Billy came into Sugar Babies—that's the name of our restaurant—the very next day and a few times after that but then we didn't see him there for the longest time maybe a year or more. The first time he came in he went over to where Inez was snapping green beans at the back booth and asked her to go fry him up a hamburger and hold the onions and she went back without saying anything to him and I remember thinking that was kind of funny, Inez always said something to everybody even if it was just to cuss at them. It was a Saturday and just medium busy and I was there on my first day on the job as Grandma's dishwasher. Twelve is old enough to have a job she said and dishwasher is what she had me do. Later that summer I got to be the night dispatcher for our cab company which was just next door in a little shed she'd put up in the vacant lot between the res-

taurant and the movie theater. I saw a cab driver shoot and kill another cab driver my first month on that job. The driver that shot the
other one was scared to death of snakes and the man he shot kept
shoving this dead rattlesnake at him only the other man didn't know
it was dead and when he finally threw it at him he pulled out his gun
and shot him in the throat. But, that's another story too.

That's how I happened to be back in the kitchen when Inez fried
up Billy's hamburger. I watched her slap it on the grill and it was
plain to see she was mad. I took out one of the big galvanized garbage cans to the back and when I got back she was just standing
there. She'd been waiting for me, I had the feeling.

She stared right at me, but didn't say a word. I didn't either, just
turned and picked up a broom and started to dig at some potato
peelings that had fallen on the plank flooring and were sticking to
the wood like peelings did, where you had to get down and get under them with your fingernails.

She put it on a bun, with lettuce and tomatoes and ketchup. Billy
wouldn't eat a hamburger with anything but ketchup. And sweet
pickles. We usually put dill pickles on most folks hamburgers but
we all knew Billy had a fondness for sweet pickles. Inez put some
chips on the plate and shoved it at me and told me to take it out to
the sheriff. Tell Miz Landon I got a bad cold she said to me looking
me in the eyes. I'll be going home the rest of the day. When I went
through the swinging door that led to the bar, I looked at the hamburger but it looked all right. I don't think I would have bit into it
though, if it was my hamburger. There was something about the way
Inez was acting.

Inez lived just out back, in a trailer my Grandma had bought
and moved there for her. When I found Grandma and told her Inez
had gone out back, she gave me a look and said something about
lazy niggers and I went back and tended to my dishes. There was a
lot of them. And the steam table. I had to wash all the pots on the

steam table before the night rush started. We weren't allowed to soak dishes at the restaurant like Mom let me do at home.

In a minute, Grandma came through the kitchen and out the back door to where Inez's trailer was and I could tell she was mad the way she was walking. She came back a little bit later and walked around the kitchen slamming pots here and there. You got fifteen minutes to get those dishes finished, she said to me and then she went out in the restaurant.

Well, of course they never found out who killed that black man out on Bryan Beach and after a week or so people mostly quit talking about it. Some things changed after all this. I don't remember Inez and Grandma and me ever again sitting around a table when things got slow like we had before. And I asked Inez more than once to pop my Dr Pepper bottlecap with her teeth but she said her teeth had gotten softer and she was afraid she'd break one.

Inez died when I was seventeen and we'd moved away to Indiana. "We" meaning my mom and dad and sister Carol Ann. They let me come back for her funeral. After all, Inez had been my nanny before she started cooking for Grandma. She's the first one ever spanked me, when I was little. She had a nice funeral and there was lots of white folks there too, not only just me and Grandma but eight or nine others mostly from the restaurant.

Two years later, Grandma died while I was in the navy and stationed in Bermuda as a cryptographer. We tracked Russian subs all up and down the east coast and intercepted their radio messages. I went on leave to be a pallbearer for her and it was the biggest funeral I've ever seen before or since. Grandma was probably the most prominent businesswoman in town what with the restaurant and cab company—she paid for every brick of the First Baptist Church all by herself, even though she wasn't allowed to become a member on account of her selling beer and wine in her restaurant, but that didn't stop people from coming to her funeral and the preacher of the First Baptist preached it even. I wore my dress whites with my Good Conduct and sharpshooter medals, and the ribbon for the Cuban crisis I was in a year before.

The funeral service was in Freeport and then we had to go to Houston where she was buried, fifty-some miles away. The funeral procession was over five miles long, must've been half the town. The *Houston Post* even ran a picture and a story about her, as our family was prominent in Texas and Grandma was first cousin of Senator Ellender of Louisiana. Billy Watson led the way in his squad car, the bubble light on top going the whole time and every once in awhile he'd let go with the siren so's it sounded like it let out a burp.

After the funeral and before we started to Houston he came up and shook my hand and said how sorry he was about my grandma, what a fine, fine woman she was and all that, and he asked me if I wanted to ride with him in his sheriff's car, lead the way. No, I said. I believe I'll ride back in the funeral home limousine with Mom and Dad and Carol Ann.

That's the way we went to Houston and this is disrespectful, but most of what I remember about that ride was that I had the worst nicotine fit all the way and couldn't smoke. That would've killed my mother if she knew I'd taken up the habit.

That's the story and I'm glad I finally got it out, told it. I loved my grandma, almost as much as my mom and dad, but I wish she could have been different in some ways. I keep saying to myself that she was a victim of her times, like everybody else, black and white. I want to write this story a different way, have it end where she tells somebody what Billy Watson did. Or didn't do. But it wouldn't be the truth, would it? All I could do is get it out the way it happened.

# Voodoo Love

E d watched Margaret from where he sat on the bed, naked except for white boxer shorts, one leg crossing the other, upside-down vees, his spine bent back as he rested his weight on his elbows on the mattress and his chin pushing against his chest. Outside their open apartment window he caught sight of men in coveralls emptying garbage cans into their truck and the odor of stale beer and coffee grounds came through the open window. "Come on, you'll like it," Ed said. "We'll go by the voodoo lady's place so you can look at the gris-gris, all the other junk she has. You like that."

"I might," Margaret said, seated before the dresser mirror, back to him, clad only in her panties. She stretched her arms toward the ceiling, her eyes on her breasts that were stretched to disappearing. "But I won't. You won't let me."

"What's that supposed to mean, 'I won't let you'?" He raised himself to a sitting position, addressed her twin in the dresser mirror.

"Just that." She tossed her head and ran her brush through it, from the bang area to the ends in the back, blonde strands pressing against her scalp and then bouncing up immediately as the brush passed. "You just want to laugh at Madame Leonine, at the tourists, show how cool you are. How smart you are." She laid down the hairbrush and turned to face him, hands palms up on her calves, the weight on her bent wrists which pushed her shoulders up close to her face, leaning forward, legs spreading slightly.

"And you don't?" He pulled a leg up, hands clasped around his knee, rocked back and forth slightly. "You like that kind of stuff, too, baby. Don't tell me you don't." He let his leg down flat on the bed and brushed something white out of his chest hair.

"Not like you."

Margaret spun around and threw her hands up as if to punctuate something she wanted to say, and then let them fall to her lap.

206

Instead of speaking, she turned back to face the mirror and picked up her hairbrush and began taking it through the back, snapping the end of her strokes, stray wisps following the brush and then falling away like cobwebs breaking off in the trail of a dustrag. She stopped her brushing momentarily and engaged his glance, her lips thin, the corners turned slightly down.

He looked away first, staring at his knee and picking at a tiny scab until a drop of blood began to seep. "Sure. And you hate it. You think that old lady doesn't have feelings."

He wiped the droplet of blood with the tip of his finger and then smeared it on the side of his leg, laughed and stood up, walked over and bent down, putting his arms around her neck and nuzzling the top of her head. He looked in the mirror and noted the contrast they made, his own black hair and dark complexion against Margaret's freckled, pale skin and Marilyn Monroe hair. He stared down at her nipples. They were small for a woman, as were his own, even for a man's. He liked their similarity.

"Oh, of course." He laughed again, the superior one he used when he needed to move a particularly tough bond issue. It was a gamble, that laugh. Sometimes it worked, sometimes it didn't. "She's a Rhodes Scholar, that one," he went on, flexing his muscles in an exaggerated pose that made her turn away, but not before he caught a glimpse of a smile. "The first ever from Jamaica. No, listen, I won't make fun of her this time. Promise. I'll ask her advice on the stock market, find out who the next president should be, stuff she's got the inside scoop on. I'll ask her to toss the chicken bones, sprinkle the eye of a toad on my underwear, whatever she does. Voodoo crap." He winked, but she didn't laugh this time, only began digging in one of the drawers for something.

"Hey, I know. I'll have her down to the office, give Mr. Barnes, some of our best clients advice on their mutuals."

She looked at him. "I'm not going."

But of course, he knew she would.

⌖ ⌖ ⌖

At Madame Leonine's, Ed poked through the shrunken heads.

"I wonder how they get the plastic to shrink," he smirked.

"Someone said she has real ones in the back," Margaret whispered, hand over her mouth, and edged back into the darkness of the shop, back under the hanging row of ritual masks, next to a tiered row of baskets of rubber snakes, plastic alligators, and cheap-looking rattles. He knew she whispered to keep Madame Leonine, who was standing in the open doorway that led to the back room, from hearing.

"Hey! You got the real thing back there?" He held up the ugly little hairy object.

He observed the rush of color that appeared in the points of Margaret's cheeks and heard her giggle. This was so . . . *Margaret* . . . he thought dryly. He stood bemused as she walked quickly over to where he stood before the proprietor, a black woman of indecisive age, hair gray as pigeons, but face unlined and smooth. Madame Leonine had the seamless skin of a doll. Her eyes, black as caves and as fathomless, never darted about or moved from whatever or whomever she turned her stare toward.

"My husband," Margaret said, her cheeks apple-red, "is a great kidder. Come on, Ed." She pushed a wispy spray of blond hair out of her eyes.

"No," said the voodoo lady, her eyes on Ed's, her voice water pouring from a gourd, "I don't have anything for you in the back room."

"I didn't think so," said Ed, turning and grinning down at Margaret.

Margaret went over to the far corner where the charms for luck, for wealth, for success in love were along with a stack of placemats with pictures of the zodiac. He felt, rather than saw, her eyes—never directly on him, always alert and aware, like a jay in the yard keeping an eye on a creeping cat. Ed knew what it was she was afraid of. That he would say something to Madame Leonine, something she considered embarrassing. He knew, too, that she dreaded those encounters, but in one sense anticipated them almost with delight. It was clear to Ed that Margaret took a perverse pleasure in the way the voodoo lady responded to him. It was more in the way Madame Leonine addressed him than in anything particular she ever said. Like she was royalty and knew it and knew that Ed knew it too. Ignorant, superstitious ninny! She had her nerve.

"I need a love potion," he said, his voice mockingly condescending. "You got anything good?"

Madame Leonine stared out the window. Outside, tourists in tank-tops and t-shirts with Mardi Gras themes strolled by, some looking in the window, pointing down to their companions to exclaim, Look at this! Can you believe *this! Come over here, honey!* Somehow, Ed knew she wasn't seeing the tourists or even the street, but something further away. What the hell was he doing here . . . he ought to grab Margaret and leave, go get a drink—

She turned slowly. "What you want is over along that wall." She lifted her arm and hand in a full gesture, like a queen indicating a point of interest on her estate. The finger she pointed bent downward like a hawk's talon. Ed had never seen another nail that long. Something like that was a weapon, an instrument for exacting pain, for tearing eyeballs from skulls, slashing flesh.

He stared at her a moment while his mind drained, and then he walked over to the bin, reached in and picked up a small clear bottle filled with liquid the color of fire.

"Which one?" he asked. There were all kinds. Red, yellow, pink, blue, Christ!

"You'll choose the right one," she said. "That's how it happens." Ed thought he detected a smile, but he wasn't sure. Her voice did something inside him, made his stomach do a physical thing that traveled up to his throat, and he looked away, quickly.

He chose another, held it up to the bit of light coming in the front window and saw the blue of summer sky reflected. For some reason, seeing the intense cobalt gave him a wrench in the stomach, like her voice had.

"Who drinks it, the lover or the lovee?" He laughed in a higher register than usual.

"It doesn't matter."

All of a sudden, Margaret turned and hurried to the front door, not waiting or explaining to Ed why she was leaving. He bared his teeth in a smile at the voodoo lady and dug inside his pocket for money.

In a few moments he came out, a small brown bag in his hand, and they started down St. Peter's, walking in the middle of the street with native instinct, avoiding hidden doorways where street people liked to lurk. Tourists tripped gaily in elbowing crowds on the sidewalks, unaware of the potential dangers.

They stopped for a little while and watched a troop of black urchins acrobatically dancing on a sheet of cardboard. There was a gang of tourists oohing and aahing and a businessman and woman or two and the music was some kind of rap thing, music Ed detested. Ed pulled Margaret's arm. They didn't toss any change into the bucket, either, although Ed sensed that Margaret wanted to. He wasn't about to waste hard-earned cash on a bunch of juvenile con artists! That was the job of tourists.

They wandered the streets of the Quarter and got into a mild argument about which was the correct term, French *Quarter* or *Quarters*, he maintaining it was singular. They had café au lait and beignets at Café du Monde, sneezing on the powdered sugar, and then wandered down Pirate's Alley, even though Ed pointed out there were more muggings there than anywhere else in the Quarter. He pointedly said Quarter, but Margaret had her way in this and they walked down the narrow street, only at a quick pace. The odors of the district assailed their nostrils—cinnamon rolls, beignets, cooking grease from the Takee Outee's, beer and wine, and under it the faint smell of vomit.

They ended up sitting at a table on the balcony of the Seaport Cafe on Bourbon Street. They always sat here, watching the tourists on Sunday afternoon. Ed drank beer and Margaret had a Coke or sometimes a mixed drink. Daiquiris mostly, strawberry.

When they got there Margaret mentioned she was thinking about having the red beans and rice.

"You can't," Ed said.

"Why?"

"Because it's Sunday. Red beans and rice are a Monday's meal. You know, washday."

"Ed, I know that, but it's not like it's a law or something. I've got a taste for red beans."

"If you want to look like a tourist, go ahead."

She didn't.

"You know, Ed, there might come a day—" The waiter came just then and she modified her sentence in midstride, fingers flying to the hollow of her throat as she uttered, "Strawberry daiquiri, please," in a small and circumspect voice to the bent-over man who scribbled on his pad.

"There. There's one," Ed said, a few minutes later after their drinks had arrived. He tipped his head below toward a man and woman wandering down the street, pointing at cabaret signs, plastic go-cups decorated with the purple and gold of Mardi Gras in their hands.

"Watch," said Ed. "Female impersonators. That's what they want. They don't have those in Iowa."

"I don't think so," said Margaret. "They want jazz. Dixieland." Strains of just that, Dixieland, floated all around them.

It was a game they played. Figuring out what the tourists would do. It was an easy game, but Ed could play it over and over, like a

child hearing the same "Three Bears" story, listening each time with
new fascination.

"Let's go," Ed said.

"Where?"

"Down the street. You know. Casey's. Wait for the tourists. Play
the game."

"Can we skip it this once? You said we wouldn't do that this
time."

He looked at her and grinned, draining the last of his beer and
crooking his finger at the waiter for another. He pointed toward the
street to indicate he wanted it in a go-cup.

"Aw, c'mon, Mag," he said. "You always say you hate to and
then you get the biggest kick."

He was standing now and she still sat. He reached into his pocket
and got out some of the change and left it on the table.

"You think I like it because I laugh," she said. "Just because you
laugh doesn't always mean you like something. It just feels mean.
They're on their vacation. How would you feel if we were somewhere and people were laughing at us?"

"I'd like to see *that*," he said. He reached down and put his hand
under her arm and pulled her up.

"You worried about *tourists*? C'mon."

They left the Seaport and walked down Bourbon to Casey's, the
first homosexual outpost, its windows full of crimson neon flamingos. That's where they went, to stand across the street, Ed smoking
cigarettes and Margaret sipping her daiquiri.

"Flamingos," he said to Margaret as they waited. "You see a bar
has a peacock or a flamingo in New Orleans, you know. It's their
code."

"How come you know so much about gay codes?" she said, her
eyes malevolently coy from over the rim of her go-cup.

"Screw you, Margaret," he said, turning and showing her the
back of his head.

Presently, a couple came sailing along, smiling and laughing and talking loudly. They had drinks in their hands, holding them defiantly, thinking, if only the folks in Indiana or Ohio or Iowa could see them now.

"Watch," said Ed, elbowing her and grinning.

"I know, Ed." said Margaret. "Honestly."

"Twenty seconds," said Ed.

"Why don't we go," she said, sipping through her straw, brow tensed and furrowed. Ed glanced at her. "Twenty seconds," he repeated. "Bet you a drink." She looked away, down Bourbon in the direction they'd come. Ed wondered what she was thinking.

The couple went into the bar, holding hands, heat moisture visible on the man's forehead, the woman smiling and skipping.

It was over a full minute, but then here they came. They were still holding hands, but this time the man was jerking the woman along behind him and she was trying to keep her drink from spilling. The man had left his drink someplace inside, along with his smile. He was mad, it was plain by his face, and the woman had lost some color in hers.

"Fuckin' queers," they heard the man say, as the couple hurried back the way they'd come, to the safety of the strip joints. Just as they crossed the street, the woman giggled nervously and the man jerked at her arm.

"See? I told you twenty seconds," said Ed. "You'd of said thirty-one, you'd of won. You owe me a drink. I'll give you a chance to catch up. Double or nothing on the next one. I'll say thirty seconds before I even see them."

"Let's go," Margaret said. She slurped the rest of her daiquiri, making a face at the sound. "I'll buy you that drink. Let's go to Deanie's. I feel like soft-shelled crab."

After streetcaring back to Carrollton at Riverbend, they retrieved their car. "Goddamn it!" Ed jumped back out of the car and then got back in slowly, letting himself down on the seat a little at a time. "We got to get one of those things for the windshield," he said. "Or cloth covers. What's the temperature, anyway? I got second-degree burns on my butt!"

"Let's go to Fitzgerald's instead, so we can watch the sailboats," Margaret said, once Ed had started the car and flipped the A/C button on high. "They'll have the softshells, too."

The waitress at Fitzgerald's said they were fresh out of soft-shelled crabs, so they asked for cold, boiled shrimp and a saucer of hot sauce to dip them into. The waitress brought another plate to put the shells on. Only a couple of sailboats were out on Ponchartrain. The wind had picked up almost to the point of being a gale, but a young man was up on a windsailing board, far out past the end of the jetty they sat staring at. The urge of the tide from the Gulf and the skiffing of the tiny tops of the waves from the late afternoon wind made the lake an undulating field of grain, crimson from the setting sun. The windsurfer nearly toppled, going perpendicular to the horizon for a long moment and then righting, and the illusion was that time seemed to slow, just then, for the almost imperceptible space of a single heartbeat.

"I'd like to try that sometime," Margaret said. "Wouldn't you?"

"Where do you suppose they are right now," he asked, after a minute. "Those tourists."

"Where?"

"In the hotel, packing," he said. He laughed and Margaret smiled, just a little, in spite of herself.

They ate shrimp for awhile, picking the shells off with deft, practiced movements, sometimes spitting out a bit of missed shell, not talking, and then Ed said, "Would you ever want to go there?"

"Where?" she said.

"There," he said, pointing up. "Up North. Where the yankees live."

"Maybe," she said. "They seem like nice folks, mostly."

"Yeah, right. Nice and dumb. They can't cook."

"I've heard," said Margaret.

"Yeah. Look in their spice racks and all you'll find are salt and pepper. They eat noodles on mashed potatoes. They call that a meal. I was in Indiana, once. Nasty! That's how they iron their shirts. Just spit and hit the iron to it. So much starch, they stand 'em in corners instead of using hangers."

"I think I'd like a drink," Margaret said. "A double. Bushmill's and water. And you know what? Salt and pepper are spices. I use them."

Later that evening, back in the apartment, they made love. The A/C was turned on high, but sweat ran off both their bodies anyway. Not from passion, but exertion. Ed tried, thinking he would get excited once they got going, only he couldn't concentrate. He realized after a few minutes he'd made a mistake by entering her too early. He'd had this idea he'd get hard once he was inside, but it didn't happen. All he could think of was her breasts. They were bigger. She must have put on weight. The very first time they'd had sex, four years ago, he'd whispered it was her breasts that turned him on the most. She said later that was one of the things made her fall in love with him and why she'd agreed to marry him, a month later. Her other lovers had never said anything about her breasts. She'd always thought they were too small, mannish almost. No, he said; I like them that way. Small breasts are sexier. Somehow, unnoticed, they'd gotten bigger and it was a turnoff. He thought about saying something, but didn't. But it ruined it, the sex. He couldn't think of anything other than her breasts being too big now.

For awhile they drank Chablis and looked out the bedroom window at the pool. A man sat in one of the lawn chairs with a portable radio beside him, drinking beer out of a long-neck. Pearl Beer. Ed could see the label.

"You put some of that stuff in my drink." She didn't say it accusingly, she just said it, stating a fact. She must have seen him do it, sneak it in, but she hadn't said anything at the time.

"Must work," he said. "Eh, Margaret? Great stuff. Only I guess *I* should have drank it, not you."

"How come you picked the blue? Why not the green? Or the pink? I thought you hated blue."

"I don't know. 'Cause I already had it in my hand. There's nothing in it, you know. Just colored water. Sugar. Bunch of bullshit! I can't believe I threw good money away on that crap. I did it for a joke, anyway, Margaret. Get a clue."

He turned over on his side, away from her, felt the sweat evaporating. It felt good, cleansing somehow.

"Then why'd you bother putting it in my drink?"

"Christ, I don't know! As a joke, I guess. I already said that. Who knows?"

They were both silent for awhile and then Margaret swung her legs out of bed and stood up. Without thinking about it, she crossed her arms over her breasts.

"I don't have any energy," she said. "I think I'll go take a swim."

"That guy out there," he said. "You know him?"

"No," she said. "He's from Chicago or something. Just moved in."

"How you know that, you don't even know him?"

"Lucille. Lucille said something about him. He's down here on some engineering project or something, she said. She said he's staying with Ernest."

"Ernest, the guy in the end apartment? The guy who never has girls over?"

"Yes."

"Oh," he said, and rolled his eyes upward. "Well, go ahead. I think you're perfectly safe, he's a friend of Ernest's."

He watched her put her towel on a chair next to the man's and speak to him for a minute and then she dove into the pool. He must have drifted to sleep, because the next time he was aware of anything, the sun was shining and there was no one out by the pool.

He found Margaret on the couch in the living room, a sheet over her nude body, lying on her back. He went over and pulled down the sheet. Bending over, he kissed one of her breasts, taking the nipple into his mouth and sucking hard. She jerked away from him, and sat up, pulling the sheet up to her neck, instantly awake.

"That *hurts*," she said, her eyes small and crusty with sleep.

"*Everything* hurts," he said, and went out into the kitchen. He poured half a glass of wine and took it with him into the bathroom and got out his shaving gear. From the bathroom, he said, "Did it hurt last night, too? It must have, way you were."

"What does *that* mean?"

He didn't answer her, only went back out to the kitchen, shaving cream still under his chin where he hadn't shaved yet. He filled up the wine glass and got an ice cube from the freezer.

"Maybe we ought to go on a diet," he said, in a loud voice so she could hear. "I can hardly get into some of my stuff anymore."

"Do you think I'm fat?" she said, her own voice lower, but still clear enough for him to hear.

That night they went to the Oriental Triangle over on Jefferson Highway. Ed drank beers, fast, one after another, and then he started in on the shots. They didn't talk much and when he wanted to order her a drink, a *real* drink, she told him, no, Coca-Cola was all she wanted tonight.

The next morning Ed had to fix his own eggs. Margaret stayed in bed, whispered in a husky voice that she had a hangover. Last night she'd switched from Cokes to Bushmill's and water and had four or five. Ed tried again to make love, but she said she felt sick from the booze. For some reason, he'd thought of the blue bottle, sitting out on the kitchen counter, and considered drinking a bit of it, see what it did. This is crazy, he thought to himself. I'm acting like I halfway believe that stuff! To his surprise, her turndown made him feel relief more than anything.

Sitting at the breakfast table, picking idly at his eggs, he stared at the blue bottle, but his thoughts were jumbled, confused.

When he got ready to leave for work, he picked the bottle up and dropped it in the trash. Halfway to the front door, he turned and came back and fished around until he found it again. He rinsed off the coffee grounds and dried the bottle on the towel hanging on the refrigerator door. He started to put it back on the counter and then had a second thought and just stuck it in his pocket.

\* \* \*

When Ed got home from work, Margaret was gone.

At first he wasn't too worried. This wasn't the first time. It was more like the third or fourth.

When two days went by and she still hadn't returned, he decided she wasn't coming back this time. For some reason this didn't bother him. Thursday, he got a postcard from her. He wondered why she'd bothered. It showed a big amusement park someplace in Tennessee and was mailed in Kentucky. She didn't say much on the back, in her jerky handwriting, just that she had left him and was going up north. Maybe Chicago. She didn't say anything about the man at the pool, but Ed knew she was with him.

She said to take care and not take it too hard. She said she'd get hold of Lucille and have her collect her clothes and send them to her when she got settled so he wouldn't have to bother. She said she was with a friend who was just giving her a ride and that they had stopped in one town and she had lunch in a diner and they had noodles on the menu and she tried them and he was right. They were bland. But filling. She wished him the best of luck in his life and hoped he'd wish her the same. She signed it, "It Wasn't All Bad, Margaret."

Actually, she'd written quite a bit, but she didn't say much, he decided. He ripped the card up and put the pieces in the wastebasket in the kitchen, on top of the coffee filter and grounds from the day before.

\* \* \*

Early Sunday morning, he got up and drove the car over to the little shopping center at Riverbend. He got change at the Camellia Grill and got on the streetcar. It made him mad to have to do that. There was no change in the glass jar on the kitchen counter when he went to get some. She must have cleaned it out. *Bitch* was what went through his mind when he had to ask the one-armed cashier at the Camellia Grill for streetcar change.

He had a beer at the Seaport Café, sitting on the balcony, the same table as the week before, and watched the people walking down below. The barkers were out, shilling the people to "come inside, see the *sex-ee* strippers, hear *real* New Orleans' jazz." After another beer, he left the Seaport and walked down different streets until he got to the voodoo shop. He hesitated only a moment and then he went in.

He thought at first he was alone in the dark room, but when his eyes adjusted, he saw the figure of Madame Leonine standing by the cash register. Quickly, he walked over and up to her.

"This crap doesn't work!" he said. "I got the wrong one."

"Of course," she said, in her singy-song voice. "Take the one you want."

"Here." He thrust the blue bottle at her and strode over and flung bottles around until he got the one he wanted.

"This is it!" he said, his voice agitated and high.

"Yes," she said. "You see?"

✻ ✻ ✻

He stood across the street watching and in a little bit a tourist couple came along, laughing and drinking out of gaily-decorated plastic go-cups. The man had on loud Bermuda shorts and a hat with a beer can on top. The woman had on a yellow halter that spilled over with breasts, and tight, yellow shorts. Even her sandals were yellow, and there was a thing pinned on her shorts, a flower or something, that was yellow, too. They went into the bar, holding each other's hands, and in a few seconds they came back out, the man first, his face red and contorted and jerking the woman behind him,

who was holding onto the yellow sunhat that was threatening to
come flying off her head.

Twenty *seconds*, Ed said, out loud, and, *I win*, and then he realized there was only a drunk a few feet away who looked at his out-
burst with a quizzical expression and then came over and asked for
a dollar in a squeaky voice.

*Get away from me*, he said.

The drunk staggered off, and it was then he noticed the street
was deserted, all the way up to Canal; people, tourists, inside, eating
lunch at all the restaurants, in their hotel rooms, screwing. Catching
a nooner. He laughed.

*What the hell*, he said, under his breath, all of a sudden, and crossed
over and went in. At the bar, he said, *make it a beer, Heineken Dark*,
and put his foot up on the railing. He took a long swallow and thought
about how good it tasted, deliciously cold and bitter. He glanced at
his watch, at the second hand, marked where it was.

He pressed his belly up against the bar and felt something in his
pocket when his trousers tightened, and it took a second before he
realized what it was. It was the bottle from Madame Leonine's. What
the hell, he thought. He reached down into his pocket and felt the
smooth cool glass and brought it out. The cap was a little hard to get
off, must have been on there a long time. He didn't even look at it,
just tipped it up and drained it, every drop. It was sweet, like sugar
water.

Then, he waited.

As he waited, he found himself staring back out through the open
door to the spot across the street where he and Margaret had always
stood. Everything looked different; reversed, as if standing in there,
in the bar, he was really on the outside, and out there, on the street,
was actually the inside. It was the light, he thought; must be getting

ready to rain. He turned his back and let his gaze settle over the scene before him, not knowing exactly what to expect, but knowing something was about to happen and that he needed to be ready for it when it did.

# Acknowledgments

"Hard Times," and "Broken Seashells," were first published in *The Analecta*; "I Shoulda Seen a Credit Arranger" by *The South Carolina Review*; "Princess" by *Whiskey Island Magazine*; "Sheets" by *The Typewriter*; "Toothache" by *Kansas Quarterly/Arkansas Review*; "My Idea of a Nice Thing" by *Breeze*; "Telemarketing" by *Flyway Literary Review*; "The Jazz Player" by the *Hopewell Review*; "A Shortness of Breath" by *Loonfeather*; "Hard Times" by *The North Atlantic Review*; "Dream Flyer" by *The Chiron Review*.